Hitler, My Father

Hitler, My Father is a gripping family drama played out on an international stage. Many have wondered how anyone could love Hitler. Now all may know.

Lorenz Meyer, a Professor Emeritus at Heidelberg University specializing in early Twentieth Century European history, traces the life of an Austrian girl, Lotte Schoener, from her eighteent' year to her death a half century later. Meyer studies Lotte's unshakable love for the despicable Hitler, whose seduction of her precedes the birth of Lotte's son and that son's eventual search for his father. Their chronicle brackets an epoch that may seem ancient to many contemporary readers. They lived i a time of unspeakable crimes against humanity, destruction of cities and entire cultures, and the final taming of the German war juggernaut. Monumental forces flow through their story, b only from a distance.

"An eerie new twist on a classic tale, *Hitler, My Father,* flashes back to the darkest days of WWII when any evil was possible. Then adds one more."

—Doug Allyn, author of *The Jukebox Kings,* an Edgar Award winner

Hitler, My Father

A Novel of World War Two

Rod Merten

Parkhurst Brothers Publishers
MARION, MICHIGAN

© Principal text copyright 2018 by Rodney D. Merten. All rights reserved under the laws and treaties of the United States of America and all international copyright conventions and treaties. No part of this book may be reproduced in any form, except for brief passages quoted within news or blog features about the book, reviews, etc., without the express prior written consent of Permissions Director, Parkhurst Brothers Publishers.

www.parkhurstbrothers.com

Parkhurst Brothers books are distributed to the trade through the Chicago Distribution Center, and may be ordered through Ingram Book Company, Baker & Taylor, Follett Library Resources and other book industry wholesalers. To order from Chicago Distribution Center, phone 800-621-2736 or send a fax to 800-621-8476. Copies of this and other Parkhurst Brothers Publishers titles are available to organizations and corporations for purchase in quantity by contacting Special Sales Department at our home office location listed on our website. Manuscript submission guidelines for this publishing company are available at our website.
Printed in the United States of America

First Edition, 2017
2017   2018   2019   2020 10 9 8 7 6 5 4 3 2 1

Library of Congress Cataloging in Publication Data: [Pending]

ISBN: Trade Paperback   978-1-62491-094-4
ISBN: e-book   ~978-1-62491-095-1

Parkhurst Brothers Publishers believes that the free and open exchange of ideas is essential for the maintenance of our freedoms. We support the First Amendment to the United States Constitution and encourage all citizens to study all sides of public policy questions, making up their minds independently. Closed minds cost a society dearly.

Cover art adapted from the poster: "Youth Serves the Leader: All 10-year-Olds into the [Hitler Youth]". Unknown artist. Library of Congress, Prints and Photographs Division, Washington, D.C.

Cover and interior design by	Linda D. Parkhurst, Ph.D.
Proofread by	Bill and Barbara Paddack
Acquired for Parkhurst Brothers Publishers by	Ted Parkhurst
Edited by	Roger Armbrust and Ted Parkhurst

112017

Contents

1

"How I have missed you, my angel."

Tante Lotte's Diary
13 March 1938

YESTERDAY WAS ABSOLUTELY THE BEST DAY OF MY LIFE!!!

It all started in the old school in Braunau am Inn, my dear Fuhrer's home town. Our church choir had been chosen to present a special concert just for him, and were we ready! The old priest, Father Sohn, wanted us to sing a bunch of old church hymns, but we knew that would not please Hitler. Only patriotic songs would do.

Our choir has many good voices, but only one great one—me! I knew that if we did well we might have a chance to actually meet him!

My only competition came from Gerta Beyerlein, that old cow. Mein Vater said I had the voice of an angel and he should know—he talks with them every day. Mein Mutter, for her part, dressed me as well as she could working night and day to finish my dress, all white with red trim and a black swastika right over my heart. I just knew I'd be fantastic, and I was!

Poor Herr Hitler did not seem too interested in our singing. Probably he was still excited by the Anschluss and all. Anyway, he applauded at all the right times and especially after my solo. He even stood when he clapped for me. I saw him whisper to one of his men and point at me.

I was putting away my music, feeling pretty good, when the man, the one Hitler had been whispering to, came up to me. He was short, stout, not at all good looking. He said Herr Hitler was so impressed by my singing that he wanted to meet me. He said this in front of everybody, even Father Sohn.

What could I do? One does not reject the Fuhrer. I did protest a little saying I would have no way to return home as the rest of the choir was leaving. He assured me that would not be a problem.

Sofia and Heidi were poking me, telling me to go, telling me that this was my chance to get out of Oberschwarzenberg, to make something of myself. Father Sohn asked the man would I be safe. The man said of course. The old priest asked him just how was I going to get home. The man said a Party member would deliver me to my home later this very day.

Well, what could I say? I said yes! I followed the man across the street to Hitler's hotel. We went right up the stairs to his room. The man knocked and we heard from inside, "Yes?"

The man said, "I have the girl."

The door opened into a fine room. Thick green carpets, creamy walls and a blue ceiling complimented the heavy brown leather couch, matching chair and a wood framed four poster bed. The sun streamed in through windows framing Herr Hitler as he sat on the couch. He rose as I entered and said, "Fraulein Schoener, how nice of you to come." Like I had a choice!

I was in awe. Was I to curtsy? Shake his hand? Faint? Or run away while I still could? All I did was to stand and stare. Never in my eighteen years of life had I expected this moment. How does one prepare for this?

"Fraulein, please have a seat."

That I could do. I sat on the chair as far away from him as I could. A handsome man gave us each a cup and saucer, served us tea and a Linz torte. He bent over the Fuhrer's cup and poured in a powder he said would "help you calm down," then took his leave. Herr Hitler sipped his tea in a most delicate manner, not manly at all. I drank only a little, afraid I'd spill it being so nervous.

The more he drank the dreamier he acted. His eyes focused above my head and his breathing slowed. I thought he was falling asleep until he said, "Come, my Geli. Sit on your uncle's lap again."

Geli? That was not my name. Who was he talking to?

"Geli, come here! I've missed you so much."

Then it dawned on me! He thought I was his niece, Geli. This was creepy. She had died years ago! Yet, he was the Fuhrer. Who was I to correct him?

I did as he ordered. Rising up on unsteady legs, I walked slowly towards the sofa and stood before him.

"Sit here, dear child." he pointed to his lap! This was too much!

"Herr Hitler, I am not Geli. I am Lotte."

I had heard that "his Geli," born Angelika Rabaul on June 4, 1908, was Hitler's half-niece. Over a six year period it is alleged that he repeatedly molested her, forced her to perform unusual sex acts, held her a virtual prisoner though well-provided for, wined and dined. On September 18, 1931 she either committed suicide using Hitler's own pistol or, as some thought, she was murdered by someone using Hitler's gun.

This seemed to rouse him from his dream. His eyes began to focus on my face which was okay. But then they slid down my body all the way to my shoes, then slowly they rose until once again he was looking me straight in the eyes.

"Lotte? Your name is Lotte? Are you sure?"

"I am quite sure."

Dreamily, he continued, "You look just like my Geli. You even sing like my Geli. Humor an old man and for now pretend you are Geli. Would you do that for me?"

I would die for this man! Pretending to be Geli was not that much to ask. I wanted to be a movie actress anyway. Why not start now for the man who could make my dream come true?

"*I was just teasing, Uncle. Yes, my Fuhrer, I am your niece, Geli. What would you have me do?*"

"*Sit here,*" *motioning again to his lap,* "*and sing to me.*"

I was not sure it was all right to sit on a man's lap even if he was the Fuhrer. But, I was not sure it was wrong either. His eyes continued to look into mine and I felt my resistance crumble like stale bread. His eyes pulled me closer until he reached up, grasped my arm and eased me down.

Immediately, I felt secure, held safe in his arms, nuzzling my head under his chin, feeling his legs under my hips supporting me. I was overwhelmed! Nothing had ever prepared me for these feelings. Sure, Erich Schwimmer had kissed me a little but that was not the same. This was so much more.

I sang to him, softly, a lullaby from my youth. I thought, perhaps, that it would have been a song Geli would have known. His hand on my shoulder tightened, then slowly released and rubbed up and down my arm. His other reached in front and caressed my waist, wandering up to feel my diaphragm move in time to my music.

I must have sung to him for over an hour. Every song I'd ever learned that did not involve church. The more I sang, the quieter he got, but the more he rubbed me. He caressed my arm, then my back, and neck until his gentle hands reached my hair.

He interrupted my singing to remark, "*You are just as I remember you. Your soft body and gentle voice. How I've missed you, my angel.*"

Here it was. The greatest leader the world will ever know touching me, a poor country girl. Or was he still thinking of his dead niece as he touched me? I had to know. Gently, I gathered his hand from my diaphragm, holding it between mine, I asked him, "*Is it Geli or me whom you are loving?*"

As if from afar, "*It is both.*"

That was enough for me. He knew it was not just Geli, but me who loved him. I turned into him, reached up with my hand and pulled him down to my lips. My first real kiss! And it was with Mein Fuhrer. The world's greatest kiss. Beyond lay uncharted territory. I rose off his lap and let him lead me to the bed.

He perched on the edge of the bed standing me right in front of himself. A simple, "Take off your clothes," was all he said, all he had to say. Buttons popped, skirts fell, shoes dropped until I was standing in just my chemise.

I was twitching, shaking, scared and shocked by my behavior. I waited for his next command. My friends and I had talked about boys and love, but we had never discussed what a real man would expect or want.

Hitler just stared at me still using his hands to caress me from my knees up to my arms and back. Why was he still dressed and me almost naked? Was he shy or just waiting to see what I would do? I took the challenge! I started to undress the Fuhrer!

First his jacket and shirt, each button was a challenge for my fumbling fingers. He sat still as I struggled. I laid his clothes on the chair next to the bed. Now what? His top was bare so I started at the bottom. Kneeling, I untied his shoes and raised each foot to pull them off and then his hose. Top and bottom were done. Now the middle. I did not know if I was to continue. This was all new to me. My parents would kill me if they knew I was undressing the Fuhrer.

Well, as Mein Vater always said, "In for a pint, in for a gallon." I raised my hands to his waist and started to work the buttons. They were stubborn but I was determined.

"You will have to help me, my Fuhrer."

He placed his hands on the bed to lift his bottom up just enough so I could pull his trousers down, and then off. He raised again and I removed his drawers. I thought to myself, "not as big as I might have guessed." Yet, he was a great man and soon would be my lover. Who was I to judge?

"What is this?" I asked pointing to a dark square smudge high on

his right thigh.

"Only a birthmark exclusive to my family," he said.

He put his hands on the hem of my chemise, caressed my knees as he raised it above my waist. He continued higher and higher until it was over my breasts which my left arm and hand immediately covered. Then back to my waist, hooking fingers into my panties and rolling them down until they puddled at my feet. My right hand plunged to cover my womanhood. I could not help it.

"Child, such modesty is charming but most inconvenient."

——

12 December 2008
Heidelberg, Germany

I put aside the diary, dusty with age. As a Professor of History at Heidelberg University, I had never seen such. Seated in my study, I was surrounded by boxes of letters, the diary of my long-departed Great Aunt Lotte Schoener, and my own research spanning almost twenty years. How many times in one's life is a person presented with documents such as these?

My wife, Hilde, poked her head in from the hallway. "What are you going to do with this mess?"

"I think I am finally going to write my book."

"Took you long enough. I've been cleaning around these piles for two decades."

"I had to wait until I retired and had the time."

"Then I'll let you get to it."

A letter from Lotte's friend Erich Schwimmer had arrived at my door in 1991. I was her only living relative whose address he could find—and the only one caring enough to record and understand her story. I planned to take a short, or so I thought, sabbatical to begin my search in Oberschwarzenberg to discover my Tante Lotte and story.

My family's history told the tale of Tante Lotte from

Oberschwarzenberg, a bumpy point of land between Czechoslovakia and Germany in northern Austria, about a hundred kilometers from Linz, itself off the beaten path, being far from Vienna—the Austria the tourists flock to.

Every relative who knew Tante Lotte had disowned her. Who wanted to admit that even a far distant relative was convinced that Adolf Hitler had fathered her child? Here I sat, almost seventy years removed from the beginning, trying to make some sense of her tale. I hoped to understand this most amazing woman within the context of her times, her village and her obsession. (Author's Note: I have taken the liberty to translate the original documents into modern English and, as a history professor, added as much historical background as necessary).

Lotte Schoener was just fourteen years old when in 1934 Adolf Hitler came to power in Germany, at first invigorating a beaten-down people ruined by hyper-inflation and fear, then taking his people down to the hell of defeat and occupation.

In 1934, however, all this history had not yet happened. It was a time of renewal for all Germans reeling from the betrayal of World War One, and the visceral fear engendered by Russia's Communists. Onto this stage stepped her dear Adolf, her Liebchen, to whom she wrote almost five dozen letters before her death.

Adolf Hitler, like Tante Lotte, began his life in Austria, not Germany. He was born in a hamlet, Braunau am Inn, quite near the German border. Having left Austria as a failure he returned to Vienna, a hero. He took time to visit his birthplace and grade school. On March 12, 1938 in a schoolroom in Braunau am Inn, a choir from an even smaller village came to perform for their new leader. The soloist of that small choir was my Tante Lotte, whose diary and letters I now reveal.

2

"I am awed by the love we shared"

13 March 1938
Mein Fuhrer, Mein Liebchen

You cannot know how very special our time together was. I will value yesterday for the rest of my life. You have transformed me from a simple village girl into the vessel of your future. Yes, my dear, I am carrying your baby. I know it is soon, but I am sure, so very sure, that I am the bearer of your glorious future.

I am awed by the love we shared! I adored you from the moment you said how much I reminded you of your dear cousin. I was honored to remind you of your dear Geli, your first love. I am pleased to take her place in your affections. I pray I can help you get over her.

I know we are meant to be together!

Your Lotte

27 March 1938
My Darling,

My heart beats with joy to be writing you. To think a poor country girl is carrying the heir to the greatest leader the world has known. Even now I can feel him growing inside me. Since you are the only man I've known, there is no doubt—you are the father. And you both are all mine.

As to your son, my dear. I will name him Adolf in your honor, of course. My Love, when can I come to Berlin to be with you? It is so hard waking up in this drab little village when the love of my life is so far away.

Please, my love, can we get together soon? I long to be in your arms, to feel you against me, to kiss you and, yes, to make love again and again. You have set my soul on fire! I yearn for no other but you My Fuhrer.

Lotte

———

The home of Dr. Erich Schwimmer
Oberschwarzenberg, Austria
3 September 1991

"Herr Doktor Erich Schwimmer?"

I greeted the old man who answered the door of 34 Schwarzenberg am Bohmenwaldstrasse. The home was not the grand house I expected of a physician, but a fairly plain two-story wooden structure, badly in need of paint. Doctor Schwimmer, for indeed it was he, wore plain clothing. His shoes were scuffed, his pants patched in the knee, and his sweater the gray of an October sky.

"May I help you?"

"Doctor Schwimmer, I am Lorenz Meyer, Lotte Schoener's nephew."

"Yes, we have been expecting you. Please, follow me."

The ancient gentleman turned round as he welcomed me to his home. I had to duck to enter as the door was in the traditional low style. He had a slight limp as I followed him through the short entryway to a small parlor. It was crowded by two cushioned chairs and a large divan, none of which matched.

"Please, have a seat." He perched on the chair to the right of the fireplace. I went to sit in the left chair, but was waved to the divan.

"I am sorry, but that chair is Lotte's," he admonished me. I noted he used the present tense. A slip of the tongue? Or just old age?

I got right to the point. "Dr. Schwimmer, I have just returned from Moscow where I was given Lotte's letters to Adolf Hitler."

The smile on his face was accompanied by a sudden gasp. Before he could respond a cute young woman many years younger than my fifty plus years came bustling in. She was dressed very smartly in a tailored suit of bright red which seemed to match her countenance. She was about five and a half feet tall, well-rounded in the hips, with wavy blond hair and Rhine River blue eyes. She regarded me with an angry glint.

"Uncle! Who is this? What does he want? I've told you a hundred times to not let strangers into your home. Your days as a Good Samaritan are long past!"

He and I both withered under this assault. The doctor was the first to recover, having experienced this performance before.

"Hilde," nodding towards me, "this young man is not a stranger. He is Lotte's nephew."

"That is hardly a good reference, Uncle."

The old man struggled to his feet, clearly in some pain. He towered over Hilde by only an inch. These two were well matched and had surely sparred before. Yet, I saw in their eyes an affection that put me at ease. I recognized this exchange as a dance that happened often, each knowing the steps and the outcome.

"Niece! This is my home! It was my father's home! I will have anyone in I wish as long as I have breath. You may apologize to my guest, Herr Doktor Professor Lorenz Meyer of Heidelberg University."

She turned without a reply and flounced back the way she had come. In the vacuum of Hilde's departure, I began my interview. I, apparently, had much to learn about my aunt.

"Before we begin, I beg you to address me as Erich as I no longer practice medicine."

"And you can call me Lorenz, if you please."

"One thing that I do not understand, Dr. Schwimmer, sorry, Erich, was how you and the rest of the village put up with Aunt Lotte."

Erich glanced into the cold fireplace for long minutes. Finally, he spoke.

"This, I am reluctant to share with you. The consequences can be far-reaching. Are you sure, Professor, that you want to know?"

I responded with more bravado than bravery, "What can the truth hurt?"

"Perhaps you are right. As you will discover, Lotte was a very strong person. She had to be to survive the abuse she received. She believed to the very end that Hitler loved her. That he never, ever answered any of her letters, never acknowledged his son, never returned to Austria only served to prove to her that it was all true.

"Her views changed a little to accommodate the end of the war. Hitler's suicide was a fake, of course, so he could escape. She still wrote to him often. That the letters remained unanswered only proved to her that he was busy trying to re-establish his Third Reich. She was convinced that there was a Nazi in the Berlin post office who intercepted her letters and forwarded them to her dear Adolf. Otherwise they would have been returned to her."

Hilde burst in. She looked directly at her uncle with nary a glance for me.

"Time for lunch, Uncle."

"Did you make enough for our guest, also?"

Again, keeping her focus on Erich, "I did not know he was staying."

"He will sleep in Lotte's room."

Then to me, "You will stay?"

"That is very kind of you, Hilde." What did I have to lose by being civil to her?

"That settles it. Hilde, please set another place and prepare Lotte's room. We have a guest!"

Hilde did a quick about face and stormed into the kitchen, her heels echoing the *tromp, tromp, tromp* of soldiers. "Do not worry about her, Professor. She spends so much time protecting me she has little for herself. I tell her she is young and should get out and enjoy life."

He gave me an appraising look. "Perhaps you could provide her a little diversion when I take my afternoon nap." With a wink he was out of his chair and heading for the kitchen. I joined him at the table as she finished placing the food. "For now, Herr Meyer, tell us about yourself. We will talk of Lotte later." Again, the wink.

"There is not much to say, I am afraid. I teach at the University in Heidelberg. My specialty is Twentieth Century Europe. Mostly, I look at the wars and their aftermath. I am single, have no pets, and live in a one bedroom apartment close to the university."

As I droned on, a funny thing happened. The doctor's eyes took on a glazed, far-away look. Was he re-living his own war? Meanwhile, Hilde was seeming to warm up to me. She even acted interested in my discussion of events decades before her birth. Lunch became pleasant rather than the battle I had anticipated.

Later, after Erich's nap, we settled into our respective seats. Erich took the lead. "You asked earlier how we kept Lotte's secret? A better question might have been, *why*. In a little town like this, it is easy to keep a secret from outsiders. Everyone living here knows all the secrets.

"As I said, Lotte was very strong in her beliefs. It was easy for the village to join in her fantasy. There are scarce opportunities for any other diversion besides telling stories. Lotte simply became a story, albeit, a living one. She was so busy telling her lie to everyone and so often that people accepted it as the truth just like Hitler had done to the whole German nation.

"In May of 1945 the American Army arrived in Vienna. By June they were in Linz. Then they arrived here, more as tourists than conquerors. Long before, however, Lotte concocted a bigger lie. She claimed that she had personally heard from friends of Hitler. She said she was given specific instructions. She and her son were to be shielded from the outside world. If any of us exposed her—well we knew what happened to his enemies. The death camps were all big news by then. Seeing how the Nazis treated innocents we could only fear the consequences if we were found guilty.

"It became very easy for us to keep the silent conspiracy in place because who really cared? It cost us nothing! And maybe it kept us out of harm. No one was willing to risk their lives to show out a crazy woman."

"The whole town went along?"

"Every last person. Better safe than sorry, as the Americans say."

"Lotte was what, about twenty-five years old when the war ended?"

"Yes."

"And she died in 1989—over forty years later. So for all those years you kept this charade going?"

"It became very easy after awhile to believe her story. It became everyone's story. It was a harmless hoax."

Hilde entered quietly, "Dinner is ready."

"After," Erich continued, "I'll give you her diary and the letters we wrote to each other during the war. You may find them interesting."

3

"I am with child—your son!"

12 April 1938
Happy Birthday, my dear!

Great News, My Lover! It is official—at least for me. I am with child—your son! I can only marvel at the glorious child growing inside me. Surely, he (I am so sure it is a boy) will grow up to be as great as his father, My lover, My Fuhrer.

You should see the way people look at me. They are beside themselves that I had all that time together with you. Especially that Gerta Beyerlein! She thinks she is so much better than anyone else. Just because she married Johann Beyerlein and he owns the only store in the whole town. She stands behind the counter like she owns the place. Well, I guess she does, but that does not give her the right to glare at me like something is wrong, like maybe my dress is too short or something.

You should see the pathetic little shop she is so proud of. It is only a few meters wide and a few more deep. And the stuff they sell! Greasy nuts and bolts, dull cloth, all kinds of shovels, cheap tea, stale crackers, and ugly shoes. Nothing like the fine stuff I'm sure you see in Berlin! Now there is a town I'd like to live in.

Because they handle the mail, just about everybody has to go there once a day "just to check." Like anybody in this town ever gets anything important! Mostly, it seems to me, they just get together to gossip. As long as this town has Beyerlein's, it'll never need a daily paper!

Before I hardly even got back to town it was all over that I had been permitted to spend time alone with you. My friends, Sofia and Heidi, are so jealous they can hardly stand it. They walk around town thinking their cheap dresses are fine gowns. They act like they are so special just because they know me. Some of the others, the ones who deny your greatness, won't even speak to me anymore. Too bad for them is all I can say. Especially for old Mrs. Zoellner. She never liked my family anyway, but now she is just mean. My friends told me that she told their mothers that she did not trust you being with me. Wait until I start showing, then her tongue will wag!

I am afraid to tell Mutter und Vater. They will not be happy that I am having a child without a husband. Might we get married? I know I would make you a good wife.

Every night before I sleep and every morning as I awake I relive that glorious afternoon. You gave me the greatest gift I could ever hope to receive—your love and your child.

I promise to write you often though postage is so high for a girl without a job. Mutter und Vater are not rich. They will not understand why I must write you. Might you send me a few Marks to help me and your baby? I hate to ask because I know you need all your time and energy to lead us into a great future—but it would help us so much.

Your love, My Dear Fuhrer, sustains me.

Lotte

Lotte's Diary
13 April 1938

You should have seen how they fawned over me at Mass. In the choir loft they all gave way as I entered. I had no solo today so just gloried in the glow. Sofia and Heidi stayed close. They don't know that I am pregnant—yet.

After church we three, we call ourselves "the Three Musketeers" even though we are girls, went on a picnic. Sofia overheard three boys saying, loudly enough so she would hear, that they were going to climb Plockenstein. What show-offs!

We knew they would never climb to the top. Not when there is still snow up there. Making sure Sofia knew the path they were taking, they set off. We followed with our food. The picnic began when they "accidentally" returned from their "climb" along the same path we were on. Good manners required us to ask them to share our picnic. The two Schuler brothers, Reinhard and Hans, and Ludwig Rodammer were happy to accept our offer.

Hans tried to put his arm around me. Very sly. Felt like a python slithering round my shoulders. Still gives me the shivers. I shrugged. He stopped, his fingers marking time on my back.

It started to feel kinda good. Then I remembered my love for you, Herr Hitler, and I leapt to my feet. How foolish Hans looked with his arm hanging in midair. Heidi laughed, he went red. She grabbed a sandwich and stuffed it in his big mouth. We set far apart for the rest of the day, unlike Sofia and Heidi. They let those boys get awfully friendly, if you ask me.

———

The home of Dr. Erich Schwimmer
Oberschwarzenberg, Austria
4 September 1991

We were seated in the parlor the next morning. I noted again the pictures on the mantle over the fire-scorched fireplace. They looked more like an altar one would see in a developing third world country immersed in paganism. There was a common theme, I noted. Every one of the dozen or so photos included at least one woman. Could these be Lotte? I stood up to examine them closer.

"Erich, are these pictures of Lotte?"

He nodded, stood also, though much slower than I. The rainy weather sharpened his pain. I held up the first one from the left. A beautiful young child held the hand of a lanky older boy.

"That was Lotte's first day of school. She was five years old. Her father, Friedrich, asked me to walk her. She was such a little sprite, always running and skipping. It was more herding than walking for me."

"Her hair looks like it might be blonde."

"Black and white photographs never did her justice. Her hair *was* blonde. Very similar to Hilde's, only curly."

"She looks like that American movie star, Shirley Temple."

"Only more beautiful."

Obviously, Erich was still in love with Lotte. I replaced the photo and pointed to the next. It showed a girl dressed in a frilly, white dress, a small tiara perched jauntily on her head and white tie shoes on her feet. That same impish smile.

"Her First Communion dress. She looked heavenly in it. That was when her dad started calling her his angel."

The next photo was of three girls, probably nine or ten years old. "That is her with Sofia on the left and Heidi on the right. Called themselves 'The Three Musketeers.' All through their teens they were either best friends or sworn enemies. It seemed to change daily. I used to take her side until I found that in a moment or a day they would be together again and I'd be the bad guy. Women!"

The other pictures, though intriguing, could wait. I was determined to know more about these "Three Musketeers."

"'The Musketeers' stayed true to each other regardless. I do not hear you saying the same about these three."

"Quite the contrary, Lorenz. I think that they were like any other teen girls—especially when they discovered boys. Except that Sofia and Heidi were a little more reserved. Lotte was quite the looker back then. It wasn't just me that was swarming round her. I loved her, but she never saw me as anything but an older brother. It was Hans Schuler that intrigued her.

"I watched over her the best I could. More than once I had to give Hans a good talking to when he got a little too friendly with her.

But, once I left for university he had a free hand, so to speak. I could only hope that her parents would keep her on a short leash. I wrote her as often as I could, warning her of boys, trying to convince her to leave Oberschwarzenberg and come to Vienna for school.

"It would have been unseemly for her to live with me, I know. But, I felt so strongly that she was wasting her time and her talent. Her voice, a gift from God, could have taken her far. Far away from here. Far away from Hitler and her history.

"My mother, Marta, had relatives she could have stayed with in Vienna, just as I was. They were rather well-to-do. Lotte would have been introduced into their fine society, perhaps become a professional vocalist. Maybe the opera, even. Traveling the world as a diva."

"What kept her here, Erich?"

"Inertia. The same thing that brought me back and kept me here. Kept us all here."

"Tell me more about the 'Three Musketeers.'"

"I think it would be best for you to speak with them. Hilde can make a few calls for you."

Hilde continued her habit of interrupting our conversations when she came bouncing in, her straight shoulder-length hair a wondrous shade of neither auburn nor blond that accentuated her oval face, graced with blue eyes that were sometimes greener, sometimes darker

"Uncle and Lorenz, please wash up so we can eat."

Like little boys being chastised by their mother, we rose without complaint, with me following my host. This was only the beginning of all I would do for her. But that was in the future.

4

"I still have the bruises"

Lotte's Diary
9 May 1938

Doktor Schwimmer told my parents that I am pregnant. I was a little in shock myself. I mean I "knew" I was carrying Herr Hitler's baby. But to hear the doctor declare it as a fact, WOW !

Mutter und Vater were outraged. Their angel had been soiled. They went on and on about how I'd shamed them. They shouted at the doctor that his son should marry me right now because they think he is the culprit!

Dr. Schwimmer asked me who the father was. I told him Herr Hitler. Boy, was he surprised! "Are you sure," he asked me. Yes, I'd only been with one man. I'm not sure he was more relieved it was not Erich or shocked that it was Herr Hitler.

Mutter started bawling. Vater made fists and pounded the desk. What a scene!

Vater beat me when we got home. He hit me really hard in my belly trying to kill my baby. I fell down and hugged myself to protect my baby. Mutter just stood there crying.

Luckily, I was able to protect Little Adolf. My bruises will fade, but I'll never forget. Mutter said I had to leave before everyone found out. I refused! Maybe Sofia or Heidi will take me in.

12 May 1938

My Dear,

Every morning I wake up feeling just terrible. At first I told my parents it was just the flu. But after a week they took me to see old Dr. Schwimmer. I think Mutter had already guessed but she knew Vater would be very mad so kept it to herself.

That old doctor put his hands where only your's had been and he asked the most embarrassing questions! He asked me if Erich, his son, and I had been intimate. No, I said, we are just friends. Then he asked me who is the father. I told him it was you, dear Adolf. He got red in the face, started to stutter and almost fainted. He asked how could that be. So I told him about the time we spent together after the concert. I still do not think he believes me.

My parents said I should make Erich marry me. Like everybody else they think poor Erich is the father just because we have been friends forever.

Vater was very mean. I still have the bruises! What a brute! Not gentle like you. They'll be sorry, won't they?

Mutter und Vater do not believe I am carrying your baby, your heir, the greatest child this century will ever know! My own parents! You can be sure, My Leader, I will never disown our son. You can depend on me! I am not ashamed! I am proud to be chosen by you.

Since I had not heard back from you, though, and I had no money, I had to struggle to find a place for me and Little Adolf (I'm going to name him after you, of course!). There is not much in Oberschwarzenberg as you know. Why, it's hardly a town at all, not like Berlin.

As luck would have it, Dr. Schwimmer offered me Erich's old room, now that he is in the army. It is very small but comfortable. I think he did it out of shame—he still thinks that poor Erich is the father. I'm afraid most of the town agrees.

Every time I go into Beyerlein's to shop for the doctor I hear the tongues wagging. There is always a bunch of old biddies gathered around that Gerta. She has been married for a whole year already and still no baby. Hah! I guess I showed her. She can have her old husband and his grimy little store. I've got you!

I do not like to I beg, so I won't. But, if you could please send me some money I'd appreciate it so much. Or bring me to Berlin where I can have a real doctor deliver Little Adolf.

Until I hear from you, My Darling, I will continue to do the doctor's housework and wait for your reply.

Forever Yours,

Lotte

The Kremlin, Moscow
13 August 1991

I had planned to go to Moscow in August 1991 to do some research for one of my classes. Timing was important at the Kremlin. No one knew how much longer the West would have access to their archives or how long the Russians would spend money to house and protect them. Once I had finished my official research, I began my personal journey. What little I knew of Lotte, I shared with every curator and official I met. None of them, I was not surprised, knew anything about such a person. Finally, after I pestered everyone as far as manners allowed, a clerk directed me to Sergei. She described him as, "this crazy old man that spends his days in the basement drinking and re-living his glory. He is entrusted with only the most mundane files."

Finding Sergei took some doing. I wandered through the maze and warrens of dusty documents uncovering ever more mundane people protecting ever more mundane files. It was much like those nesting Russian dolls. Every nook and cranny revealed another until I found him, not sober but not too drunk.

There he was, Sergei Androvsky, former KGB officer, and long-time archivist of the least important documents in the Kremlin.

"Mr. Androvsky, I am Professor Meyer from Heidelberg. I was told you might help me locate some letters. . ."

"Please, you must call me Sergei," he interrupted.

". . . Written by my Aunt to Adolf Hitler."

"There were bags and bags of letters."

"These were sent from Oberschwarzenberg, Austria b.…"

"Lotte Schoener?"

"You have them?"

"Da."

"Sergei, just how many of my aunt's letters are in your collection?"

He leaned back in his straight back chair balancing on the back legs. His slightly sour breath, flavored by cheap vodka from his ever-present flask, whistled through his bushy, Stalin-style mustache. Heavy lids partially occluded his rheumy eyes, ringed in red, searching like beacons through his thick glasses. After another deep sigh, he bent to his task, pawing through a cheap, cardboard box sitting between us on the heavy, steel table. He pulled out a thin bundle of letters, held together by a faded red ribbon.

"Herr Meyer, this is our whole collection."

The bundle had a tag attached, handwritten in Cyrillic, unintelligible to me, but not to the boozy archivist. He continued, "It says here," pointing to the tag, "that there are fifty-eight documents enclosed."

"All from my Aunt Lotte to Hitler?"

"Da, da, Herr Professor. They date from 1938 through 1989."

Sergei seemed to drift away, his eyes glassing over, his trembling fingers now strong and stable. Having interviewed many veterans, I assumed, and was correct, that Sergei had a story to tell, and there was nothing I could do to stop him. Not if I wanted my aunt's letters.

"Tell me, Sergei. Did you enter Berlin before or after Hitler died?" His row of battle ribbons gleamed bright on his more than ample chest. I recognized several from WWII, and one specifically given to the soldiers who took Berlin.

"You are most perceptive, Herr Professor. Yes, I was there the day the monster took his life. My regiment was the first to enter the Reich Chancellery. My platoon was assigned to gather up every scrap of paper we could find. Of course, by the time we had entered we were, how the Americans on TV say, 'feeling no pain.'

"On the ground floor we found a door with a plate announcing it as Postal Amt, the Nazi's post office. It was closed and locked, but could not withstand the force of the victorious Soviet army! One kick and we were through. The door crashed against the wall, shattering the glass panel. That was the only damage that we did that day, except for that poor little clerk we found cowering in the closet."

I raised my eyes at that.

"You have to understand, Herr Professor, we had been without the comfort of a woman for several months. We had fought through the winter, sleet, mud and bitter cold. We'd lost several comrades. And there huddled on the floor, crying like a baby, wearing a swastika armband, was the only Nazi we could find to take the brunt of our anger."

"Did you join in the rape?"

"Herr Professor, you wound me! I had my orders! The others, well, they had orders too, but the little office only needed me to collect every scrap. I wanted to take the time to study every morsel. Here we were in Hitler's post office! There were boxes of military orders, bales of civilian correspondence, and it was all *mine*."

"Did you read them?"

"I tried to read, but I could not concentrate with all the shouting and screaming. I just gathered it all together into sacks and waited for my men to finish with that poor little Nazi!"

"What happened to her?"

"Who knows? We left her in her tattered uniform curled up in the same closet she had been hiding in."

"And the documents? Were my aunt's letters there?"

Sergei held up his hand signaling that I was pushing him too fast. Damn! I needed to know while he was still mostly sober! He reached for his flask, twisted off the cap. He offered me a drink, which I refused. He proceeded to tip it to his mouth and gurgle down several ounces. His eyes closed as his mouth grinned. I was losing him!

"Sergei." He looked up quickly. "You must finish your story! I need to know!"

"Da, da. Your aunt's letters were there in a small folder. It had a label, 'Liebchen'. It contained thirty one letters, all from some little town in Austria. Naturally, I had to read them."

"Thirty-one? I thought you said there were fifty-eight!"

Again, the hands high, telling me to slow down. OK, I could take the hint.

"Sergei, please continue."

"As I said, there were thirty-one in the bundle. Most unusual that such a monster would be getting love letters. But, as I read them it became clear that your aunt, you will excuse my frank language, was crazy. She had a totally skewed view of the monster and the war. Yet, she sounded harmless. We were very busy fighting the Nazis, you understand. And after the war, we were busy re-building Europe and fighting the Cold War."

"The other twenty-seven?"

"Letters addressed to Hitler continued to arrive at the East Berlin Post Office. Naturally, they were confiscated and sent here so that I could add them to my archives."

"When did they stop?"

Sergei turned the bundle over, extracted the bottom letter, and held it up for me to see. It was postmarked November 20, 1989.

"How could that be? Tante Lotte died late the previous evening!"

Sergei said nothing, just opened the envelope, and unfolded the yellowed sheets. The date was November 19, 1989. Then he showed me the last lines.

> *"It is late and I am so very tired. I am stopping here, Mein Fuehrer.*
>
> *"You are forever in my heart, Liebchen!"*

5

"Damn them all!"

Lotte's Diary
14 May 1938

Sofia said I cannot stay with her! How dare she! We are the Three Musketeers—all for one, one for all. Well, I guess not.

I got on my knees and begged. She still said no. She would not even ask her parents for me. Why? Because I said it was Herr Hitler's baby? She called me crazy. Said I should stop covering up for Erich! Unless I told her the truth she wanted nothing more to do with me. Can you believe that?

Heidi turned her back on me right on the street. I ran up to her, swung her around so she had to look me in the eye. She answered my request with a solid, "nein," all the time looking to see who was watching. She said I was crazy, too, and that I was an embarrassment to her and the whole town.

Lot of good being a Musketeer did me. Damn them all!

———

Lotte's Diary
15 May 1938

Vater told me not to go to Mass. I reminded him it was a mortal sin. Vater pointed at my belly and said I already committed a big mortal sin.

I went anyway. Maybe I should have listened to him. Frau Zollner kicked me out of the choir. Right in front of everybody! Let's see how they get along without their best soloist! The best around. The one presented to der Fuhrer.

I loved being in the choir.

———

The home of Dr. Erich Schwimmer
Oberschwarzenberg, Austria
5 September 1991

Early Thursday morning the phone rang. Hilde was the first to wake up and make her way down stairs to the vestibule between the dining room and living room. I could just barely make out her voice, sleep-deadened as I was. After a few sentences and questions, she padded up to my room, knocking softly and calling my name, "Lorenz?" My sleep-addled brain thought she was asking to come in, to crawl under the sheets. A man can dream, can't he?

"Lorenz. The phone. It is for you."

I got up and opened the door hoping she would enter. Instead, she stood, the hall light haloing her blond hair. I'd like to say it was charming, but actually it was more Medusa-like. The light cast her whole face with shadow furthering the effect. Luckily, being smitten frosted my view with a tinge of forgiving lightness and joy.

"Wake up, Lorenz! It is long distance. Sergei from Moscow!"

I decided it could be a couple things: Sergei could be dying, he could have some news for me, or he could be drunk. Whatever it was, he deserved my attention. I'd be nowhere without him.

Hilde led me down the stairs, her rump a beacon steering me onto the shoals. Hers was a trap I did not wish to avoid. She handed me the phone and asked without saying it, "Coffee?" I nodded, grateful for every moment I could spend with her.

"Lorenz, my friend."

Sergei sounded too bright to be drunk or dying. Much better than I. Of course it was barely 7:00 a.m. here. In Moscow it was two hours later.

"Sergei. A little early in the morning for me. Can I call you back in a few hours."

"No need my friend. Just wanted to tell you I mailed a package of letters to you that a colleague discovered. I sent it via Beyerlein's. I hope that is alright." That meant the whole damned town would know, but it was a little late to complain.

"I'm sure it will be OK. When did you send it?"

"Tuesday."

"Thank you, my friend. I'll let you know when they arrive."

I followed the aroma of brewing coffee and frying bacon. This woman was sure getting to my heart.

——•——

Interview with Gerta Beyerlein at her home
Oberschwarzenberg, Austria
5 September 1991

"She thought she was so great. Called herself Frau Hitler! Can you believe it! Never married, never even engaged. Well, we called her Hitler's bitch."

I was shocked! I was not used to old ladies talking like this. "What did you say?"

"You heard me right. We called your Aunt Lotte just what she was, Hitler's bitch!"

"She did not actually call herself a bitch, did she?" I asked plaintively.

"Not exactly, but she certainly made sure everyone knew he was her," Gerta held up two fingers from each hand like quotation marks, 'lover and the father of her child.' The less kind of us called them Hitler's bitch and bastard right to their faces! But, not I."

Gerta Beyerlein, the widow of Johann and mother of Egan, was a tall, hard-edged, stork-thin "paragon of virtue," in Hilde's words. I saw and heard nothing that would convince me differently.

Hilde had been kind enough to phone Frau Beyerlein last evening to set up this interview. As the town's head gossip for several decades, she was critical to my understanding of Lotte. I had to try to get her beyond vitriol and into facts.

"Frau Beyerlein, it is obvious you and Lotte were not great friends. But, I would really appreciate you helping me understand how things were in Oberschwarzenberg before the war, back when you were growing up. If it pleases you, I will quote from you if ever I write a book. Would you like that?"

Her stormy aura started to dissipate. Her steely blue eyes softened, her mouth transformed from a frown to almost a smile. Clearly, she had an ego that needed stroking.

"Professor, that would be most wonderful."

Relaxing into her over-stuffed leather chair she said, "I apologize for calling Lotte Hitler's b-i-i," her hand raced to her mouth as surprise replaced humor in her eyes. "Please forgive me, Herr Professor." To break the tension she offered me a cup of tea. Not my first choice, but I did not want to offend her. With a nod from me, she rose, creaking like an old garden gate, and strode through a door that I presumed led to the kitchen.

In her absence, I stood and wandered around the parlor. Chintz curtains, a little faded and tattered, braced every window. Blue, painted walls were punctuated by black and white photos of her family and primitive watercolors of local scenery. The carpet was a faded gray background with faded roses surrounded by faded greenery.

Hearing her approaching footsteps, I quickly seated myself. She brought in our tea in what I suspected was her fine china. She handed me a cup and took one for herself.

"Frau Beyerlein, just relax and tell me about your life here."

Leaning forward in her chair, she began, "Before the war, Oberschwarzenberg was a very quiet little hamlet, not much smaller than it is right now. My parents were farmers from up near Donabauer, above the river." (The Weissbach River runs through Oberschwarzenberg at a lazy pace most of the year. That changes with the Spring melt of the snow on Plockenstein, the mountain that towers over it.)

"I was the youngest of three, with two older brothers. I guess you could say I was a little spoiled. My mother made sure I was not forced to help around the farm like my brothers. I just stayed at home, played in the yard and went to town with her when we needed things like tea and sugar.

"Every day, including Sunday, my father and my brothers, Waldemar and Ludwig, rose at dawn to begin their day. My mother was up before them, fixing their breakfast. I got up well after the sun had begun its march across the sky. Mother made me my own meal and served it to me on my own plate."

"Why did she treat you so special?"

"She wanted to make sure I did not grow old before my time, like she did."

"Didn't your brothers resent your special treatment?"

"They never said anything."

She yawned and looked at her mantel clock. There was much more I needed to know, but I sensed she was wrung out from our chat and a return engagement would be better than forging on right now. Besides, Hilde awaited me.

————

Having bid Frau Beyerlein, "Auf Wiedersehen," I walked back to Erich's for a late lunch with Hilde. The afternoon sun painted the homes and few businesses with a golden halo. I spent a few moments in front of Beyerlein's Gemischtwarenhandlung (general merchandise store). It was not large, and its paint was flaking. The three steps up to the porch had seen better decades. The weathered wood steps were cracked and gray with age. I would not have trusted them to hold some of the more *zaftig hausfraus*.

I figured I had a few minutes and should buy some sort of gift to repay Erich's hospitality. Perhaps I could find something worthy of Hilde, too. So, up the steps I went, listening to every groan, hoping to not make a spectacle of myself. The porch was crowded with two benches—one on either side of the chipped white door.

Pushing through, I entered another era. The walls, ceiling and floor were all crammed with merchandise. Scythes, crocks, and drindls competed with televisions, microwaves and blue jeans. And between these opposites were two long rows of groceries. Some things I could identify, many had labels in languages other than German. I hoped I could find Erich a bottle of wine with an understandable label and good vintage.

I wandered down the aisles amazed at the variety and the dust. At the far back, behind a counter piled high with cloth, cases of beer, and pantyhose, stood Egan Beyerlein, proprietor. It was no stretch to believe he was Gerta's son, given his lanky build. Apparently all he got from his father was this store.

"Need something?" he inquired.

"Do you have wine?"

He pointed to a shelf I had passed earlier. There at knee level were a few dusty bottles. Bending down, I rubbed the dust off the labels with my hankie and found a decent Reisling. The seal looked good and there was no sediment. I wiped off the rest of the bottle and started to look for Hilde's gift. Retracing my steps to see what else had been missed I located the perfume on a very top shelf nestled between bottles of bleach and boxes of cold cereal. Picking out a scent would be easy seeing as how there was only one to choose from.

I walked the gauntlet down his dusty aisles with my purchases arriving at what passed for a post office, about one square meter of Egan's counter backed by a wall of cubbyholes stuffed with mail. Of course, being a visitor I had no box.

"Herr Beyerlein, you have a package for me?"

"And you would be?"

"Lorenz Meyer. I am staying with Erich Schwimmer."

"Mother said you were coming to see her today."

"Do you have a package for me?

"Where would it be from?"

"A friend in Moscow."

"Are you a Communist, Herr Meyer?"

"I am a college professor. If you would not mind?"

Egan bent at the knees, rummaged under the counter, before standing. "I believe this is yours."

Slower than the flow of the Weissbach River, he handed it across.

I placed my purchases on the counter prepared to pay Heidelberg prices. Surprise! Looking up from the butcher paper serving as his calculator, he stared at my handful of money, grinned and quoted an amount almost double of what I expected. Like magic, two or three townspeople appeared to watch the outsider get taken. Vacillating between making a scene and taking my medicine. I opted for the latter.

The golden glow dulled as I continued my journey. A few people nodded in greeting but kept on their way. Nearing Erich's, I saw Hilde out raking the yard. Even from a distance, she looked good. The golden glow brightened considerably. She looked up, saw me and waved. I was really beginning to like this girl. I handed her the perfume.

"Do I smell that bad?" she chirped with a smile.

She took both the perfume and the wine into the house. I followed enjoying the view. "Supper'll be ready in an hour, but there is a little lunch left."

"I guess I'll wait for supper. On second thought what are my choices?"

"Lunch was meatloaf sandwiches and cold sauerkraut. Supper is roast beef, potatoes and onions, squash soup and strudel for dessert."

"Supper it is. Where is Erich?"

"Finishing his nap, I presume."

"Guess I'll just stay here and watch you cook."

Grinning, she said, "Suit yourself."

And I did.

Only later did I open Sergei's package.

6

"I long to be in your arms again."

12 June 1938
Mein Fuhrer,

My friend, Erich, the doctor's son came back from Vienna for a short visit. He, too, is amazed I am carrying your child.

When first I told my parents, they accused me of being with Erich. How could they think such a thing? That I would give myself to someone so inferior to you?

Don't get me wrong. Erich became a doctor just like his dad. And he's in the army. It is just that we have been friends forever. He could never compete with you.

Little Adolf makes himself known every morning when I get sick. Dr. Schwimmer says this will pass in a short while. I can only hope. But, my lover, it is a small price to pay to be the mother of your son.

I long to be in your arms again. To feel your strong body warm in my embrace. How I miss you. Life in Oberschwarzenberg is so very drab. Could I please come to Berlin? If even just for a few days?

Your Lotte

———❦———

Lotte's Diary
14 June 1938

How blessedly ironic! Mutter und Vater kicked me out of their house. But, then they have had to come to work everyday in Paul's *house, now my home!*

I can see that Vater is not amused. He says no more to me than necessary, which is not much as he works outside most of the time.

Mutter, on the other hand, works in <u>my</u> house and she has come around a little bit. She asks how I am feeling and offers home remedies for my morning sickness.

Paul tried a few times to make Vater take me back or at least be friendly, but as they say, "You can always tell an Austrian but you cannot tell them much!" I think once he sees his grandson that he will be kinder. Who will be able to resist Little Adolf when no one escapes from his dad's charm?

The home of Dr. Erich Schwimmer
Oberschwarzenberg, Austria
5 September 1991, late evening

I sat at the desk in Lotte's room and opened the first of the letters provided by Sergei.

Büro der Oberinspektor
Deutschen Nationalen Post
No. 12 Wilhelmstrasse
Berlin, Germany

Gauleiter Hermann Strauss
Protectorate of Austria
38A Viktorstrasse
Vienna, Austria

16 May, 1938

I am writing you on behalf of Deputy Reichsfuhrer Bormann regarding a spurious claim against der Fuhrer made by one of your citizens. Normally, one of my assistants would handle this matter, but apparently this is serious enough that I need to get involved. As if I have the time!

My office is deluged by letters from all over the world mailed to

Herr Hitler. Herr Bormann's people are charged with sorting through this Alp every day. Only a few are forwarded to der Fuhrer. Most are answered by secretaries and other functionaries, if at all. The few that are threatening or otherwise inappropriate are forwarded to my office.

Thus I am contacting you to investigate this Lotte Schoener of Oberschwarzenberg. I've included a carbon of the copy I had transcribed from her longhand letters.

As you can see, she makes severe and possibly embarrassing statements regarding the paternity of her unborn child. Herr Bormann confided that der Fuhrer and this girl were together earlier this Spring in Austria. He assures me, however, that other than tea and conversation, there was no possibility that she is carrying his child.

Nonetheless, I charge you with the responsibility of determining the validity, if any, of her claim. Further, and this is directly from Bormann, you are to do whatever necessary to see that this matter is settled — and does not become an issue in the future.

Yours,
Bruno Stockmeyer

Gauleiter Hermann Strauss
Protectorate of Austria
38A Viktorstrasse
Vienna, Austria

SS Sub-Gauleiter Spiekermann
412 Archduke Ferdinandstrasse
Linz, Austria

25 May, 1938

Wolfgang,

As I told you last week, you must get on this right away. We need to know if this Lotte Schoener is as crazy as she sounds. Orders from far above have charged us to investigate and handle this matter with the greatest speed.

Go there at once. Phone me upon your return. Then send me your report.

This letter serves as all the authority you will need.

Hermann

———◆———

I could not believe that my Tante Lotte had been investigated by the Nazis! Had Berlin really taken her seriously?

I had to share this with someone. I knocked on Hilde's bedroom door. Muffled by the wood, and possibly sleep, she responded.

"Yes?"

"Hilde, are you awake? I have to talk to you."

"Give me a minute."

Scraping noises, rushed footsteps, and squeaking closet door hinges filled my five minute wait. How could anyone take so long to get out of bed and answer the door? Turns out I had a lot to learn about women, and especially, Hilde.

Her door opened slowly. Shyly, if a piece of wood could feel such an emotion. She was backlit by her table lamp crowning her hair with a golden halo. She wore a dressing gown, a very short one, that lured my eyes to take a tour far south of her eyes and smile. Every centimeter of her 1.87 meters attracted my vision like cheap iron to a magnet. She didn't just look attractive, she smelled enticing. Her perfume zapped up my nose numbing my amygdala and flooding my prefrontal cortex with dopamine.

For the uninitiated, I was in love.

In retrospect, I'm pretty sure she knew the effect she was having.

"Lorenz, what is it?"

I was working hard to re-engage my professorial brain. I was sure there was a good reason for knocking on her door. There must have been. I'm not the sort that goes round interrupting people's sleep.

"Lorenz, are you feeling alright?"

"Uh...."

I regularly mesmerized classes of post adolescents with my oratorical skills. With Hilde, I was tongue-tied.

"Come in and sit down. I'll get you some schnapps."

She turned and I followed her scent into a near-spotless room. She directed me to a hard-backed chair near her bed, still warm from her body. Returning, she offered me the glass and watched as I sipped a little.

"You must tell me what is wrong," she insisted as she sat across from me, folding her legs under her, perched on her bed.

Without thinking, I gave up. Rational thought lost out to emotional mush.

"Hilde, you certainly smell ... good."

She had the good grace to not laugh out loud, or act shocked. She smiled and the room was bathed in an opalescence. Her cheeks blushed like a late-season Winesap.

"Is that why you interrupted my sleep? To tell me about my smell? "

All my advanced degrees and I'm mumbling like the village idiot.

To her credit, Hilde took pity on me. Obviously, talking was not my strength tonight. Whereas, following her lead was pretty easy.

"Come sit with me on the bed, professor."

———

I awoke in my own bed with no idea how I got there. I vaguely remembered some letters, going to Hilde's room, then sitting on her bed.

A knock at my door and a cheerful, "Lorenz?"

"Come in, Hilde."

She entered looking as good in her house dress as she had last night in her gown. "I will leave you to your reading."

I picked up Sergei's package to inspect the rest.

SS Sub-Gauleiter Spiekermann
412 Archduke Ferdinandstrasse
Linz, Austria

Gauleiter Hermann Strauss
Protectorate of Austria
38A Viktorstrasse
Vienna, Austria

7 June, 1938

Report regarding Lotte Schoener:

Lotte Schoener is the eighteen-year-old daughter of Hanna and Friedrich Schoener. Both appear to be loyal. He is a veteran. They are both employed by the town's doctor.

Lotte is pregnant. I confirmed this with Dr. Schwimmer, also a veteran. He has taken her in because her parents are ashamed of her. No one in Oberschwarzenberg accepts her assertion that der Fuhrer is the father of her unborn child. Yet, she persists in calling it "Young Adolf" and sending letters to Berlin.

I spoke to her for over an hour. She is convinced of her little truth, even telling me when and where she met der Fuhrer. The town priest, Father Sohn, confirms the meeting, but violently disagrees with her assertion.

Her own parents told me that the culprit is one Captain Erich Schwimmer. They were childhood friends and clearly things got a little out of hand before he left. The whole town seems to agree.

I suggest that I continue my investigation. I may have developed an informant, one of Lotte Schoener's friends, who may be of great assistance.

I fear, Hermann, we may have much to fear from this girl.

Heil Hitler,

Wolfgang

Gauleiter Hermann Strauss
Protectorate of Austria
38A Viktorstrasse
Vienna, Austria

Büro der Oberinspektor (Office of Inspector General)
Deutschen Nationalen Post (German National Post Office)
No. 12 Wilhelmstrasse
Berlin, Germany

14 June, 1938

Sir:

Regarding the matter of Lotte Schoener. We have determined that she is probably not a credible person, but could be a threat to der Fuhrer. We intend to maintain a vigilant investigation.

Heil Hitler,

Hermann

Gerta Beyerlein's home
Oberschwarzenberg, Austria
6 September 1991

I returned to Gerta Beyerlein's home. I usually dislike grumpy people, but she intrigued me.

She opened the door before I could knock. Her angular frame was clothed in a blue wool skirt that contrasted nicely with a sunny yellow blouse. Her blue hair hung free. Quite a change from yesterday.

We resumed our seats surrounded by the aroma of tea already poured. We both took sips, replaced our cups and looked at each other. Then she spoke.

"Professor, I am not proud of the way we treated your Lotte. You must understand that those were hard times. Many of us lost our bearings, doing and saying things we would live to regret.

"When Lotte was growing up, she lived on the wrong side of the street. Her life was much poorer and harder than mine, than most of my friends, than anyone in the whole area.

"Her father never had a real job." She read the protest in my eyes. "Oh sure he worked for the doctor but we all knew that was charity. Something to do with the first war. He did little except brag on his daughter and her wonderful voice. It was unseemly for him who had so little to spend so much of his time championing Lotte.

"Everyone knew I sang better. I'd even had lessons!"

"Her diary and Erich both agreed that she, indeed, had a great voice," I said. "She must have been quite talented to have been presented to Hitler."

"I did not say she could not sing, only that her father made too much of it. And after she came back from Hitler, even Herr Schoener changed his tune!"

"What was Lotte Schoener like before Hitler?"

"Before she became Hitler'...." She paused for a sip of her tepid tea and forgiveness. "Again, I apologize Herr Professor. Old habits die hard.

"Lotte was one of the most beautiful girls around. Even I had to concede that to her! She was a strawberry blonde, curls all over the place, framing a roundish pixie face and a ready smile. What did she have to be so happy about?

"She had very few friends. We made sure of that!" Another sip of tea and another change of mood. "I meant to say that she just did not fit in with my group. She did have a few friends, Heidi and Sofia. You should talk to them. They knew her better than the rest of us. And, of course, Erich paid her a lot of attention. But, you knew that. They were thick, those two."

"Meaning ...?" I asked.

"Meaning that where ever you found one of them you usually found the other.

"And that was wrong?"

"More like most unusual, I should say. They stuck up for each other like they were from the same family." Again, she saw protest in my glance. "You must understand how things were here!"

"That is why I am here, Frau Beyerlein."

"Well, yes you are. So let me continue, please."

I nodded. Now I was getting somewhere I thought.

"Things were very bad here after the war. . ."

"World War I?" I asked.

"That is what I want to tell you about," she snapped.

Again, I gave her a nod.

"My parents told me that, unlike our German cousins, we had enough to eat, but our central government was gone. Our village was afloat in a sea of uncertainty."

I couldn't help thinking, they must have read my thesis!

"Even up here in the mountains, things were not clear. We had to rely on our Burgermeister to keep things under control. We still had our church, our farms, and homes. Johann's father had his store— the center of our community." Now she was on a roll. Her eyes got brighter as she recalled those times through her parent's eyes. "People met there daily to get their mail, perhaps read a week-old newspaper, and try to make some sense of the world. The few war survivors told what little they knew of the outside world, but for the most part we just kept on living as we had, hoping we could survive.

"The '20's flowed into the '30's. I was getting old enough to see for myself what was happening in Germany. Chaos! We hoped their problems would not get past the Gegenbach River and bedevil us. Of course, that was not to be."

"Did Oberschwarzenberg lose many men in the first war?"

"For such a small area, I think we did. The churchyard has graves of over a dozen of our young men, mostly boys. My mother lost her brother, my Uncle Xavier. He was going to be a poet, such a gentle soul.

"Even after, the veterans seemed to have a very hard time, except for my Johann, of course! He got right to work in his daddy's store. It was like he had never gone away.

"The others returned in body but not in spirit." Downcast eyes and a shamed tone. "Us kids called them ghosts, even though they were our fathers, brothers and uncles.

"The only blessing that war brought was the arrival of Dr. Schwimmer just in time to deliver me." I started to laugh until she added, "Unfortunately, he brought along his Jew wife."

7

"Everything was fine until the circus came to town"

12 July 1938
My Darling One,

Great news! The morning sickness has finally run its course. No more stale biscuits! I got so tired of those dry as dirt things. Every time I went to buy more I had to put up with Gerta's stare! How I wish there was another store. But at least I am a true woman while she remains barren. Serves her right!

Things sure have not changed much here. They never do in Oberschwarzenberg. I read in the doctor's "Wein Gazette" of your great triumphs. The world is beginning to know what I already do—that you, My Leader, are the greatest man alive. And that you were sent to deliver us from the Jews and the communists and all the others who are not like us! Even those old Beyerlein biddies say they are impressed by you. And, as you know, they are a tough group to get any praise out of.

Little Adolf is getting stronger. I am convinced that I can feel him growing inside me everyday. I have begun 'showing,' as the rustics say. Only the memory of our blessed afternoon makes it possible for me to survive in this horrid place.

Before Erich left, he told anybody who would listen that he was proud to be an Austrian and a German just like you. Erich believes in you even though his mother was a Jew. He is not responsible for his *mother, is he? She is dead now, so it does not matter. Does it?*

I go to Mass every Sunday just to show people I am not ashamed. I sit on the aisle so everyone can see me, especially that old futz of a priest we have. No one sits with me.

Even Heidi and Sofia have abandoned me.

I'm sure that, if I named Erich as the father, things would be much easier for me. But I refuse to live a lie. My baby is yours and so am I!

I hate to ask, but if you could send a few Reichmarks it would help so much. The doctor tries but he doesn't have much either. I don't know what I'll do when I cannot wear my few clothes any longer. I know the women here will not help me.

I fear your son will be cold without blankets and sheets to warm his tiny body.

If money is too much to ask for, perhaps you could send a bolt of cloth or a few of your old shirts. I'm not much at sewing but the doctor will help me.

I have so little that even the postage for these letters is a burden. If you can't though, I'll make out somehow.

Yours forever and forever,

Lotte

━━◆━━

The home of Dr. Erich Schwimmer
Oberschwarzenberg, Austria
6 September 1991

"I walked today to the cemetery," I said. "I saw a headstone for only one Schluckbier, a woman named Lena. What is the story behind that?"

Erich and I are back in his parlor in our appointed seats, talking.

"To tell you about Lena is to tell you about my mother, Marta," he responded.

"If it is not too painful I'd like to know."

"First, my mother fell in love and married a Gentile who went to war leaving her pregnant, then having to raise me on her own for two years. My father, Paul, came back from the war wounded, unable to love her like he should or to father more children. Then he got it in his mind to leave Vienna based on a letter from his army pal. She had to turn her back on her culture, her synagogue, parents and extended family and friends. In short, her entire life. She knew no one in Oberschwarzenberg, and other than the Schoeners, she had no friends. In her isolation, she focused all her energy, aspirations and hope upon Lotte and me. That pretty much sums up her life. Sounds dull doesn't it?"

"Surely there must have been some excitement here."

"A town on the way to nowhere, Oberschwarzenberg, rarely had visitors beyond the kith and kin of its residents. That changed on the second of April, 1928 when the Schicker's Zirkus Bayerische arrived. It was traveling from Germany to Linz for a week of performances, then on to Salzburg, and with luck, Vienna. Where before, they would be taking a one-to-two-day train ride, they were now reduced to traveling the dusty roads at the slow plodding pace of the old days. The circus had never really made big money but it had managed to travel in a little luxury. Now, in these troubled times, it rarely made enough to feed the people and animals."

His eyes aged in reverse until he was barely a teen. "Imagine the excitement, the stunning wonder of it all, when eleven wagons—all painted in cardinal scarlet, sunset violet, and new-mown-hay green, and decorated with paintings of clowns, tigers, and trapeze artists— were pulled up the hill coming into town by big brutes of horses. Except for one, if you can believe it, that an elephant was harnessed to!"

"The news of it raced up the street until it reached our home. My father and Lotte's father were out on rounds near Gut, almost twenty kilometers away, so our mothers took us out to see what was happening. The dust cloud blocked the sun, the noise silenced the sparrows.

"Lotte and I looked at each other. We'd never seen anything like this before. No one else in town had either, except for Marta. She knew. The circus was an annual event in Vienna.

"I kept running out into the street to get a better view. Lotte, barely eight, tried to follow me, but she was restrained by our mothers—one holding each arm.

"The creaking of the wheels and the plop-plop-plop of the horse's hooves grew until they reached our house. As the first wagon neared, it stopped! At our house!

"The horses snorted and stomped. A woman big as a house stared out the side, giving Lotte a case of the giggles. Me, I just stood and stared. "

The driver yelled down, 'Is this the doctor's home?'

Mother nodded, the rest of us silent.

The driver leapt down brushing the dust from his clothes, stomping his feet to warm them. He repeated, "Is this the doctor's home?"

Mother regained the use of her voice. "Yes."

"Is he in?"

"No, he is out on rounds."

"When will he return?"

"Before supper. Why do you ask?"

"One of our performers, Lena the Fat Lady, is sick. Back up the road a piece a farmer said Oberschwarzenberg had a doctor. Might we wait until he returns?"

I answered for the whole town and shouted, "YES!"

"The Burgermeister, with a worried face, and Johann Beyerlein, a money-making glint in his eyes, rushed over. Mother introduced them. This was too big an event for them to remember they didn't like each other.

"The Burgermeister quickly ordered the wagons to move off the road and into the meadow bordering the church. Father Sohn would be unhappy, but wasn't he usually? Beyerlein made sure Herr Schicker knew he could depend on Beyerlein's store to supply all they needed—for a price, of course. While the men dithered, my mother helped the huge sick woman into our parlor.

"Lotte, her mother and I, like most of the children and adults, followed the wagons down past the church. Father Sohn was standing head to head with the Burgermeister in front of the church. Both men's faces were beet-red, arms flailing, with only Johann to separate them.

I still get excited every time I think of those days. I was busy watching the circus when much of what I am going to tell you occurred. All I know is what my father and Lotte's mother told me."

———

This is the story as Erich heard it:

"Can I get you some tea?" Marta asked the obese Lena. She was a good hostess even if she had few opportunities to show it.

"Yes, thank you. It might help settle my stomach. Better make that two cups."

Lena gazed down and patted her whale-like abdomen, "I've got a lot to settle," she chuckled. Marta gasped, then joined in the laughter.

"Here you go." Marta handed Lena a large steaming mug. The two women sipped, each searching for something in common to base a conversation on. Finally, Marta moved into medical mode having helped Paul several times. "You are not feeling well?"

"It is just a cold or something. Herr Schicker worries too much. Yesterday, I felt much worse, couldn't keep a thing down. At least today I can drink a little."

A few hours later, Paul finished his examination of Lena. He pronounced, "You appear to just have the flu. You'll feel much better tomorrow."

"That is a relief. I lost my mother to the Spanish flu after the war. Even now, we hear reports that it has re-appeared in Germany."

"If you'd like, you can stay here for the night and I'll examine you tomorrow just to make sure."

Thus Lena Schluckbier, the circus fat lady, spent the night in Erich's home. Erich was sent to sleep at Lotte's, so that Lena could have his room. Marta, ever the good hostess, saw to Lena's every need.

Lena complained throughout the long evening that she was feeling worse, that the doctor's powders were not helping. She was feverish and chilled. The physical effects of the Spanish Flu—though similar to those of the seasonal flu—could be quite severe: abnormally high fever that might lead to extreme fatigue, fainting or coma, terrible stomach upset, extended episodes of nausea, vomiting, or diarrhea, and chronic respiratory difficulties which could lead to the development of deadly pneumonia.

Marta stayed with her through the night covering her with a quilt or sponging her heated flesh with cool water. Around 4 am, Lena became quiet and Marta fell asleep confident that she was over the worst of it.

At 7 am, Paul arose to check on his wife and his patient. Lena was not breathing! She was cold to the touch. Paul pulled the quilt over her face, woke Marta and walked her back to their bedroom.

Marta asked Paul, "What did she die of?"

"I fear it was the Spanish flu," Paul replied.

"We must get her out of our house immediately! We must clean the room and burn her bedding! I'll not put Erich at risk!"

"I'll need to see Herr Schicker. We are going to need some help getting her out of here."

And that is how Lena Schluckebier, the circus fat lady, came to be buried in Oberschwarzenberg. But that is not the end of Erich's sad tale. Marta contracted the flu and died on Thursday. Lena and Marta were Oberschwarzenberg's only flu victims this time.

The townspeople, not to their credit, said it was God's judgment because Marta was a Jew. Even Father Sohn agreed. It did not help that Good Friday was the next day, with Easter on Sunday, or that Catholics still blamed the Jews for Jesus's death. Rather ironic, really. The whole cross thing, dying for everyone's sins, rising up to heaven, etc. The whole Christian religious system depends on someone having to kill Jesus. Seems like they should be thankful. Without the Jews, they would all be going to a synagogue.

Following Rome's dictate, Father Sohn refused her burial.

————

Erich's eyes were sprinkling his cheeks. Hilde arose quickly and got him a glass of water and two pills. He dozed off as Hilde told me to come with her. I followed her to the kitchen enjoying the view as always.

"It is always hard for him to talk about her. He and Marta were very close. She was, perhaps, a little over-protective, but she felt she was in hostile country. She is buried out back."

8

"Who is to help your son if you do not?"

12 August 1938
My Leader, My Lover

Your son continues to grow right on schedule. Dr. Schwimmer says my pregnancy is about half over, and both of us are doing well. I am not so tired as I was last month.

This summer has been peaceful here in Oberschwarzenberg. We know so little of the outside world, only what we read in the doctor's paper. Paul is the only person in the whole village to get one. Plus, he has a shortwave radio that I get to listen to sometimes. I especially enjoy hearing your speeches! Your voice is as enchanting on the radio as it was that spring afternoon when we first met.

Vater is still angry and will not talk to me. He even crosses our dusty little rutted road to avoid me. Mutter, though, is starting to take an interest in her grandson. Just yesterday there was a bundle of clothes on our doorstep. I'm sure I remember seeing her wearing some of them. And they are her size so they should last me until Little Adolf is born.

Everyone in town still believes that Erich is the father. I think he is scared to come home for a visit.

How silly these people are, blaming poor Erich when they should be proud that one of their own is carrying your heir! Poor Erich could never father such a child as this. Only you! You were my first and only!

The Beyerlein biddies keep on talking when I go to the store.

Heidi came over last week for a talk and a stroll. We both walked but she did most of the talking. But that was OK. I miss her so much.

Perhaps, I'll hear from Sofia, also. I sure hope so.

I'm working up the nerve to ask Father Sohn about baptizing Little Adolf. I hope that is OK?

The Burgermeister came to see me. He thinks that he can convince Erich to take responsibility by writing to his commanding officer. I explained to him that Erich is not the father and to leave him alone. Around here, the Burgermeister sees to it that even the most worthless father provides for his children, or at least his family does.

Who is to help your son if you do not? Is there any of your family I can ask for help?

I think Erich suffers more than I. His own father and the whole village still think he is responsible. I guess that until Young Adolf is born there is no way to convince these people. I'm sure Little Adolf will look just like his father. Then everybody will know for sure!

Should I write to your supporters in Linz for help or will you send me some money for your son? Even better, bring us to Berlin to be with you!

Lotte

———

The home of Erich Schwimmer
Oberschwarzenberg, Austria
7 September 1991
After Supper

Once again, Erich and I are sitting in his parlor. Lotte's seat remains empty but I sense that she is near. I start the conversation on a topic I want to know more about.

"So, Erich, your father was injured in the first World War?"

"You know, Lorenz, like many veterans he talked little of those days. When I returned from my war we talked about much but never his wound.

"I think, however, it was a wound that went far deeper than any bullet could reach. I'm not sure he ever really healed. Whatever it was, he took it to his grave."

I changed the subject. "Help me, Erich, to understand your relationship with Lotte. It is obvious that you cared for her deeply letting her live with you all those years, having a chair just for her, yet you two never married."

"I was always," raising his fingers as quotation marks, "her 'big brother.' I was almost six years older. While her parents were working for my family I took care of her. I was there for her first crawl, her first step, her first words. I changed her diapers, taught her the ABC's, how to count, her colors. Everything!"

Quiet, thick as a cloud, surrounded us, but Hilde saved the day. Thank God she was a good eavesdropper. She moused her way into the room, sat in Lotte's chair, and talked to Erich in a voice the tone of good scotch. She carried a thick sheaf of papers in her left hand.

"Uncle Erich, let Lorenz read about how your parents came to live here."

To me, she said, "Talking about his parents often upsets him. Years ago, just after I came here, I asked him to write about his life, his family and Lotte. This is the result."

She held up the bundle, neatly tied together with a green ribbon. "I am not a writer, but I did my best, given that I had to base it on Uncle's memories."

She handed me the bundle as Erich nodded his assent.

1315 Schopenhauerstrasse, Apt. 3B
Vienna, Austria
3 February 1919

"We must leave here," Dr. Paul Schwimmer told his wife, Marta. "We must leave right now!"

"How can you say such a thing? My whole life—our friends, our family—our whole life is here in Vienna!"

Marta and Paul were seated in the dining room of their tiny, two bedroom apartment near the medical school. It had been their home since their marriage in 1914. The furnishings reflected the fact that Paul was a poor doctor. Just recently discharged in November, and still a little unsure of himself as he recovered from a two-year-old wound, he had yet to establish his practice. His parents were not in a position to help the couple, and Marta stiffly refused to ask her parents for help. She had spent too many years trying to become independent of them.

"You, my dear wife," Paul said softly, taking a stab at being conciliatory, "just do not understand."

"I understand much has changed since you got back from the war," Marta challenged. "You've changed, Vienna has changed. Everything is different. Yet, it is my home. I will not move!"

An unwelcome silence settled between husband and wife. Huffing and puffing in unison, glaring at each other, never actually seeing each other, they sat, the table a no-man's-land. Seconds morphed into minutes, breathing slowed, tempers cooled. Finally, Marta said, "Talk quieter, my love. You'll wake Erich."

Paul nodded, unsure of his ability to talk right now.

"His whole life is here," she continued. "All his friends, all his cousins. His grandparents. Everything he knows is here in Vienna. What can be so important that we have to leave?"

She put her hand on his arm and rubbed it lightly. "I know it has not been easy for you, but the war was not kind to us who stayed home, either." Her attempt to gentle him, almost in an erotic way, only served to fan the flames of his anger.

"Have you forgotten what the Communists did to me, to us? Now they are here in Vienna! Never will I live with such beasts!"

After World War I, Austria had been proclaimed a republic. At the Vienna city parliament elections of May 4, 1919, the Social

Democratic Party gained an absolute majority. The city underwent many changes. Refugees from Austrian Galicia (now West Ukraine) had settled there. Many former soldiers of the Imperial and Royal Army came to stay, while many former Imperial-Royal government ministry officials returned to their native lands. The middle classes, many of whom had bought war bonds, which were now worthless, found their families plunged into poverty. Flats were overcrowded, and diseases such as tuberculosis, the Spanish flu, and syphilis raged. The Social Democrats were hardly communists, yet this was a time of extremes, black and white thinking and action.

"My darling Paul, you know that you are still my husband, the father of my son, the greatest love of my life."

Paul stood abruptly, turned from her towards the window flooded with the setting sun. Marta rose and moved to embrace him from the back, just like she used to do before the war.

"Paul, you must talk to me. I want to know what is wrong."

Paul turned into her embrace, holding her tightly as he did when they had fallen in love. For the first time in two years he felt the stirring of love, or at least the memory of it, as she melted into his embrace. In his mind he was still a whole man, young and capable, a skilled physician fresh out of college, claiming Marta Rosenberg as his bride. He was swallowed by the memories of that time so long ago, just five years ago, a lifetime.

A memory surfaced like an ugly sulfur bubble in a volcanic cauldron, its heat and stench sweeping away the loving memories. Paul's arms dropped to his side, his body going stiff. Marta felt him drifting away from her, back to the war, back to July 1917.

She still remembered every word, every letter of the telegram that heralded her new life, one she never hoped for, never expected, never wanted—but accepted. Her darling Paul, one of Vienna's finest young doctors, had been injured in an artillery barrage in Galicia in what became known as the Kerensky Offensive, Russia's last WW I assault.

Initial Russian success was the result of powerful bombardment, such as Austrian troops had never witnessed before on the Russian front. The Austrians did not prove capable of resisting this bombardment, and a broad gap in the lines allowed the Russians to advance without encountering any resistance. But the German forces proved to be much harder to root out, and their stubborn resistance resulted in heavy casualties amongst the attacking Russians. Their advance collapsed altogether by July 16. On July 18 the Germans and Austro-Hungarians counterattacked, meeting little resistance and advancing through Galicia and Ukraine as far as the Zbruch River. The Russian lines were broken on July 20, and by July 23, 1917, the Russians had retreated about 240 kilometers.

Now after all her efforts to help him recover his virility, he seemed to want to destroy her world, uproot her and her son, and separate them from all they knew. "Paul, tell me why we need to leave. I'm just a woman," she said in a tone guaranteed to get a response, "who does not understand all this political business."

"Dammit, Marta. You know you are smarter than me. Your father teaches at the university. We attended college together. Don't act like you don't understand."

"But, Paul, I do not. Why now, all of a sudden, do you want to leave our home? Was it that letter?"

Paul had wondered when she would bring it up. It was the letter, of course. But so much more. Memories of what had happened, things he had done. Things he had almost forgotten. That damned letter had changed everything.

Paul reached into his coat pocket and removed the envelope. He handed it to her as if it was a papyrus from an Egyptian tomb. She noted it had been opened gently. Inside was a single sheet of cheap paper. She held it up to the window letting the setting sun's feeble rays limn out her fate.

Paul, my friend

Good news. My wife, yes I am married, Hannah is with child. I am to be a father!

I vowed I would never hold you to your promise. After all, in war people say and do things they later regret.

There was no job for me when I got home. Hannah was waiting for me. Even with the way I am she continues to love me.

You remember all the stories I told you about Oberschwarzenberg? Well, they were all true. You must come and visit!

Friedrich

9

"He is going to be such a good little Nazi."

12 September 1938

My Darling, Adolf

I wish you could feel what your son is doing to me. Every day he kicks his feet out like he is one of your goose-stepping stormtroopers. He is going to be such a good little Nazi.

All day long we talk together—well actually I do the talking but I know he is listening. I tell him what a great leader his Vater is, and how you are working so hard to make the world a better place for him to grow up in and to rule.

Little Adolf is such a bright child just like you must have been. I'm teaching him his ABCs. Already he can count up to one hundred.

My Dear, I get so lonesome without you. I know you are busy but if you could see me for even a day it would be a dream come true. Then everyone will know that we are in love. We can go on a picnic if the weather is good. You could feel your son. I just know you are going to love him as much as I love you.

Faithful to you only,

Lotte

—◆—

The home of Dr. Erich Schwimmer
Oberschwarzenberg, Austria
7 September 1991

I looked up from the yellowing sheets to ask, "I'm not sure I understand, Erich. How did that letter get your parents to move here?"

"Schoener and my father had been comrades in the war. That line about not finding work was a cry for help now that his wife was pregnant. The vow was the bond. If either asked for help the other was duty-bound to help."

I continued reading as Hilde described Erich's suppositions about his father's time in battle.

Galicia
15 July 1917

"Mein Gott, that was a close one!" Friedrich Schoener was more interested in the barrage than he was in assisting Dr. Paul Schwimmer.

"Schoener, help me, please." Paul struggled to cut the pants leg off a young soldier, writhing in pain.

Schoener turned from the medical tent's flaps, recalled to his duty and friend, seeing the bloody straw floor, surmounted by the stench of blood, guts and disinfectant. With a last look at the real war—out there—that he was being spared—except for the endless river of wounded and dying boys passing through his tent.

He grasped both of the soldier's feet as another orderly, Frahm, held the arms. With practiced ease, Paul finished his cut, spread the pants, exposing a gaping, dirty, plum-red wound.

"That is not such a bad one, is it," Schoener asked as he did thirty or forty times every day. The medics never saw the really bad ones—who died before getting medical help—or the minor injuries who were treated closer to the front.

Schoener had started the war like many peasants—a horse man. The Austrian army depended on beasts and men. Of the two, it seemed the generals valued the horses more. Many soldiers spent their careers as grooms, drovers, country vets and go-fers rather than fighting the enemy, the Russians.

With peasant guile and persistence, Schoener had moved from tending the beasts to attending Paul. These two unlikely comrades, a Vienna physician and a farm laborer from Oberschwarzenberg, bonded not on background but on their shared destiny. After three years of war their futures were in doubt. This battle, the Kerensky Offensive, could be it.

"Hold him tight!" Paul cleansed the wound. He knew it would be hard on his patient, but necessary if he was to save the leg. He surveyed his meager medical supplies—no anesthetic or alcohol to dull the pain, and only primitive wrappings—not the first time they had been used.

He muttered, "Lord, help this young man," as he cleaned the wound cutting out bruised and torn flesh, removing as much dirt and debris as he could see in the tent's permanent twilight.

"Next."

——————

The pain and misery always slowed at dusk. Paul and Friedrich sat before a small fire enjoying the respite. Artillery shells continued to thunder. They spoke about their homes and families—never about their work or the war.

"Know what I miss most?" Friedrich asked.

Paul knew better than to answer.

"I miss hiking up to the meadows at the base of the Plockenstein to see …" There usually would follow a thirty-minute monologue about the beauty of Oberschwarzenberg and his fiancée, Hannah. But, not this time. A fierce whistle rent the air just before the artillery shell burst. Schoener and Schwimmer were both tossed in the air, landing twenty-five meters apart covered in dirt. All Friedrich could see was a hellish pit where their tent had been. He arose to search for his friend.

Paul was lying in the bottom of a ditch, slumped against the bank in a couple inches of muddy slime. He lifted his friend, blood gushing down Paul's leg.

1315 Schopenhauerstrasse, Apt. 3B
Vienna, Austria
3 February 1919

"Schoener saved my life. I owe him more than I can ever repay."

"You sent him a package of sausage last Christmas while we ate potatoes. Isn't that enough?"

"Marta, he needs more."

"The letter does not say that."

"One must read between the lines. Friedrich is too proud to ask."

"He sounds happy. He is becoming a father. What more can he want? You have done enough! Think of me," Marta continued. "Think of Erich! We cannot survive in such a place as Oberschwarzenberg."

"It is in Vienna that we cannot live! The Communists have taken over. They took my, m …" Paul shuddered at the memory of his wound, "…and now they are taking our homes!"

"Surely it is not that bad. This is not Russia. No one stops you from being a doctor. No one is taking our home."

"Soon they will. I know them. You don't!"

"You are as stubborn as that peasant who wants to take you from me. If you must go, then I go with you."

She reached up to her man, hugging him tight. Running her hands through his early gray hair, she thanked her God, Yahweh, for delivering Paul back to her.

Life without him had been hard on her and Erich. She had missed her man every moment. She would not lose him again. Besides, they could always move back to Vienna after he had paid his debt.

———

I looked up to see that Erich had drifted off. Hilde helped him onto his feet and guided him to bed. She whispered she would be back for a nightcap.

She returned with a bottle of schnapps and two glasses, placed them on the coffee table and joined me on the couch.

"Please pour," she ordered. And I complied. Keeping her happy was becoming very important to me.

"What should we drink to?" she asked.

Thoughts rampaged through my brain. Her warm thigh pressed harder against mine clouding my neurons with all sorts of feel-good chemicals. I'd forgotten the question. I sat numb and dumb.

She raised her glass. I followed suit like an automaton. Then I remembered. A toast!

"To us?"

Hilde smiled. "To us."

10

"That is what I want— to be Frau Hitler"

12 October 1938

Dearest,

How could I have been such a fool? Why would I ever think these peasants could understand?

I am so very tired of all the gossip about me and your baby. Every time I go to Beyerlein's, all I hear are whispers. I know what they call me. I hear it all the time. Hitler's bitch! And not just the gossips, but everybody!

Do they not know that even a great leader can also be a great lover—my lover? Someday, we'll make them sorry they ever treated me this way.

Why I let you seduce me I'll never know. My life was so easy. A routine without change. Everything in its place.

Now all is different. And it is your fault! And you cannot even find five minutes to write me or a few Marks to bring me to Berlin to stand at your side as your wife? Yes, that is what I want—to be Frau Hitler, the mother of your son. Nothing more, nothing less!

Do not forsake me!

Your Lotte

————◆————

Lotte's Diary
15 October1938

    This pregnancy is lasting forever! No more morning sickness, but the pressure is beginning to tell. I cannot get away from the abuse. I have no money. No car, no nothing. I'm stuck here without friends, only a little family support and nothing from Herr Hitler. Not a note. Not a pfennig. Surely he has not forgotten me.

Letter from Erich to Lotte
18 October 1938

    Dear Lotte

    I wish I was the father of your baby so we could be together now. I'm sure I could get leave if I was. Captain Gnabbe is very friendly and helpful to his men.

    Our regiment, according to the rumor mill, is to become a German Army regiment. I fear, but it seems possible, that we may become an SS unit. I don't know what they will do with me. I'm hoping the Captain can smooth things out. I really like the army and would hate to leave. There is no better place for a doctor. I am treated well and will be needed if we ever go to war.

    I'm hoping to be home for Christmas. Maybe I'll be there for the birth.

    Your friend

    Erich

Church of St. Polycarp
Oberschwarzenberg, Austria
8 September 1991

    "Perhaps you should come to church Sunday. You'll get a chance to see just about everybody who lives around here. Afterward, I'll bring you home and you can meet my friends. You will find I am not the only one."

This offer had concluded my talk with Frau Gerta Beyerlein. I think my face had mirrored my emotions at all she had to say about Lotte. While Lotte had had her problems, she was still family! I was starting to feel a little protective of her. Though back in Heidelberg I'm sure I would be telling her story to my colleagues just to hear them laugh and scoff as intellectuals are wont to do.

Thus, I found myself standing on the fine old white-washed church's steps on a sunny Sunday watching the believers arrive, while I waited to enter last.

The bells tolled the beginning of the service and I was swamped by a rush of latecomers. An older gentleman in a black suit held one of the two doors for me. And what doors they were. The pair had weather checks, gaping pores and chipped trim pieces. They were freshly painted, though not too well.

An unfamiliar hymn rang out from the choir loft where Lotte's star had shone so brightly. I had not been in any church recently, but trusted I'd remember enough to not embarrass myself. The rear of the church was filled to overflowing, the front pews occupied by Frau Beyerlein and the rest of her troupe, their families, and others there just to be seen. The middle four rows had only a scatter of worshipers— mostly ancient women wearing black.

Even the front pews turned as one following the priest's gaze as I walked quietly to the first available space. Naturally, the wizened gnome chose not to cede her aisle-side perch, forcing me to step over her feet and the kneeler.

Putting at least a meter between us, I sat just as the choir finished and everyone's gaze moved from me and, toward the altar where it belonged.

Father Sohn now slept in the church cemetery with most of his generation. His replacement, Father Jung, had all his hair, blondish, and was tall and slim. A real Aryan!

I remembered to stand, sit and kneel at all the right times, earning a smile from my neighbor. The sermon, "Embracing the Prodigal," actually was pretty good. This priest had a modern outlook, though judging by my pew-mate's face, not a popular one. Small towns live on their sameness, pushing out those who dare to be different. Not banishment as in the old days. Today, these good Catholics used more subtle methods to let a person, like Marta or Lotte, know they are not welcome, even in church, even after all Christ is alleged to have said about loving one's neighbor.

Well, so be it. I was not looking to live here. In fact, I was pleased to be completing my duty to Lotte's memory. One could easily be dead and still drawing breath in such a place.

Gerta and her group waited for me on the walk. After thanking the priest for a nice homily, I joined the threesome—Gerta and the Musketeers: Sofia Rodammer and Heidi Schuler. They talked among themselves on the two block walk. Gerta opened the door and we trooped into her parlor. It was crammed with four mismatched chairs in a lumpy circle. Each of the women went to a cushioned one like they belonged there, leaving a hard wooden chair for me.

And off they went telling how bad they now felt about their treatment of Lotte and her son. I let them rattle on, only interested in Sofia and Heidi, Lotte's erstwhile friends. At the end of the apologia, I spoke with them. They agreed to meet for "a little coffee, some strudel, and a talk" at Frau Rodammer's home.

I might have stayed longer, but had promised Hilde a drive up the mountain to see the sunset.

———

"One thing I do not understand, Hilde, is what you are doing here in Oberschwarzenberg?"

We were seated on a blanket overlooking the town, having finished a cold chicken picnic and a bottle of Beyerlein's best. We were starting to get comfortable with each other. She was even wearing the perfume.

"Put your arm around me and I'll tell you."

Hilde was such a refreshing change from the women I seemed to attract and chase back home. Most were either wanting to be my intellectual better, financial better or looking for someone to save them—sort of the old knight in shining armor played out in high-rises and city bars.

Hilde wore common clothes very well, listened without challenging everything I said, and was a great cook. What more could a man ask for?

The sun had set and the sky blinked with thousands of stars and a gibbous moon. A slight fragrant breeze ruffled her blonde tresses tickling my lucky arm.

Turning to me to make sure I was listening and then back to the scenery, she began. "Paul's family, the Schwimmers, and Marta's were not happy about the marriage. But there was nothing they could do. Over the years, they became acquainted with each other. By 1939 or so, they were actually friendly.

"In 1940, many of the Jewish families in Vienna were rounded up, put in cattle cars, and relocated to concentration camps. Marta's whole family was sent to Mauthausen.

"Peter, Paul's brother, sent him a letter asking him to intercede. Along with Lotte and her father, they set out for Mauthausen, almost a hundred kilometers from here. They arrived just after the train unloaded.

"Paul went right up to the gate to ask if he could speak to the commandant. Recognizing one of his former patients, Hans Schuler, now an SS guard, Paul pleaded with him. Schuler would not help, and even threatened them with his gun. There was nothing an ordinary guard could do. Hans had his orders just like everybody else.

"Peter was my grandfather. He swore that not another Jew would be taken from Vienna if he had anything to say about it. He did not, and the deportations and killings continued. What he could do and did was to watch over Erich, his last link to the Rosenbergs. My father continued the watch. When it became clear that Erich was getting too old to live by himself, the family sent me here. I've been here two years and I will stay to the end!"

"What does Erich think about all this watching?"

"He does not know and you must never tell him!"

"My lips are sealed."

And, indeed, they were. By a kiss!

———

Sofia Rodammer's home
Oberschwarzenberg, Austria
9 September 1991

I was pretty sure Gerta was not Spiekermann's spy because he had said his spy was Lotte's friend. That left just two suspects, Sofia Rodammer and Heidi Schuler.

As I walked down Schwarzenberg am Boehlenwaldstrasse, across the bridge spanning the Weissbach River and past Beyerlein's store, I marveled at the town's cleanliness. With its granite sidewalks, its wide paved main street, and picture postcard homes this indeed was a little bit of heaven.

The Rodammers lived in a two-story home, one block off the main avenue. A nice little place, white stucco, blue tile roof, yellow trim and a bright red front door. The path was lined with late-blooming flowers, mostly mums, in shades of purple and yellow.

Knocking on the door, I wondered how the widow Rodammer was able to maintain her home and yard. Hilde had told me that Ludwig, her husband, had passed away over a decade ago. She had a daughter who lived nearby, perhaps that was the answer.

The door opened to what I can only describe as Father Christmas in drag. Wearing heavy boots laced up well above her ankles, shrouded by heavy blue woolen pants, and topped by a red and black flannel shirt stood a burly woman with short gray hair and a few straggly gray chin whiskers. Her eyes matched her pants.

After scanning me from feet to head, the look on her face said that I was found wanting. As she was in her early seventies, I did not take her evaluation personally.

"Frau Rodammer?" I asked.

"Please come in young man."

She led the way into a room filled with two sofas, bedraggled and faded, somewhat like their owner. Seated on one was Heidi Schuler. A coffee table between held a carafe and a few cups, creamer and sugar, and a few rough and lumpy, not to say stale, blobs of brownish dough, perhaps cookies, perhaps not.

Sofia guided me to a largish, lumpish, faded-to-lavender chair perpendicular to the sofas. Sofia sat to my left.

The chair swallowed the back half of my body. Sofia sensed my situation and did nothing to help. Actually, I'm sure, she was well aware of her chair's predilections regarding posteriors and had purposefully put me there. Sort of a one down in a power struggle I was only becoming aware of.

Heidi wore a bright, emerald green dress that showed a lot of old lady leg, though I noted her's were in pretty good shape. A pair of delicate mules graced her feet. The bodice showed a lot more cleavage than one would expect from a senior citizen. Her skin was not too wrinkly, so she brought it off. Her face had no facial hair, was softly sculpted on high cheekbones framing chestnut eyes topped by a mop of red hair straight out of a bottle.

I nodded to her. "Thank you both for agreeing to see me."

"After all, we were Lotte's best friends," Sofia said.

"Yes, 'The Three Musketeers,' according to Lotte," I concluded. "All for one, et cetera."

Sofia answered, "Before the war we were very close indeed. We were like sisters, playing together, going to church and school together. As long as our parents knew where one of us was they knew where the other two were.

"Remember, Heidi, the tea parties in your yard. All summer long, we spent every afternoon drinking tea like rich society ladies." Heidi picked up her coffee cup, extending her pinkie to demonstrate. "Life in Oberschwarzenberg was so much easier. It was peaceful here. There were only a few dozen children, so we all knew each other."

"Five days of school and one for church only left us afternoons and Saturdays for play. We spent most of our after-school time at Sofia's," Heidi said.

"My parents," Sofia said, "were very understanding. And strict. We knew how to behave back then. Not like today's kids. Mostly hooligans, if you ask me."

"Dear," said Heidi, "please let me tell the story. I'm sure the Professor knows about such things. He teaches them every day, don't you Herr Professor."

I just nodded in counterpoint to Sofia's harrumph.

Heidi continued. "We lived less than a kilometer apart. Of course, poor Lotte lived on the wrong side of the river, but we loved her anyway. We took her under our wings, trying to help her learn the important things schools do not teach."

Sofia interrupted like a ripe blackhead, "Like manners."

With a nod to her friend, Heidi continued. "Poor Lotte always felt like she was not quite up to our standards."

"She wasn't." Sofia was getting riper. "How could she hope to compete? Parents working for the Jew doctor, hanging around with that Erich Schwimmer, no shoes to wear during the summer." Accusingly, she bobbed her face at Heidi, adding, "It was only because you insisted we include her that I even played with her. She always smelled, too."

"Just because I had manners does not make me weak, does it

dear," Heidi asked.

"Well, I never. . ."

"Perhaps if you had. . ."

Time for a professorial intervention. In the interest of fact-checking, I began with the events of when Lotte became pregnant.

"I'd like to move ahead to your late teens, specifically 1938."

With an icy glare from Sofia, Heidi began again. "What were we to think? Our dear little Lotte, a tomboy most of her life with a voice as smooth as her skin, declared she was pregnant. Well, that was not the surprise. She had developed an interest in boys just like us, especially Hans Schuler. And she had been unnaturally close to Erich. Seven month pregnancies were not unknown.

"It was her contention that Adolf Hitler was the father. We were okay with Erich being the father. After all, his father was a doctor, if a poor one married to a Jew.

"Naturally, we were stunned," Heidi continued. "At first we were a little jealous that she had been picked to sing to the Fuhrer. No one could fault her for her voice, but, really! All the way from here to Braunau, just for an afternoon.

"Of course, we were there too. We did not have her talent but the choir was about the only thing happening here. So we sang the best we could, showed up for practice and Sunday masses.

"We get there and we sing for him. Lotte does her solos. We could all see his eyes light up at her."

"Why her?" Sofia asked. "She was so second class. Not dressed well or with good manners like us."

"When that man came to her," Heidi continued, "and asked her to go with him to see Hitler, we were all so jealous. Father Sohn tried to argue but they told him that Lotte would get a ride back. We could all leave on the bus they had provided for us."

"Coffee, professor?" Sofia asked. Control was important to Sofia as she tried to deflect Heidi's monologue again. I nodded for the coffee, but kept my focus fixed on Heidi. Perhaps if Sofia got angry enough I could get some deeper truths from this pair.

"A few days later she tells us she had sex with Hitler," Heidi said.

"Remember, Heidi," Sofia asked, "that picnic the next Sunday? She was making out with Hans like everything was back to normal."

"Actually, I was kind of focused on his brother, Reinhold. And I seem to remember that you and Ludwig. . ."

"At least we married them," Sofia said. "She just played him along like she did with Erich. All the time, it turned out she was pregnant. She refused to name either boy as the father."

"She was in love with Hitler, or so she said. Claimed he was the father."

"We all know that she was *verrückt im Kopf* (crazy in the head)."

"One of you spied on Lotte for the Nazis," I changed the subject.

The two were taken aback. I had not shared my suspicions with anyone, not even Erich or Hilde. For once, I wanted to see how these people would react when caught in their perfidy.

Heidi and Sofia locked eyes like a bull and its matador. Sofia was the stronger physically, though Heidi had the strength of character often hidden in girls trying to attract boys and later to keep their husbands. I was neither, so she let me have it.

"What gives you the right to even ask such a thing? We would never do such a thing, especially to our friend, Lotte. Would we, Sofia?"

Sofia looked like a slow-motion movie of a building imploding. Her eyes sprinkled, mouth quavering at the edges, turning her face down in shame. Heidi turned her anger on her old friend.

"Look at me! Is what he says true? You betrayed me? Why?"

"I did not hurt anybody," Sofia answered. "I just told him about how things were here. He wanted just a letter every month about what Lotte and her little bastard were doing."

"Never did I see you mail a letter except to Ludwig."

"He picked them up in person."

"Who is this he?" Heidi demanded.

Sofia looked to me for help. I have to admit I did get some pleasure in her baring her treachery to her best friend. I swear I did it for Lotte.

"Back in 1938 your town was visited by the Gauleiter from Linz, Wolfgang Spiekermann," I informed Heidi.

"He talked to me and Sofia, wanting to know about Lotte and her pregnancy." She nodded to Sofia, "We told him we did not believe her. We told him the father had to be Erich for sure, or maybe Hans. Then he went away." She nodded again to Sofia. "Isn't that right?"

"Why don't you tell Heidi what really happened," I said.

"I cannot. It is all so long ago. What can it matter now?"

I took a leap of intuition.

"Permit me. Heidi. Your friend Sofia, one of the 'Musketeers,' was not just Spiekermann's spy. She was also his lover. From 1938 through early 1945 she met him every month to share her information and her bed. Even after she married Ludwig. Even while he was losing his arm in Russia."

"I don't believe you!" Heidi rose and walked to Sofia. She knelt to hold her in an embrace much more intimate than would be expected of two senior citizens. Tears cascaded down both faces, washing away the years, transforming them back to the teen lovers they had been. Lotte had never really been one of them. She had just provided them a cover and an excuse to get together without raising suspicions.

Heidi broke free to order me out of the house. I left with a smile, my duty done.

11

"We are connected forever in love."

12 November 1938

Dearest Adolf

I look like I swallowed a Zeppelin! I have truly lost my girlish figure. Now I look like a hausfrau, not at all beautiful. I'm hoping I get my figure back. I know you do not want to be seen with someone like me.

Dr. Schwimmer says I am doing fine. Yesterday, he let me listen to Young Adolf's heartbeat. Like yours, his beats for a strong Germany. It seems he kicks harder each day. If he wants to be born—I am ready. It seems like I have been pregnant for years.

Everyone in town, especially Gerta and her gossips over at Beyerlein's, are calling our baby a bastard, Hitler's bastard. Just because we are not married. Don't they know there are deeper unions than marriage? We are connected forever in love. I will never forget our first time together. You were such a sweet lover. Kind and gentle. Always making sure I was comfortable. Even if you did call me Geli once in a while. I know you love me.

I sure wish we could be together. I miss you so much.

Forever Yours,

Lotte

Lotte's Diary
15 November 1938

Today was a perfect day. I waddled out of the house over to Mutter's. I'm allowed over when Vater is gone. So there!

She patted my tummy just as Little Adolf was kicking up a storm. She agrees that he is going to be a big baby. She checked with Frau Keller, the midwife, about the gender of my baby. She noted how low I am carrying him when she saw me on the street last week. She is convinced that Little Adolf will be a boy. What else?

Lotte's Diary
22 November 1938

Vater and Dr. Schwimmer went up to Dornbau today to deliver Frau Bronner's baby. Paul said it will be a rough delivery. Her baby is "breech," which means it is coming out backwards. There must have been a lot of breech births around here because there are sure a lot of backward people.

I sure wish Herr Hitler would come to spirit me away from this hellhole. Or at least take responsibility for his baby and me. It is mean to make me live with my doctor like a pauper. No husband, no money, no respect.

———

The home of Dr. Erich Schwimmer
Oberschwarzenberg, Austria
10 September 1991

Over breakfast, I spoke with Erich. "According to 'The Three Musketeers,' she was also close to a Hans Schuler. Hilde said he was a guard at Mauthausen where your mother's family went. What do you know about him?"

"It would be better for you to find out about him on your own. I cannot be objective. You have met Heidi Schuler?"

"Yes."

"Then talk to her."

⎯⎯⎯

Frau Schuler's Kitchen
Oberschwarzenberg, Austria
10 September 1991

Heidi Schuler answered the door, brushing flour off her hands and onto her apron. Today she was a hausfrau and angry.

In my calmest voice I asked, "I hope yesterday's contretemps will not stand in the way of my asking you a few questions."

"You are contemptible, but courtesy is a requirement I was taught early."

"As you know I have been in town now for a short while," I declared.

"Not short enough!" snapped Frau Schuler, a woman of few words.

"And the name of one man, Hans Schuler, comes up every time I ask about the war years."

"Yes?"

"People say, 'Talk with Frau Schuler. She knows,' when I ask them for more."

"Yes?"

"Do you know him?"

"Yes." A sharp tone had entered her voice. I was onto something. What made Hans Schuler stand out among all others?

"Tell me about him."

"No! His story is better not told!"

"What?"

"No! I said no and I mean it! Hans is as dead as his memory!"

I raised my hands, palms out, trying to calm her. A large man came storming into the kitchen. Yes, once again I was seated on a hard wooden chair.

"You will leave my wife alone! She knows nothing."

I was not falling for this. All these people knew what was happening during the war. If anything, they chose not to know while using the wares made by slave laborers in concentration camps, fighting the war with prisoner-made weapons, even spreading their bones and ashes for fertilizer.

"Who are you," I demanded.

"I am her husband, Reinhold Schuler."

I turned on him. "You have the same last name. Are you sure you are not Hans?"

He charged me, knocking over the chair between me and his wife, to face me squarely. I was seated so he was looking at my semi-bald pate and my eyes took in a view not-soon-forgotten of a fat belly busting through the buttons of an old plaid shirt, red and black—Nazi colors.

I raised my palms seeking to calm him without saying anything else that would upset him. Not the best idea. He grabbed both my hands at the wrist and jerked me out of my chair. It toppled, crashing to the floor. For a fat guy he was strong and fast. And unwashed. And a stranger to toothpaste and mouthwash.

I may be an intellectual but I had not forgotten the skills needed to survive while growing up in the Vienna's roughest area. I knifed my right knee hard into his crotch. It was like a cartoon. Slow motion. His eyes shot out of his face, then snapped back into their sockets, his hands jerked back like they had been shocked, and his mouth curled up in pain. He bent at the waist, just missing me, then crumpled to the floor breaking both chairs.

"You have killed him!" Frau Schuler screeched. She shifted her bulk from her chair to the floor by his head.

"He is not dead, though he may be wishing he was. I fear he will not be of much use to you in the bedroom for a week or so. Although, I suspect that will not be a problem."

Poor woman. Her strong man put down by a teacher. They were both sobbing. Him in pain, her, maybe overcome with concern for him, or just the loss of two of those damned chairs.

"Now! Frau and Herr Schuler, I want some answers. Where is Hans Schuler?"

Funny. A few minutes ago I hardly cared. Hans was just another loose end. Now, I had to know.

"Where is he!" I repeated.

Frau Schuler looked up through watery eyes, red-tinged with hate. Her mouth betrayed her eyes. "I will tell you, then you must go!"

———

The home of Hans Schuler
Oberschwarzenberg, Austria
11 September 1991

I asked Hans, "Tell me how you became such a mystery man."

"Self-preservation, Professor."

Hans Schuler lived in a hovel. It was more than a hut but far less than a home, made of rough stone, situated up the mountain from Heidi's.

"One day a stranger, Sergei Androvsky I would later learn, came to town nosing around asking questions. He seemed overly interested in Adolph Schwimmer, Erich's and Lotte's boy. He was taking pictures of the whole town, but mostly of the boy.

"He asked Gerta about how the veterans were doing. Well, she started naming them off starting with the dead and ending with me and Erich. She told me later that he had pulled out a notebook as she talked checking off a list of names, even reminding her of a couple she had forgotten.

"When she mentioned my name, he made a note, then closed his book, asking if I lived in town. Did I have any relatives in the area? Of course Gerta told him about my brother."

"A day later he knocks on Heidi's door asking after me. She tells him I never came home from the war, and she thinks I became a POW or died.

"Sergei goes back to Gerta Beyerlein. Now the store is full of people. He asks what happened to Hans Schuler. No one speaks, not even Gerta."

"Why?"

"Because I told 'em not to. Professor. No one was to know my real purpose. They just knew that I had some powerful people behind me."

"How?"

"When I got back from Mauthausen, the village was in a sad state. Several houses were destroyed by that bomber that crashed in 1944. Every family still had an outhouse out back. The main road was rutted dirt. I made it known that I could really help the town if they just kept my secret."

"That's the same sort of thing Lotte told everyone when she first got pregnant. They believed her because they had nothing to lose. Why'd they believe you?"

"Because they had everything to gain! I put in the sewage system, rebuilt homes, and paved the road. I kept my promise and they kept theirs, Except for that loudmouth, Gerta Beyerlein!"

"After a week of the silent treatment, Androvsky left. For the next year he came to town for a week every month. I decided to find out what this Commie bastard wanted. I asked big mouth Gerta to deliver a note from me the next time he came to town."

"What was in the note?"

"Simply that I wanted him to come see me. Up here. Told Heidi to give him directions. About two weeks later he knocked on my door.

"I listened to that little Commie bastard for over an hour. Seems they took Lotte's story seriously. They wanted someone to keep track of little Adolf."

"Why you? There must have been a lot of people willing to spy for a few dollars."

"I guess you could say I was a little more motivated. This Russian, Sergei, said he had the power to wipe me out of the official records. It was like I never existed. No war crimes for me. Of course, I did not really need his help. I already had protection and an assignment and money to make a change in the town and regain some respect.

"As you know, Lotte wrote many letters to der Fuhrer claiming her son was his. Absurd, I know. When I returned home in May 1945, there was an order waiting for me at Heidi's. I was to keep track of Lotte's son. Enclosed were several thousand Reichmarks and an address in Switzerland where I was to mail my monthly reports.

"When that Commie showed up, I was already in the spy business. I did not need his money but only a fool spies for free. His offer of immunity did interest me. Every month I copied my Swiss report to Sergei in Moscow.

"I had spent so freely fixing up the village that by 1948 I was broke. I added a note to my Swiss report asking for more money. Said I needed it to maintain my cover. They bought it. Every few months they sent me a few thousand Deutschemarks. Adding that to Sergei's stipend, I enjoyed a comfortable life.

"In 1957, Adolf Schwimmer turned eighteen and left town. Sergei intercepted Lotte's letter to Hitler telling him that her son was on a journey to find his father. I thought I was out of a job here but the Swiss and Russians both wanted me to monitor Lotte's letters and activities as a means of trying to keep track of her son."

"Who was getting your reports at the Swiss address?"

"I never had a need to find out."

"Didn't you wonder, though?"

"Sure. But not enough to put my income at risk."

"Are you still spying?"

"When Lotte died so did my income. Luckily, I had saved and

invested wisely." He spread his hands out showing his whole hovel to me. "As you can see, I live comfortably. Just me and my books."

"These were people you were killing, Hans. In fact, many of them were Germans and Austrians. Quite a few were from assimilated families who had no knowledge of their Jewish roots. Dammit, man, they were Christians. Just like you. And you killed them!" I admit I was trying to provoke Hans into coming clean about the thousands he had murdered. In a voice far too calm, Hans answered my charges.

"Herr Professor, these people you mention were Jews by law and heritage. Therefore, they were a danger. They had to be exterminated. I was only following orders."

"You would have killed Erich? A boyhood friend? The son of the doctor that brought you into the world, though he might regret that now," I challenged.

"Herr Professor, have Erich tell you how I saved his life before you judge me so severely. Besides, you must understand the people and times. Not just your research. I personally swore allegiance to Hitler. My life was his to do with as he saw fit. I went to Mauthausen following his order. I did not always enjoy my job, but I did it. I was not a shirker like some. I transferred to Auschwitz to better serve Germany and Hitler. What I did had to be done. If not by me, then someone else. I did my duty. No one can take that away from me.

"Hatred of the Jews was the norm back then. All over the world, not just Germany.

"Why would I respect a person, in fact a whole race who walked to their deaths. Never a protest. Never fighting back."

The words of Hans Schuler, a guard at the Mauthausen and Auschwitz, startled me. "They could have overpowered us, yet did not. They just waited around eating our food, waiting for me to put them out of their misery.

"Yes, that is what I did," he added in a wondering tone. "I was an angel of mercy! Ha, ha!"

Several of his chins joined in the mirth. Schuler was one of the fattest angels I could imagine. His belly bulged over his pants.

"Are you listening to yourself? Do you really believe what you are saying?"

"Of course I do."

"You are aware that I am writing a book."

"About your crazy old aunt Lotte, I've heard."

"And the whole world will know what you said and how you acted."

"The whole world agreed with us back then. Much of it still does."

I raised my hands to signal I wanted him to stop. He ignored me and went into a monologue.

"The Jews knew where they were going. When we took away their stores and jobs, destroyed their synagogues, rounded them up like cows and put them in cattle cars with slats for walls, straw and shit on the floor, open to the weather. CATTLE CARS! Are you hearing me? They must have known.

"Supposedly, they were a smart race. Is that the way you treat someone you respect? Does anyone respect the cow? No, we just use her for milk and then meat! Why would I respect anyone who accepted such treatment."

I had to say something. "Are you saying it was the Jews own fault they were slaughtered?"

"It was not mine! They came to Auschwitz like animals. So we treated them like animals. They never complained. They never rebelled. What was I to think?

"The Americans," he mused, "have a saying: 'if it quacks like a duck and walks like a duck then ...'"

"Whether they fought back or not—they were still people. Human beings. Did they not deserve to be treated better?"

"Professor! How can you know how things were?"

"I have researched ..."

"Sure you have your textbooks and your research, but what do you really know of that time?"

"I know enough that you are full of shit!" Oh, oh. "Excuse me, I meant you are ignorant." Not much better. "No, I mean, I have studied the Holocaust for years and I know that they did fight back!"

This got his dander up. His calm face filled with righteous indignation. His glare dared me to continue my defense. I did.

"There are several examples. For instance, the Warsaw Ghetto uprising."

"And ..."

At a loss for further instances, I tried, "Well, wasn't that a sign they were human beings deserving respect and life?"

"That late in the war they finally wake up? Warsaw was in 1943. Already four million Jews had been taken care of. It was too little—far too late!"

"How about when the Jews took control of the camps?"

"Again, too late. Had they done that in 1939 or 1940 then that would have been something. Then they could have held their heads high. They would have been men! Instead, they were sheep!"

I needed a break, time to marshal my intellectual forces to beat this rustic killer.

"Could I have a glass of water, please?"

Hans scraped his chair back from the kitchen table. He wandered the few feet to the sink, rinsed out a glass, filled it with tepid, cloudy water. I took the time to assess where this interview was headed.

"That was me, Herr Professor." I followed his pointing finger to a portrait hanging over the hearth. A good looking young man in uniform smiled shyly back at me.

"That was taken in 1940 just after I enlisted."

"Why the SS?"

"Why not! They were the only group fighting our enemies at

home and in the field. Not like the regular army. No, the SS secured
the homeland and fought to protect it.

"I liked working in the camp," he continued. "Little chance of
getting hurt. Many of my comrades left Mauthausen for the Waffen-SS,
only to die in Russia. Of what value was that? They should have stuck
to their camp jobs. There we accomplished something!"

"Murdering innocents?"

"Herr Professor, they were not so innocent. One had only to
read the paper or listen to the radio. The Jews were responsible for
much that was wrong in Germany and the world. Jews used banks to
steal from us, they were corrupt lawyers and bad doctors, they were
insidious writers and demon-artists. Nothing that generated wealth,
just money changers. Just parasites really. We proved that."

"How?"

"Simple. The world runs just as well without them as with them.
They were not needed."

I was struggling just trying to process this rubbish. "You actually believe that anti-Semitic crap Hitler and you Nazis spouted?"

"You would do well, Professor, to not disparage der Fuhrer.
He saved us from the Versailles burden and almost won his war. He
brought most of Europe to its knees to acknowledge his greatness.

"I did my own research after the war."

He pointed to the opposite wall covered with books. Many of
the titles I recognized from my own research.

"I have much time to study and read."

He arose and lumbered over, searched for a moment, then
pulled out "The Protocols of the Elders of Zion," a much discredited
invention from Czarist Russia. No one took it seriously, at least no one
intelligent.

He opened the book and removed a sheet of lined yellow paper.
Closing the book, he took his seat. The sheet was filled with writing
but in such small script I could not read it. I did not have long to wait.

"I have here, Professor, some of my research. Quotes. Actual words of great men." He paused.

"And ..."

"For instance," he stroked down with his nicotine-yellowed index finger seeking the right one. "Here. You have heard of Henry Ford?"

"Who hasn't."

"Ford wrote on May 22, 1920, 'If fans wish to know the trouble with American baseball they have it in three words—too much Jew."

"That is out of context and Ford retracted all his anti-Semitic writing and speeches and apologized to the Jews."

"Recanting his lies or lying about recanting? Matters not."

"It does matter! People change their ideas. They learn and grow."

"Again, matters not. What is written is written."

"You are wrong, Herr Schuler."

"I think not, Professor. Would you be more interested in looking at actions?"

"They certainly speak louder and stronger."

"Neither Roosevelt nor Churchill acted on information the Jews gave them about the concentration camps. On April 10, 1944, two Jewish prisoners, Rudolf Vrba and Alfred Wetzler, escaped from Auschwitz. They passed a thirty-two page report of what was happening to Jewish officials in Slovokia. Their information became known as the Vrba-Wetzler report. On June 15th and June 20th, 1944, the BBC and *The New York Times* issued the first reports describing the mass murder taking place. Those were based on the Vrba-Wetzler report."

"To my knowledge, their report could not be substantiated."

He tented his big paws under his chins. Using a voice suggesting incredulity, he went on, "Amazing isn't it, Professor. With all of the Allied spies, saboteurs, commandos and Resistance fighters, they could not get confirmation! I think they chose to not try."

"What could they have done? They couldn't bomb the camps. Think of the prisoners who would be killed or injured."

"Once again your knowledge is limited. On 18 February, 1944 the RAF bombed the Amiens Prison. A surgical strike, very effective. I'll not bore you with the actual bombing, just the results: of the 700 prisoners, 102 were killed, 74 wounded, and 258 escaped. Are you telling me they could not have done the same to Auschwitz or Mauthausen? The Allies could have saved thousands of your precious Jews!"

What had happened here? My goal had been to confront Schuler, to get him to take responsibility for killing human beings, unarmed children and adults. Instead, he had put me on the defensive. I said my good-bye.

12

"They had better watch out"

12 December 1938

Mein Liebchen,

It is almost time for Little Adolf to be born, My Dear. Dr. Schwimmer says it will be any day now. Myself, I'm holding out for Christmas. Wouldn't that be so appropriate? Another child of another god born on Christmas. Born to be the savior of his people. Not those dirty Jews, but the great German nation. He will be such a wonderful gift for us and the world.

I fear, my Dear, that I am getting a little frightful as we get closer. Out here it is not unusual for the mother to die while giving birth. Who would take care of our son? My Vater has abandoned me and Mutter does not have enough money for two families. I may have to rely on the good graces of my doctor so we are not put out into the street. It is far too cold for that!

My own mother had trouble, female trouble, with my delivery. She could never have any more children. How tragic it was because both her and my father wanted a large family. She never really recovered. And Erich's mother could have no more children, either. But this was due to her husband, the doctor. I know I want to give you many more children.

I would ask you to pray for me and your baby, but I know you believe in something far greater. Even though I do not always understand. Please pray to whoever you will. I am afraid I'm going to need all the help I can get.

I will take it as a sign if he really is born on Christmas! Of course any other birth date will be fine. I know I cannot dictate to our son. He will arrive when he is ready—and not a minute sooner.

I keep hoping you can be here for his birth. It would mean so much for me to once again be in your presence. And that would show all those naysayers that you, not poor Erich, are Little Adolf's daddy.

You are mine, forever

Lotte

Lotte's Diary
13 December 1938

I know now why Herr Hitler is leaving me here. I finally figured it all out. It is a masterful plan if ever there was one. He wants his son to grow up in a small town far away from the decadence of a big city like Berlin. And Oberschwarzenberg is about as small and far away as one can get and still speak German! So here I will stay, even though hardly anyone likes me anymore.

I'm as big as a house. Mutter's old clothes barely fit. Which is good because I never leave the house anymore. Dr. Schwimmer does not want a repeat of my mother's experience and neither do I. He ordered me to stay in bed as much as possible. I get bored but it is a small price to pay. Every afternoon, Mutter comes in to talk with me. She goes to Beyerlein's to get the latest gossip and delivers it here to me.

I'm still the talk of the town, I guess. Since she threw me out she has once again been accepted into Gerta's little group so they tell her everything. They still refer to me and my baby as Hitler's bitch and bastard. They'd better watch out. When Adolf comes to visit his son, then they'll know. Maybe I'll tell him what they said. How mean they were to me. Let them explain to der Fuhrer!

The home of Dr. Erich Schwimmer
Oberschwarzenberg, Austria
11 September 1991

I thought it would be helpful if I understood a little more about the mothers of Erich and Lotte. I asked him, "As a physician, what do you make of this letter about Lotte's mother?"

"Something went wrong, very wrong, during Lotte's birth. I'm sure my dad did everything he could, but it was not enough. At least Hannah lived. However, she could have no more children. I only learned that much when I overheard my mother and Hannah having one of their afternoon chats when I was about ten."

"Did you find out why?"

"No. At the time I was too young to understand such things. And later, it was never spoken about when I was around. All I knew was that neither woman could have any more children. After the war I had all I could do to take over my father's practice. When I had time to look at Hannah's file, I found that she had a very rough time of it. My father diagnosed her as suffering from placenta previa."

"Your mother and Lotte's mother talked often?"

"Almost every day. After Frau Schoener completed her housekeeping duties here, she and mother sat down for an hour or two to talk. My mother was so lonely she welcomed the attention.

"I heard them both say more than once how lucky they were to have each other and each others' child. From the day of Lotte's birth, Marta joined Hannah in taking care of her. It was good for both parents. My mother had a little girl she could dote on, and the Schoeners had the son they would never have. That is why Lotte and I were so close."

———————

The home of Hans Schuler
Oberschwarzenberg, Austria
12 September 1991

It is a fine Fall day in the mountains, far too nice to be cooped up with this madman. Yet, here I am. Listening to the most vile accounts of a former SS concentration camp guard.

Was I getting mesmerized? What else did I want to know about this lout? Every word he spewed disgusted me. And intrigued me. Could there be value in baring this man's black soul for all the world to see. Might this not cause others to think before they said or did the same? I certainly hoped so. I hated to think I was wasting my time up here when I could be with Hilde.

As a fallen Catholic myself, I wanted to know what role his faith played in his life of killing.

"Herr Schuler, will I be seeing you at Mass Sunday?"

"Absolutely not!"

"Hans, you grew up Catholic in a Catholic town in a Catholic country. How can you turn your back on all that?"

"Der Fuhrer was against religion and I have no need for it. No doubt you have already met Father Jung. What a fraud! Wanting to be treated like a man when he dresses like a woman!"

"You seem very angry."

That opened the floodgates. "You think I am angry? Oh, dear Professor, I am much more. I am the avenger of lost souls."

"You? The killer of thousands! How dare you speak of lost souls!"

"Now, who is angry, Lorenz?"

Taking a sip of tepid tea, I tried to collect myself. Once again, Hans had managed to provoke me! What was it about him that made me forget my scholarly dispassion? Three deep breaths and I was ready to try again. "Perhaps, if you told me more about this avenger business."

Cool as the water of the Weissbach River, he began another of his outrageous tales, more so because it proved to be true.

"Were you ever an altar boy, Herr Meyer?"

Not wanting to interrupt his flow, I just shook my head.

"Thought not. I was. Back in 1930 when Father Sohn was brainwashing the locals. My parents could hardly contain their pride when I was chosen to serve. You should have seen them. Every Sunday and holy day I served, they just sat in their pew and beamed. I'm sure they hoped I'd become a priest.

"I was only ten years old when I became a junior server. There were two or three of us boys all striving to become full-fledged altar boys. The older ones made it clear that Father Sohn made the choice based on our holiness and obedience. I thought I had little chance of advancing. Those were not my strong suits.

"Father Sohn offered to take me under his wing. He said I was a lot like him when he was my age. 'Rebellion is starting to color your judgment,' was how he put it. He told my parents that if they wanted to be proud of me that I would have to spend several hours after school with him every Wednesday. He would see that I learned to be obedient.

"You should have seen the strange looks I got from the regulars when they found out. What I thought to be jealousy turned out to be pity. Not one of those bastards tried to stop me. None of them told me what would happen! Just let me be led like a lamb to slaughter!

"That first Wednesday I knocked on his door ... that was the end of my young life. That old man came to the door dressed in pants and a shirt just like any other man. He welcomed me with hot tea and cookies. His first bribes!

"Not much happened that first day. He asked me a lot of questions about church. Said he was finding out what he needed to teach me. What should have been a warning passed over my head without a pause. He made it exceedingly clear that I was to tell no one what we talked about. He threatened me, saying my whole family would burn in hell if I ever told. Since there was not much to tell, I went along."

"Hans, you are using some unusual language. Bribes. Pity. Warning. What do they have to do with becoming an altar boy?"

"Everything and nothing. Being alone with that bastard were

the most terrifying moments of my life. The warning I missed was him asking if I knew where babies came from. Being a farm boy I had started to figure it out a little. You have to understand that parents did not speak of such except to use the old stork or cabbage patch stories. We were on our own to learn the biology of the matter. I told him what my parents said. He laughed. 'My poor boy,' he said, 'you have a lot to learn. You are so lucky I chose you above all the other novices.'

Hans tried a sip of his cold tea, made a face and went to the kitchen. He returned with two cold beers. "Professor, will you join me?"

"Sure. Why not?" I had never been known to turn down a cold beer.

We clinked bottles as Hans said, "To the lost souls." He drank deeper than me, finishing half of his bottle while I sipped mine. I wanted to be hospitable but sober for the rest of his story.

"I have asked myself why he chose me. I was not the brightest, the most religious, the strongest, or the best-looking, and certainly not the richest. When I asked him later, he just said some shit about God's mysterious ways.

"Every Wednesday for the next month I met with him. Always tea and a treat. Cookies or strudel. His housekeeper was a great cook. The village priests always managed to live well, no matter how poor their parishioners. Sohn was no exception. Always with the questions. Getting more personal all the time. My parents should have known what that bastard would do to me. I wanted to tell them. Hell! I wanted to shout it from the altar!"

"Are you trying to tell me that Father Sohn abused you?"

"You are perceptive!"

We both took a beer break. Finishing his, he got himself another, then continued.

"I am sure I was not the first, nor the last. I finally understood those looks I'd gotten. Starting that second month, he drew me deeper into his depravity until I lost myself. First, it was just him putting his arm around my shoulders as we sat side by side talking. Then it was a hug when I left. Then another when I arrived. To my shame I enjoyed the contact. Like good Austrians, my parents were cold and distant. I do not remember my dad ever hugging me. His only reward for me was to not hit me!

"Sohn acted like he really cared about me. Like water to a desert; I just soaked it up. Soon, he showed me how to rub his cock through his pants. Then he was rubbing me. He said that I now knew how good it made him feel. What can I say? It did feel good. Even if I did not really know what was happening.

"After a few months he met me at the door wearing his cassock. He took me into his study. All the drapes were closed. He shut the door and locked it. By then I was in too deep. He made me reach under and feel his naked penis. I stroked him for only a few minutes when he spurted. I did not know anything back then. I just removed my hand, covered with his mess. He handed me a towel and went on as if nothing had happened. Before I left, he rubbed me again. Fair is fair, is what he said.

"Things progressed quickly. Soon, he raised his hem and had me see what I'd only imagined. I know now that he was not particularly well-endowed. But, to my young eyes it was enormous. Especially compared to mine. I was getting pretty good at this, he said. I wonder now what his housekeeper thought about those towels. Certainly she must have suspected something.

"Just before I was to leave he had me drop my pants. I watched as his hand grabbed hold and stroked me til I shot a little dribble. He used the same towel. Some sort of a bonding experience.

"This went on for a few months until Spring. He had made me taste his stuff before using the towel. I can assure you, Lorenz, it is a taste not easily forgotten."

Hans stopped for a gulp of his beer, threw his shoulders back and soldiered on.

"I started to think this was all wrong. But, who could I tell? Who would believe me? He was the priest. He knew everyone's sins. He was too powerful.

"In June, he made me a real altar boy. He told my parents that though I had been promoted I still needed his help. Of course, they agreed even though it meant that I'd miss evening chores. The one time I wanted my dad to say NO, he crumbled like everyone else.

"Despite my naivety, I was finally beginning to understand. I saw couples holding hands, married people in quiet conversations sprinkled with laughter. I observed our dairy cows and our bull. Every time it was a male and a female. Never two males. I asked Sohn about this. He said what we had was so special that God only shared it with a blessed few. Still, I wondered. And my misgivings grew.

"I was just beginning to notice girls. Not really in a sexual way. Just that some of them had nice smiles. Others smelled nice. I told Sohn. He told me again how special we were. He reminded me that I'd go to hell if we stopped. So would my whole family.

"It's funny. I'd wanted to be an altar boy so I could belong to a group. A peer group they are called now. And now I found myself more alone than ever. The others shunned me. It was like they all knew. Some were jealous that I got so much of Sohn's attention. Others treated me like I had some disease. Like they were afraid to get too close. That it might be catching.

"I could not tell anyone and I could not stop. There only seemed to be one way out. I had to find him a replacement. So help me God, I did not want to, but I had no choice. I found him another lamb."

"Did anyone ever reveal what Sohn was doing?"

"Threats of hell meant a lot back then. Besides who would've believed them?"

"So, you stopped your homosexual ways, joined the SS, and killed Jews?"

"As you say. But there is more to the story. I became an avenger. Punishing the men like him. I especially enjoyed it when they sent homosexuals to me. I beat them senseless, kicked them until every bone was broken and put them into a trundle and shoved it into the furnace. You should have heard those beasts wail from the fire. I hope they all are enjoying the eternal flames of hell.

"After the war, I set things right with Sohn and six of those altar boys. They all suffered like me. They begged me to kill them."

———

"Hans, I have heard some unbelievable stories about Auschwitz guards. Did you play soccer against the inmates like the others?

"Of course!"

"I am confused by your motives and the outcomes."

"Professor, what is not clear? All we wanted to do was to have a little fun."

"Fun? Toying with their lives?"

"Let me tell you about a memorable game we played, if memory serves me, in mid-July, 1943. A train car-load of gypsies were mixed in with a bunch of Jews. It took a while to get them all unloaded and processed.

"We started with the Jews. Gruber's job was to unlock the doors and slide them open. He thought he was so damned important just because he had the keys! Opening the door was like opening a dam on the Don. They flooded out, crying for food and water, keeping their families together. Just made it easier for us. We told them there would be plenty to eat and drink after they were deloused.

"They had to line up five abreast. We must've had about a thousand of them. Then they marched by the doctors. Only a few were healthy enough to work. The rest were gassed."

"And the gypsies?"

"Most of us had not seen a gypsy in a long time. They used to wander the countryside, dirty beggars and thieves. Their women did these seductive little dances luring us country folk into sin. Then Herr Hitler started arresting them, putting them into concentration camps. Soon, we saw no more gypsies. Until now. Now, we would see just how seductive their women could be! And their men would start doing the first honest labor of their lives!

"It was already past noon and we were getting hungry ourselves. Corporal Kleib told us to go get some lunch. He ordered a few of the regular guards to watch the gypsies. He invited the train staff but they acted like they did not want to get any closer to the gypsies than they had to. Off we went. All the way to the mess we heard those gypsies wailing.

"We were always hungry after a processing and the cooks did not let us down. Wiener schnitzel, dumplings, apple strudel and plenty of beer. I tell you, it made it awful hard for us to go back to work. But, orders are orders.

"For only four carloads they sure made a racket!

"Gruber got out his keys and the routine started. These were in pretty good shape, only a few sick and old. We got them all lined up, walked them past the docs, and separated them. The ones to be gassed were sent through the gate directly.

"The men were separated from the women and children. The latter were marched through to their barracks. We noticed the men had that shifty look common to them and were not too skinny. We sorted out about twenty and had the rest sent to their barracks and locked down.

"Our lunch had settled and we were feeling pretty good. Nothing like a little exercise to build up our appetites for dinner! We marched them over to the soccer field.

"Heine, our team mascot because he was barely five foot tall, handed them their uniforms while we changed. They were fed a little. We did not want to upset their tummies. Heine had them pick a captain.

"Gruber led our squad onto the field. As we warmed up, Jagen-hoffer, our captain, met with Gruber and the gypsy captain to go over the rules. Their captain went back to his team and spoke some sort of babble. I tell you, they were not happy.

"The teams lined up, Gruber blew his whistle. That Gruber! He could really blow a whistle!

"We easily outplayed them. Some acted like they'd never played before. Soon, we were up 2-0. They subbed in this big guy, all of 220 pounds and over six foot. Before we knew what happened, they had tied the score. Then they got a little cocky. Blocking our shots, tackling us, really getting into the game. It became a brawl.

"Poor Gruber blew and blew his whistle but we were out of control. Finally, he pulled his gun, fired a shot. That got everybody's attention. Gruber ordered two guards to bring that big guy to the side-lines and tied his hands behind his back. Next, he ordered Heine to bring him a rope.

"Making a noose, he handed the rope back to Heine and told him to toss it over a tree limb and to get an apple crate. We were starting to see what he planned.

"He marched that big guy over to the tree, made him stand on the crate, put the noose over his neck. Gruber shouted at their captain loud enough so everyone could hear. 'Your lot will do no more fouling.' He kicked the apple crate over. We won 8-2.

"Afterward, the gypsies had to carry the body to the crematoria and place it in a trundle. Gruber, himself, pushed it into the flames.

"Professor! Close your mouth before you catch a fly. We let the rest of them live. And their women. Well, we enjoyed playing with them, too."

"Wasn't it against the law to have intercourse with a non-Aryan?"

"In Auschwitz, we made our own rules. Who was to complain?"

13

"What a happy baby we have!"

Lotte's Diary
14 December 1938

When I woke up today there was a beautiful baby bed in my room. There was no card or bow so I just know it was Vater. Finally! I knew he would come around.

When I was younger I could get him to do anything I wanted. I'd give him a shot of sad puppy eyes and he'd cave in every time. I remember the time I wanted that little red dress from Beyerlein's. As usual, we did not have much money. But I really wanted that dress! Every day after school, I'd stop in at Beyerlein's just to look at it. I knew several other girls wanted it, so I had to work on my father quickly.

Finally, I followed my usual strategy of enlisting Mutter, though she was reluctant. Then I told Marta about the dress, about how much I wanted it, how happy it would make me. I really laid it on. I knew that with Mutter working on Vater and Marta working on the doctor that something good would happen.

I was so upset when I got there the next day and the dress was gone! Mr. Beyerlein would not tell me where it was or who bought it. I just knew that Gerta or one of her crowd had beat me. All the way home I was fighting back the tears.

Walking into our house, I plodded to my room and there it was!

My red dress hanging on my closet door. I tried it on right away. It fit pretty good. Without a thought I crossed the dusty road and went to Erich's to show off the dress and especially to thank Vater. You should have seen the look on his face. He was so proud of how good I looked. It made all the conniving worth it.

Vater said he found some money in the road. Sure, he did! I'll bet that Marta told the doctor to "loan" the few marks to him so he could save face. He took the found money to Beyerlein's and bought the dress while I was at school.

26 December 1938

My Lover!

A miracle like no other.! A gift unsurpassed! A blessing for all the world! Your child, your son, your heir was born early on Christmas Day!

The son of another god graces the earth! Bethlehem right here in Oberschwarzenberg!

Sadly my parents do not share our joy. My own father refers to our son as a bastard. Many in town still think Little Adolf is poor Erich's child. Impossible! He is all mine—and yours!

It would mean so much to see you again. Even though he is little I know Little Adolf would just beam with joy if you were to come home to us. Be Joseph to my Mary and come soon.

Your son is hungry—again! I feed him almost every hour it seems but I do not begrudge him, not the heir of My Leader.

Dr. Schwimmer promises to take a picture of us. I'll send you a print as soon as I can afford it.

Your Lotte

PS—Little Adolf also has a small, squarish birthmark on his upper right thigh.

27 December 1938

My Dearest Fuhrer

I have spent days and days crying for joy! Me and your baby—we made it! This was the best Christmas ever!

I so wish you could have been here to see your son enter the world. He came out crying and hungry. He has a full head of dark hair just like his daddy. I could see it in his eyes—he had his lebensraum! Now you have to get it for the rest of us!

And is he ever hungry! It seems that he never stops nursing.

I am so lonely without you! Mutter comes over every day to do the cleaning and cooking. Even Vater has stuck his head in a few times. But, they are not you!

I need your help, my dear. I am trying to decide if I should have Little Adolf baptized. I am Catholic and so were you. Should I deny our child the baptism we both had? Please, tell me what to do.

My parents insist that I go through with it. Paul agrees with them. I think he still thinks Little Adolf might be Erich's son. Probably most of the town does too. Someday when you come to see your son they will all know, won't they!

Your son takes up so much of my time I hardly have time to write you or even write in my diary. Mostly, I find that for the few days before and after I write you I'm able to find a few quiet moments. The rest of the time I'm busy!

I thought Sofia or Heidi would come by but they are probably too busy with the holidays and all.

I'm wishing all the best to you, my dear. I'll see you soon.

Your Lotte

Lotte's Diary
1 January 1939

Today was a hard lonely day for me. I had the chance to see just how hard these people can be. Even the priest, Father Sohn, continued to show his hate for me and my son. As if I was the first girl to come up pregnant! I guess, though, I might be the first in a while to not have a husband when the baby was ready to be baptized.

Paul, to his everlasting credit, stepped up to take what he thought was his son's rightful place. It is traditional for a baby to be baptized on the Sunday following its birth but that old fart refused to even consider it—until Paul took him aside. I do not know what was said but I do know that old priest came to me all red-faced and asked me if he could do the baptism following the regular service. Who was I to refuse?

Paul sat with me during the Mass. It was his first time in a pew at St. Polycarp's since Marta died. Mutter und Vater sat behind us. I spied Vater making funny faces at Little Adolf. I guess he was trying in his rough way to make amends. We will see how things turn out between these two. As for me, I am ready to forgive his atrocious behavior if he will only apologize. But you know these peasants.

All through the service I could feel the stares of everyone, especially Father Sohn. Instead of a sermon about the joyous season he focused on what he called the wanton behavior of today's children. Not like in his time, he said. Sure. Back then they did not have wireless or cars. They were primitive. Not like today.

I tried to stand to receive communion but Paul pulled me down. I guess it was a good idea as I had not been to confession in a while. Sohn might have refused and I would have been shamed in front of the whole congregation. But I have not sinned in so long. Certainly God cannot think that carrying the Fuhrer's baby is sinful! But, I suppose, most of these good Catholics would part company with their God on this issue. So we sat giving everyone a chance to stare at me and my baby on their return from the communion rail. Bunch of smug hypocrites! I think they were mostly jealous that here I was—the vessel chosen by our Fuhrer, my Fuhrer and lover to carry and nurture his only begotten son. Well, damn them. They'll see. Little Adolf will be as great as his Daddy! So there!

At the baptism after the rest of the congregation had already left,

Paul and my mother took their places standing on either side of me and my baby. Vater held back staying in the background but close enough to hear all that was said. When it came time for us to tell the priest the baby's name I still was not sure what to say. I wanted to say Adolf Hitler, Jr but was pretty sure that would be the final straw for Sohn. Paul came to my rescue telling him the baby was to be called Adolf Paul Schwimmer. I only hope Der Fuhrer is pleased.

Lotte's Diary
12 January 1939

Finally, my son is taking a nap and I have time to write.

Paul has truly come into his own. He was born to be a grand-father, even though he isn't. But I will take all the help I can. He even changes Little Adolf, which makes him a hero in my book. Not like my own Vater. He still refuses to see me or my son—his only grandson! Mutter has been coming into my room to coddle and coo. I think she would move in if he allowed. Between Paul and Mutter I actually have it pretty good. I just wish Sofia and Heidi would come over.

The home of Hans Schuler
Oberschwarzenberg, Austria
12 September 1991

"Perhaps you think it was easy getting up every morning to kill Jews?" Hans Schuler snapped.

I sat shocked at such a question. Of course, it was rhetorical. I did not have to respond. "Even in the summer, it was cold when we rolled out of bed. Those damned Jews could not be kept waiting! We were something to see, twenty young Aryans, looking smart in our SS uniforms, marching to the mess hall. I have to say we always had good food, even in the end. Always eggs, bacon, potatoes, bread, and plenty of hot coffee. All served by the cutest Jewish girls we could find. They were great waitresses. They had to be, you know!" A conspiratorial wink I did not acknowledge.

"I am shocked that you still speak that way after all those years and deaths," I interjected. "These were people you were killing. In fact, many of them were Germans and Austrians. Many were from assimilated families. They had no knowledge of their Jewish roots. Dammit, man, they were Christians. Just like you. And you killed them!"

I admit trying to provoke Hans into coming clean about the thousands he had murdered. In a far too calm voice, Hans answered my charges. "Herr Professor, these people you mention were Jews by law and heritage. Therefore, they were a danger. I only followed orders."

"You would have killed Erich? A boyhood friend? The son of the doctor that brought you into the world?"

"Herr Professor, you must understand people, not just your research. I personally swore allegiance to Hitler. My life was his. I did not expect to enjoy my job, but I did it.

"Please, we have discussed this! Hatred of the Jews was the norm back then. All over the world, not just Germany. Working the trains made us feel alive. Patriotic … for our Fatherland."

Shaking my head, I did not stop his recital of brainwashing.

"Corporal Schlechter always started our day fresh. He liked to have a clean gas chamber. Cleansed of the filth of yesterday by the Sonderkommando. They were inmates forced to cooperate in the death of their friends and families. They actually had it pretty good. We had to keep them strong. They were fed daily and had their own barracks.

"Whenever they failed Schlechter, he would order us to whip them until they bled, then throw them into the chamber, letting them die in the filth. Then we would have to get someone to clean up that mess."

Hans turned philosophical. "Like soldiers waiting for combat we drank, smoked, or played cards. Then far off, the train whistled, warning us. Sergeant Hubinger would order us to our feet but we took our time. We knew it would be seven or eight minutes before our work began.

"The cattle cars arrived stuffed with dead, sick and living cargo—all mixed together. Usually we had 2,500 to 5,000 arriving at a time. Usually one or two trains a day to process. And here is the funny part: they had to buy tickets to ride the train!

"After we had them unloaded and processed a couple of us would be detailed to make sure we had enough Zyklon B gas. We liked using it. Poison gas was always more effective than carbon monoxide or trying to shoot that many prisoners. The gas was always used in the larger concentration camps. We could process two thousand Jews in twenty minutes.

"We had to make sure that it was connected to the shower heads correctly. More than once the plumbing was sabotaged. Damned Jews."

"Towards the end of the war, we worked as hard as we could to finish our work, especially eliminating those like the Sonderkommandos who knew too much. But there was a limit. We could only process a few thousand a day. The real bottleneck was the ovens. We should have been able to process over ten thousand corpses a day, but the technology just was not up to it. They were poorly designed from the beginning. The bodies had to be trundled to them on handcarts! Hadn't they ever read about Henry Ford and conveyor belts? Then each body had to be shaved. And then fed into the ovens one at a time. When the ovens broke down, we would be playing catch-up for days. Then the ashes and bones had to be processed. We bragged that nothing was wasted!

"When the Communists started to close in on Auschwitz, we had to march the leftovers to other camps. Naturally, I went with the contingent destined for Mauthausen."

"Your war was over. Certainly you could see that. Why not just free the Jews?"

"I could not. To do so might have meant my death."

"How so?"

"The SS was looking for deserters. No soldier was safe. I kept marching with the Jews so it looked like I was still following orders."

"But, you were still killing Jews!"

"Sure, some of the weakest failed to arrive. But, that's life, isn't it, Herr Professor?"

"It was the middle of the winter! How did you feed these people? Where did they find shelter?"

"We had to struggle just to take care of ourselves. We could not muster much sympathy for the Jews. It was their own damned fault! To answer your questions, though. We were lucky to have our winter uniforms to keep us warm. Every town we went through was only too eager to feed us and provide shelter at night. Unfortunately, there was never enough of either for the Jews. You should have seen the rags they wore. More for a summer stroll. Some did not even have shoes! And slow! We could only do fifteen to twenty-five kilometers a day. You'd thought they'd be in more of a hurry. The important thing is we made it back to Mauthausen. It was like old times for a few days. Lots of my friends were there. And there was still plenty of food and booze for us. The Jews were happy to just get inside the barracks where they were out of the wind and cold.

"The Allies got closer. We had to destroy all the records we could and finish the processing. I regret to say we were not successful. By May 4th it was obvious that the Allies were very close so I took off. Rumor had it that the Communists might take the camp before the Americans. I had no wish to fall into their hands, so I headed home.

"For a while I was treated like a hometown hero, but then the propaganda started, the lies spread, the trials in Nuremburg where Hoess lied his ass off. Almost overnight I became a pariah. Old friends shunned me. Even my own family! Only Heidi and my brother stood by me. They exiled me to this mountain, to keep me safe during those dark days. I've come to love my little hovel."

Badly in need of a break, I stood, "Enough for now. Tomorrow?" He nodded as I gathered up my tape machine and notebook. Hans smiled as I left. The bastard!

Just seeing Erich's house in the distance brought me relief. Hans' craziness had invaded my very being. Hilde's cooking and Erich's friendship both could help me fight this insanity. I could not help seeing Hans and his cronies eying up the girls, whipping the Sonder-kommandos, and lolling around waiting for the first train.

Hilde opened the back door before I could knock. I must have looked terrible because she threw herself into my arms, forcing kisses onto my parched lips. Her warmth slowly brought me back to the present. Sitting with Erich in the living room, we talked low to hide Han's story from Hilde's ears. I played back my tape letting him use my ear phones. Erich's face went from calm to anger then tears stained his stubby cheeks. He yanked the ear phones off his head and stood.

"Jesus Christ, Meyer, you are not going to let this filth be printed. Can it even be true?"

"I'm not sure what I will do. Does his voice not have the right to be heard?

"No it does not!"

Hearing his shout, Hilde flew in from the kitchen. Erich gathered up his jacket storming out the door.

"Now what did you do," she demanded.

"He wanted to hear what Hans told me. So, I let him listen."

14

"That boy sure has an appetite!"

20 April 1939

My Dear Adolf

Happy Birthday! It seems hard to believe that over a year has gone by since that afternoon we made love. You have made me the happiest girl in the whole world!

Wow! Your son is growing every day! He is such a good baby. He hardly ever cries. Feeding him has become my only job.

Little Adolf is almost four months old. He's not walking yet or even crawling, but he sure likes to laugh! What a happy baby you have.

Paul looks him over almost every day and agrees with me. We have a great child!

Mutter comes over and takes care of Little Adolf some afternoons so I can take a nap. She is really loving your baby. He is her first grand-child, you know.

Even Vater has started to come in to tickle him or coo to him. Sometimes I look up from feeding Little Adolf and there he is standing in the doorway just smiling. He has even started calling me his angel just like he did when I was younger. I sure missed that!

Still no word from my friends For eighteen years we were the Three Musketeers, without the swords and mustaches! Wherever there was one of us the other two were not far away. Except for now. Well, once the snow goes and I can take our baby out more I'll see how things are with those two.

I hope you are not angry with me, my dear, but I went ahead and had Little Adolf baptized. Father Sohn was not very happy to see me. He is such a sour puss!

When he asked me for Little Adolf's name Paul stepped in and told him "Adolf Paul Schwimmer". He refused to say your name! Can he do that?

I'm sorry, but I had to accept his decision. But, I know our baby's real name and I'll make sure everyone else does, too.

I saw from the doctor's newspaper that you had a very good spring. I wish you many more victories, my dear.

I'll love you always.

Until I see you again.

Your Lotte

Lotte's Diary
21 April 1939

Little Adolf weighs almost six kilos! He is growing so fast! Of all the babies in town he is the strongest and most handsome. Of course, so is his father.

22 April 1939

I sometimes wonder if I dreamed this whole thing up. Did I really make love to Adolf Hitler? Did I really have his baby!

23 April 1939

Tomorrow, if it is not too cold, I am going to take Little Adolf over to Beyerlein's store just to show him off. And, on Sunday, I just might take him to church again now that he is baptized. Mutter und Vater are becoming more interested in Little Adolf. It's about time! He is their grandchild, after all. I am the only one who can give them more, so they better start treating me better.

Paul continues to treat me like a guest. He lets me do nothing around the house but care for Little Adolf.

Erich wrote him a letter last week saying he will try to get a leave. Paul thinks that once Erich sees Little Adolf he will come to his senses, admit he is the father and marry me. Boy! Are they in another world!

Erich is not Little Adolf's father, Herr Hitler is. I would not marry Erich, anyway. It would be like marrying my own brother, if I had one. Very creepy!

I'm very interested in seeing how Gerta's gossips act when Little Adolf and I enter the store. If Sofia or Heidi are there, we will have to have a little talk. I'm tired of being left out of everything.

The home of Dr. Erich Schwimmer
Oberschwarzenberg, Austria
13 September 1991

"Herr Professor, I trust you slept well. Uncle Erich and I have already eaten."

Hilde's eyes flashed to the kitchen clock. My eyes, grainy with the sand of a good sleep, followed hers. Could it already be after ten? No response was necessary, expected, or would have done me any good. Diversion, however, could work. I had little enough to lose. "Fraulein Hilde, your beauty is as the rising sun, your eyes two pools of sparkling water, and your outfit very fitting." This last as my eyes took the Southern route from her face to her feet with a layover at the twin peaks and valley of pleasure.

Hilde's face began to match the red of her blouse. With a very tiny smile creasing her full lips she turned to her stove to finish my breakfast. Apparently there was a way to her heart.

My efforts at softening her harsh shell had begun that first night when Erich offered to let me stay. The only bed available was in Lotte's room. To my surprise, Erich offered me that bed and Hilde had barely raised an eyebrow. Before I knew it, she was wishing me a good night.

Following breakfast, Erich and I took to our regular seats near the fireplace.

"Your Lotte and I were friends from her birth. My father had delivered her, of course, as he was the only doctor within forty or fifty kilometers. I was born a few years before her while my parents still lived in Vienna.

"We were the only children in the area without siblings. She needed a big brother and I wanted a little sister. Our families lived across the street from each other and our fathers knew each other from the Army. So, it was only natural that we became close.

"Our mothers, on the other hand, had little in common. My mother, Marta, was from Vienna. Her family was well-to-do. She grew up immersed in the capitol's culture and in her religion"

I must have given him a questioning look because he halted long enough for me to ask, "How did her religion ..."

"She was Jewish!" He huffed with vehemence. "My father was a Catholic. Not so uncommon in Vienna, but unheard of in the more rural areas. When they married neither of their families were pleased, but they at least accepted the couple. When the war came, my father enlisted. As a doctor he was made an officer and spent his time tending the wounded.

"When I was born, he could not be spared so she had to go through the whole thing alone."

An undercurrent of anger rutted his worn face and reddened his cheeks.

"This town, my dad's 'beloved heaven on earth,' as he often called it, never accepted her. She was as Austrian as anybody here, but she would always be an outsider. Even though my father presided at their births and deaths, healed and cured them, never turned anyone away whether they could pay or not, they would not accept my mother. Throughout her life the townspeople barely even acknowledged her, only enough to take her money."

Erich, by now, was shouting, his hands death-gripping the arms of his chair. He was leaning forward, his eyes menacing me like I was one of them. "My father seemed unaware of these snubs. Had he been aware, he would have written the whole thing off as women and their ways. But it was much deeper, and it was personal!"

Hilde roared in from the kitchen, her skirt flaring in her back-wash. She glared at me as if this angry shouting was my fault. She swept past me, falling to her knees, grabbing Erich's hands.

"Uncle, Uncle. You must calm yourself. That is all in the past. It is all best forgotten!"

"She remained true to her faith until …" tears crowded Erich's eyes as his voice caught, "… she died."

Hilde held onto his hands as he slowly melted, relaxing until he slumped back into his chair. His eyes stared at something a thousand miles away, reliving decades past. She motioned to a table on the other side of Erich with her chin and eyes as a guide. She ordered me.

"In there … Pill … Get me two!"

Scrambling to obey I maneuvered around her feet and his chair. I opened the drawer to see a forest of medicine bottles. Some brown and tall, some smaller and clear and one small green one.

"Hilde! Which one?"

"The green bottle!"

That sure made it easy. I gripped it to open it. Sweating hands fumbling this simple task. Finally, success.

"How many pills?"

"I told you! Two. And hurry!"

Nothing like more stress. I tipped the bottle, eight small white footballs avalanching into my palm. I focused on rounding up the spares and returning them to the bottle. I'm nothing if not focused.

"Stop playing around and give me two!"

Wiping my hand on my pants I managed to pick up two and hand them into her outstretched palm. She clawed her hand closed, then opened it as she put it near his mouth.

"Water!"

I scanned the room, saw none and headed to the kitchen. Hearing her tell him, "Uncle Erich! Take these!" I grabbed the first glass I saw, added water and raced back, only sloshing a little. She grabbed it out of my hand and offered it to Erich. He took a large swallow washing those two pills deep into his gut. His eyes slowly dulled until he closed them, dozing with rabbit soft snores.

——

"What was that all about?" I questioned softly.

We were both kneeling, breathing hard, the adrenaline beating its retreat.

"Professor, you must understand that Erich's whole world was changed by Hitler and his war. From the day he moved here he has had a challenging life. There is much you need to learn. Let me educate you."

With that I sat back to hear her version of the life of Erich Schwimmer, MD.

"I know, Professor of History specializing in the Twentieth Century ..." she drawled, then snidely continued, "... that you know this era in an academic sense. Here is how that time affected real people. My uncle's parents came from Vienna. His father, Paul, trained to be a doctor. His mother, Marta, was a socialite used to wearing fine gowns to the opera and dining at the best restaurants. At that time there was a large population of Jews there. They were the cultural elite. Her family, the Rosenbergs, were minor philanthropists and strong supporters of education. Marta's father, Samuel, taught medicine at the University. Samuel Rosenberg saw some prospects in Paul, took him under his wing, and sometimes into his house. The inevitable happened. Marta saw Paul, Paul saw Marta, and the die was cast.

"Neither side, Rosenberg or Schwimmer, were overly pleased, but at that time such unions were not so unusual, so they all agreed to get along. It was expected that Marta would give up her religion and convert. When she declined, they had to move the marriage ceremony to city hall. Neither church nor synagogue would bless their union.

"Marta remained a rebel even when they moved here. Unlike Vienna, there were no Jews, no culture, nothing she could or would be interested in. She concentrated all her efforts on taking care of her husband and son.

"As Erich told you, Paul was oblivious. It was not until Erich returned to school after Marta's passing that it was brought home to him. On the very first day, he came home in tears. Several children had taunted him, calling him a Christ-killer and half-breed. Erich did not understand. He was just a boy.

"One of the unavoidable facets of being a small-town doctor is that eventually you get to know where most of the townspeople's skeletons are buried, you know of most of the pregnancies, acknowledged or not, also about any sexual diseases or other shameful maladies. The doctor-patient relationship meant something to Paul, but his son meant more.

"The next day he went to Beyerlein's and told a few of Gerta's gossip mongers that he was very upset about the treatment of his son by their children. So upset that he might just violate that oath unless things changed and quickly. In less than a week, Erich was happy at school."

15

"My friends, Sofia and Heidi, are the worst."

22 May 1939

My Dearest Fuhrer

You should have seen them over at Beyerlein's today. I thought Gerta'd die when she saw me with Little Adolf. She is still NOT pregnant. I hope Old Man Beyerlein isn't depending on her for an heir!

Sofia and Heidi were there too. They are not married yet, but Paul has heard some talk about the pair of them. I am not a gossip monger like some of these women, but let's just say that they are not as pure as the driven snow anymore. At least I was a virgin when you and I made love. I had your baby and am not interested in any other man.

Anyway, Johann was tied up working in the back, so Gerta had to take care of me all by herself. I had a small list from Paul: a pound of salt, two pounds of sugar, a pound of coffee, a half-pound of tea, and a box of washing powder; and a few things I needed for myself: perfume for when you come to visit, and new hose because Little Adolf made my feet get bigger.

Gerta forgot to be mean and asked me if I wanted help carrying this stuff home. I agreed that I needed help so she had Edgar Volk, the local do-no-gooder, help me. I could see Gerta was not happy which made me very glad.

I'm going to have to look for Sofia and Heidi at church.

Your Lotte

Lotte's Diary
28 May 1939

Church was a disaster. Little Adolf was fussy and cried most of the time. Only my parents would sit with me. It was like we had the plague or something! All the time I could feel eyes boring holes in my skull from the back and from that old priest from the front.

Paul had tried to talk me out of going. He and Erich never went after Marta died. But, I was sure that at least at church I would be accepted. The Prodigal Son and Mary Magdalene stories went through my head as I dressed. On the walk there, Vater even carried Little Adolf. A first. But when we got there he gave me the baby and made me walk in first. Vater und Mutter followed about three meters behind.

I felt like turning around and running out. But, I was not going to give in that easy. I had just as much right to be in church as all the rest of them. So I walked down the aisle until I came to a pew with empty seats on the aisle. I entered the pew and settled myself down with Little Adolf while my parents straggled in. My Vater, the great brave war veteran, afraid of a bunch of hypocrites. And Mutter was not much better. I made them step over me to get into the pew.

About halfway through, I'd about had enough. So had Little Adolf. I stood up to leave right during the sermon. I made a big deal of making sure I had everything. I let Little Adolf wail. Damn those Catholics! I walked out with my head high, looking at all of them as I strode by, daring anyone of them to make something out of it.

No surprise. They all sat still and pretended they did not even notice my leaving. Not one of them gave me a sympathetic look or even a smile.

I'm going to ask Paul to help me like he did Marta and

Erich before.

The Home of Dr. Erich Schwimmer
Oberschwarzenberg, Austria
14 September 1991

It is evening, Erich and I converse in his sitting room. Lotte's chair remains empty. I have a sense she is here making sure I plumb the depths of Oberschwarzenberg, burrowing down to the truth about these model citizens and their bloody past. In doing so, her own complicity is revealed, which I hope is bringing her peace. Surely, she was in no position to disparage these people. Not if she truly mothered Hitler's son.

"Erich, you and Hans Schuler were both in the SS. Not exactly honorable service. You a doctor and him a death camp guard. How do you account for this?"

"I was a doctor, Lorenz, in the Austrian Army. It is not my fault it was subsumed into the SS. As you know, I barely escaped with my life."

"But, that was after six years of serving Hitler. Your unit was in every major battle. In Russia, your army killed thousands, probably millions, of civilians, POWs, and Jews."

"It was the Einsatzgruppen that did all that killing, Professor."

"Perhaps, but they were following in your footsteps. You, doctor, made it possible."

Erich deflated right before me, showing every one of his years, plus a few more. I actually felt a little sorry for him, but I had to understand how mostly decent soldiers could so easily kill the defenseless. In wars, civilians are often killed as collateral damage, but not as policy. Not like the Nazis.

"What you say, Herr Professor, is true. I am responsible. My crime is even greater given that I was half-Jewish." He stiffened his posture regaining the bearing of a twenty year-old army officer. "At least, I did not work in the camps. Not like Hans."

This was not the first time I had heard these former Nazi soldiers and sympathizers use this phrase. As I had already talked with Hans, I could accept their assertion—but only on the surface. They *were* all complicit in the war and atrocities except the would-be partisans, Paul Schwimmer and Friedrich Schoener, and not until after their encounter with Schuler at Mauthausen.

"What makes you better than him?"

"I did no killing! I only let soldiers, enemy soldiers, die untreated as I was ordered to. We only had enough medical supplies for our own. I had no choice. The wounded Russians, most would have died anyway, could not be treated at the expense of my own comrades. It was that simple."

"And your Hippocratic Oath?"

"Soldiers follow orders even if they do not like them. I had no choice!"

"This is the same thing I hear from everybody. Even Hans says he was just following orders."

"The difference with him is that he enjoyed his duty. He never made an effort to transfer out. Right to the end, he killed."

"Was there ever a consequence for participating in the Nazi's killing machine?"

"Isn't it enough that my dreams are haunted by their faces? I feel my mother's shame in me every day. My father blamed me for the murder of her family. Hans did it. Not me! My father did not come right out and say anything, but it was always in his eyes. He served in the Kaiser's army. Surely, his hands were not without blood. Perhaps his wound placated his conscience. Lotte understood me. She accepted that I had to follow orders. She trusted me with helping raise her son."

"Adolf Hitler's son!"

"What of it. Are the sins of every father to be visited upon every son? I did my best to raise him to be a moral, mature man. It is not my fault he went to find his birth-father. He was my son, too."

Hilde, the ever-present peacemaker, interceded with coffee and strudel giving us an opportunity to calm down and re-group. Watching her pour and serve almost distracted me from my duty. Every time I saw her I fell more deeply for her. I could only hope she felt the same.

She moved behind her uncle's chair and spoke to me. "Perhaps it is time for us to all go to bed." Her wink promised more than a night's good sleep. Of course, I agreed.

The home of Dr. Erich Schwimmer
Oberschwarzenberg, Austria
Morning of 15 September 1991

I would like to say that I woke up in Hilde's bed. Would I ever! Seems her suggestion about going to bed could not be taken as anything more. I did wake to the smell of coffee and bacon—almost as good.

Erich was already seated at the small kitchen table. Upon hearing my footsteps, Hilde had poured me a cup. I joined Erich as we waited for our eggs and pancakes to accompany the bacon.

"I think, Lorenz, that today I should tell you about my army years. But, first, we eat!"

And eat we did. Eggs over medium with just a little bit of runny yolk, pancakes as soft and fluffy as duck feather-filled pillows, maple syrup made by the Herzog family, warm butter and cold cream from the farm of Reinhold Schuler, enshrouded by a coffee fog.

I quipped, "If you keep treating me this good I'll never leave." They both nodded their approval, Hilde adding a wink. After eating more food than I like to admit, I pushed back from the table. My mind was so fuddled with large doses of endorphins. I knew I could not hear his story without first going for a walk.

"Hilde, would you care to join me for a walk?"

She looked to Erich who smiled his assent, and joined me on the stoop.

"Which way shall we go?"

She answered, "Up."

We did not climb far up Plockenstein before I needed a break. In a little copse of golden-leaved aspens, I collapsed unto a large, flattish rock. The cold penetrated deep into my posterior, but her presence tight against my thigh sent warmth flooding.

Perhaps it was the confluence of all the physical that had me risk the emotional.

"May I ask you a question?"

"Certainly, Lorenz."

I had mentally composed whole paragraphs to describe my feelings, my ideas and fears. In her presence my words and memory escaped like spooked deer over the ridge. I was left with the simple truth.

"You are confusing me."

"How so?"

No apology. No help. I just had to forge on like the strong man I hoped to be.

"We have kissed. We have talked. We have held hands. We have flirted. Yet, I do not know what you are thinking about me or us? You talk volumes with your eyes and words, but I understand only the occasional sentence or two."

"Why don't you just say what you mean, then."

I thought I just had. I've never been known for my subtlety in my professional life, just my personal. Well, in for a pint in for a gallon.

"Hilde, do you love me?"

There it was. I had conceded her the key to my happiness. Yay or nay, my future was in her answer.

"I might."

Here I was baring my soul, smitten to the core, already dreaming of buying us a house back in Heidelberg—and she ventures that she *might!* She might what? Love me? Not love me? I guess my face must have telegraphed my paranoia.

"Lorenz, you sweet dope. Of course I love you … think. *It's been only ten days.* A girl can't be sure that fast."

My brain sighed in relief. I had made the first cut. Whatever it took, I was determined to make her love me. But, first, I had to come up with a response. Certainly, a "thank you" would not be appreciated.

"That's reassuring. I hated to think I was the only one in love."

I reached my arms round her pulling her into an embrace. Our lips met, sealing the deal with a kiss instead of a handshake. Then a few more for the addenda. And a few more for just the joy of it. Then a lot more.

It took us almost three hours to complete our half-hour walk. Our faces were red with heat, our bodies sweaty with joy as we returned to Erich's. I cannot remember the weather or what we talked about but I know it was good.

16

"Stay strong, my love"

4 July 1939

My Dear,

The weather here is just grand! The days are sunny and warm. Every day I take Adolf out to play on the lawn or for a walk along the river. He is beginning to almost crawl—always East. Ha! Ha!

He is eating some solid foods now, mostly potatoes and berries until we have a better variety later in the season.

I think I am experiencing something of the way the world is treating you right here in Oberschwarzenberg. These people are just plain mean! The women stare at me like I am carrying the plague when all I have is your son. My friends, Sofia and Heidi, are the worst! I was sure they would understand what I did, what we did, and love my son as I do. They still do not have any children of their own. But, NO. They have their own sad little lives and no time for me. Well, it is their loss!

The men are even worse. Even my school friends are obnoxious! They all think that now that I have a baby and no husband they can have their way with me. Well, they are wrong! I would not have any of them even as a gift! None can ever match you, my love! None ever will! You know I'll be faithful to you for as long as I draw breath!!!

Erich was home for a few days. As always, it was grand to see him. He is looking so strong and trim. The army has done him good. He got real attached to Little Adolf in that short time. Naturally, tongues *started wagging. They still believe that he is the father. Fools!*

Every night before he falls asleep, I tell your son all about his daddy so that when you come to visit he will already know you. I even have one of your pictures hanging over his crib!

Stay strong, my love. Little Adolf and I pray for you all the time.

Yours forever,

Lotte Schoener Hitler (has a nice ring to it, doesn't it)

The Home of Dr. Erich Schwimmer
Oberschwarzenberg, Austria
15 September 1991

Erich started his story after lunch.

"Thanks to the Anschluss and Hitler we were assimilated into the German Army as one of four SS regiments. So you see, I really had no choice about serving in the SS. It was necessary for me to stay under the command of Major Gnabbe, because he and I were friends and because he agreed to overlook my parentage. Doctors were needed far more than some stupid pronouncement by the Hitlerites. By their standards, I was Jewish even though I was a Catholic—because my mother was a Jew.

"A year after enlisting, August 1939, we became the *Der Fuhrer* unit. By October, we were folded into the SS-Verfugungs Division. I have to admit that it was exciting, being a part of such a large operation. We had gathered near the Holland border by March. Those were good days. We all knew this would be a short war. Who could stop us? The Poles had tried, but failed rather quickly.

"Our camp was near Bad Bentheim, north of Munster, an area not so different from Oberschwarzenberg. Most of my comrades had served together for several years already. I was a newcomer and I had been there for over a year! As a doctor, I had little to do for those few months of preparation. I inventoried my medical supplies, trained my orderlies, and made sure my horses were well-fed and ready.

"Hitler declared war on 10 May and we were soon in the thick of it. Everyone sees Blitzkrieg as a fast and painless way to make war, not like my father's static war of trenches and inches. From the propaganda, I had expected a few casualties, mostly minor. What I got were severely wounded soldiers, many of whom died. For this, I was not prepared.

"My very first patient, Sepp Hubinger, a man I will never forget, was really just a kid, a few years younger than me. He was brought in to my field hospital by a pair of stretcher-bearers."

Erich paused.

"I think, Herr Professor, that the story written by Hilde will be more complete than anything I can remember now." Erich picked up the sheaf of paper and handed it to me.

———

2nd SS Panzer Field Hospital
Oldenzaal, the Netherlands
10 May 1940

"Here. Here. Put him down here," I ordered.

The two klutzes carrying Hubinger were getting mud all over my operating area. In their defense, they were as green as I. One is never truly ready to face the dead, although they are easier to deal with than the wounded.

"It is his leg," the older one explained.

Poor Hubinger was moaning, his pain severe. Blood was gushing from below his right knee, not so fast that it was his femoral artery, but bad enough that I had to act quickly.

I yelled for my orderlies. To Herbst, "Cut his pants leg." To Knappe, "I need bandages and antiseptic!" Away they scuttled to do their duties. I quickly slipped on gloves, turned to the table and was greeted by a blood-smeared leg quickly becoming white. Poor Sepp was squirming like an eel from the pain.

"Herbst. Ether." In a few seconds, Sepp calmed.

"Knappe, clean the wound." I could see nothing behind the screen of blood.

A quick probe showed the bullet had entered the front of his shin just to the outside of his tibia and exiting through the back of his peroneus longus muscle. "Look, Knappe. Not too bad of a wound. He might limp for a while but he will serve again."

I excised the skin and entered his leg to repair the muscle, then sutured the skin, front and back. "Knappe, bandages." I wrapped the wound well and stepped back.

Herbst shouted, "Doctor!"

I had forgotten about him. I wished to bask in my first successful operation, not deal with him. I turned to him.

"Yes?"

"Doctor. Something is very wrong." Knappe piped in with a shout of his own.

I froze. I could not understand. I had just sewn up the leg. He came in with a leg wound. I treated a leg wound. And now he was breathing very slow and shallow.

"You damned fool! You gave him too much ether!" I barged into Herbst, pushing him away, feeling Sepp's throat for a pulse, trying to remember the cure.

"I did as you ordered."

"Then, why is this man dying?"

Knappe pointed to Sepp's shirt-clad abdomen. The field gray was quickly turning a bloody purple. Where had all that blood come from?

I grabbed a scalpel and cut through the shirt. There, just below his left nipple was a tiny hole about the size of a leech. A steady flow of frothy pink seeped. I cut into the wound making it bleed more. I needed room to probe. I inserted my finger trying to figure out what my eyes could not believe. Sepp's breathing decreased as my finger moved faster and deeper.

"Ouch!"

Dammit. I had not just found the culprit but had wounded myself in turn. I could not take time for myself, grabbing a forceps I dug back in and yanked out a piece of shrapnel. No bigger than a small diamond but much more jagged. I held it up to the light to examine it. With a loud gasp and a body-long shudder, Sepp died.

As I realized that I had missed a tiny critical wound while treating a larger perfunctory one, the stretcher-bearers brought in another case. I could only glare at the older one, as if it was his mistake rather than mine. Sepp Hubinger would not be the last to die at my hands.

17

"Please do not forget Little Adolf."

12 October 1939

My Dear Lover

Your son is wearing me out! He learned to crawl over a month ago and never stops! Mutter und Vater are over here all the time helping me corral the little bugger.

And does he eat! Everything, and lots of it. Cheese, sausage, apples, grapes, porridge, and then whatever I am eating, too. Paul says he is far above average in every category. I would expect nothing less from your son, would you? And Little Adolf has never been sick, not even a cold, thank God.

You should see the way Paul reads him a story every night. Little Adolf just sits in his lap and looks at Paul as he reads. It is so very easy to see the love they have for each other. My heart aches because he should be feeling that way for you. And you should be doing the reading.

Christmas is not so far away and neither is your son's birthday. Please do not forget Little Adolf. I know you are busy, but it would mean so much if you could send him even the smallest little gift. Just to show him you really care about him—and me!

I know you are busy defending Germany against those Poles. How dare they attack us! And then the other countries blame you and attack you! The Communists attacked Poland, too, not just us! Well, I do not pretend to understand all this political stuff. I'm just concentrating on being a good mother for your son. If I do not get time to write sooner then let me wish you a Merry Christmas right now.

> *Please remember us, darling.*

> *Lotte*

The Home of Dr. Erich Schwimmer
Oberschwarzenberg, Austria
15 September 1991

This evening, I continued reading Erich's story:

"The wind, snow, sleet, and the ungodly cold in Russia wore us out.

"I treated my first frostbite case a century ago on 6 November. I've treated hundreds since. The worst was a week later when the thermometer read -80 degrees F! Of late it has warmed to an average of just -20 degrees F. Occasionally it is almost up to zero.

"I do not know how much more of this I can take. The battle for France seemed so easy.

"Knappe died outside Yelnya in August just before we took Smolensk. He spent his day off visiting comrades near the front—much too close. I shall miss his dry humor and calmness, but envy him his peace. Now, I have only Herbst.

"There is so very little I can do. I have no medicines, no cures for the cold, no hope. This struggle started out so well. In less than two months we had Smolensk and two months later we were headed to Moscow. By 18 October we were within eighty miles, by 23 November, thirty-five miles, on the 27th just nineteen miles, and by 2 December just five miles. By then we had been battling the winter for over a month. Then the Russians hit. Back here I am, far away from my beloved Oberschwarzenberg.

"We, the few survivors, ghosted away our days awaiting the finishing blow that will destroy us and our hopes. I have come to realize that the Russians I was taught to despise are not so different.

When I was permitted to operate on them they bled and screamed just as us. Most, Russian and German, just died.

"There are rumors, more of them than soldiers to repeat them, that winter clothing is on the way, replacements are on the way, food and medicine are on the way. Nothing ever comes.

"We had been sent to France to refit as a Panzer-Grenadier Division. From April to December we were in Evenos in Vichy, France. These were the best months of the war I was to know. The weather was near perfect, sunny and warm, enough rain to keep everything green. We enjoyed trips to the Mediterranean for holidays and the people of Vichy treated us well. They had not directly experienced Blitzkrieg. Their leader, Petain, had made peace rather than keep his people in a silly war they could not win.

"The merchants were doing well supplying us and selling their surplus to Germany. Not like the Russians, from whom we stole anything we wanted and killed them just for living. Here, we were heroes. The men respected us, the women appreciated us. My practice consisted of treating VD, hangovers, the occasional abortion, sprains, and broken bones from daily soccer matches.

"We were flooded with new recruits hungry for fighting, but relieved to be training far away from the Eastern front. This changed in November."

———

"'Herbst!' Long before the whole Jewish thing came up, he had been, at best, sullen. Since, he was disrespectful, but knowing what he knew, I bought his silence by accepting his behavior.

"Again, 'Herbst!'

"He oozed out of his cot, put on his boots and slowly stood before acknowledging my presence or command.

"'What do you want?'

"We must prepare to move out. I need your help.

'Why in the world would we leave. Evanos has everything we

need.'

"Orders.

"Herbst kicked his way through the empty wine bottles, muttering darkly about Jews and war, to the wash basin.

"Where is Gugel?" I asked.

"'How should I know?' He plunged his face. When he came up for air, he muttered, 'Probably in the mess.'

"With all the sarcasm I could muster: Shall I go get him, then?

"Giving as good as he got, Herbst rejoined, 'Be my guest, Herr Doktor.'

"It wasn't hard to find Gugel. He was a true Bavarian, enjoying food and drink, weighing three hundred pounds. His only saving graces were his obedience and competence, the two things lacking in Herbst.

"I approached his table where he was holding forth with a dozen other soldiers. One spotted me and yelled, 'Attention!' The assemblage arose as one and saluted. I returned the salute.

"'Herr Gugel, if you please. We are moving out.'

"Groans from his table mates proved they had not yet been told. I turned, knowing Gugel would only be a step or two behind.

"For the next several hours we packed up my hospital, stowing it all on wagons."

———◆———

"After leaving Evanos we were sent to Russia. After helping to capture Kharkov, we were thrown into a massive assault into the Kursk Salient, a huge bulge in the German front line around the area of Kursk and Byelgorod. We pushed upwards of forty miles into the bulge's southern sector, but were pulled out of the battle when the offensive was called off. Then we were soon sent back to try to halt a Soviet counterattack. Our unit launched its own counterattack against two Soviet tank armies, where it helped destroy much of the Soviet armor, up to eight hundred tanks. The Wehrmacht lost at least five hundred tanks. Further Soviet reinforcements stopped our counterattack.

"It all sounds so neat. Each of those thirteen hundred tanks contained a crew up to a half-dozen men and boys, all of whom were either dead or grievously injured. The lucky were killed outright. Those that lived often became POWs who were often shot out-of-hand, or perished from disease or starvation.

"I only heard stories. I was too exhausted to go on the "field trips," as Herbst liked to call them, to see the carnage. Upon his return, he shared his tales with Gugel and anyone else who would listen. No matter how hard I tried to sleep, I always seemed to overhear. Never were they happy. The worst involved a Russian T-34 tank that had been hit by one of our 88s. The shell had entered the tank's side and instead of exploding ricocheted around the interior turning the crew into hamburger.

"Herbst thought this the funniest thing he had ever heard. I could only pray their end had been mercifully quick.

"The worst cases were the burns and gut wounds. I did not have the equipment to heal these poor boys. I could only dispense my dwindling supply of morphine to keep the pain down until they died. What a mockery my Hippocratic Oath was becoming!

"May God forgive me, but the only good to come of out of this— other than our return to France—was the death of Herbst. A Russian sniper picked him off as he was kneeling on the turret of a wrecked Russian T-34 tank for a picture. My *Mischlinge* status was now safe."

18

"I'm not sure he understood"

8 December 1939

Dear Erich

How very brave of you to volunteer to serve our Great Leader. If only I could. I would follow your footsteps into the army, but I would step forward to make the battle my own, not relegate myself to the sidelines as a medic. I try to not be too critical of your decision, my Eric, but you must know how very valuable every able-bodied soldier is to our struggle. Though, I suppose, in your own way you are helping. I'm sure the wounded thank you for helping them return to the glorious struggle.

Germans everywhere, according to the newsreel Little Adolf and I saw at the town hall, celebrate the great victories of Mein Liebchen. Even your poor father smiles proudly at the mention of your name. He says, "My Eric, finally a doctor!"

The Burgermeister says to everyone who'll listen how smart we were to join with Germany before the war. He says, "That way, Herr Hitler, will know we are loyal Germans." Even though we are Austrian, but then so is our wonderful leader. So!

Christmas without you and your friends will be a somber affair. I know you never really celebrated like the rest of us because of your mother. But, as she is now gone, perhaps you can forget her misbegotten ways. Really, Der Fuhrer would appreciate it. And so would I.

Little Adolf sends you his best, as do I.

Your friend,
Lotte

————◆————

3 January 1940

Happy New Year!

My dear, you missed such a wonderful Christmas. Your son got so many gifts. He is still playing with the few he did not break. Ha, Ha! I explained to him that you were too busy with protecting us to get him a gift. I'm not sure he understood.

I really need your help, dear. What am I to teach your son about the Jews? I think I know what you believe. I always listen to your speeches. But, you see, I am living with Dr. Schwimmer. He is a good Austrian, a veteran of World War I just like you. But, he married a Jew and had a son with her. Paul's wife, Marta, died quite some time ago and he never re-married. He actually buried her out in the backyard. I know that sounds strange, but he had a good reason. I know this is complicated but that is how my life is. Sorry.

So you can see my dilemma. If I teach Young Adolf your beliefs then he will come to hate his "Uncle Erich" who has always been my friend. He might even dislike Paul because of his marriage. If he was ever to say some of the things you do, I'm sure Paul would kick me out. Maybe if that happened you might bring me to Berlin to live with you. But right now I cannot take that risk. You understand, don't you dear?

Your Lotte

19 January 1940

My Brother Erich,

The mood was a little subdued here. Frau und Herr Stolz received notice that their oldest son, Hans, died in the service to his Fuhrer just before Christmas. We had not heard from any of you boys in so long all we could do was to write and hope. For the Stolz family, hope ran out when they got the letter. Their Hans had been wounded in Poland, not a bad wound really, just a little wound to his leg. But it got infected by terrible Polish germs and had to be cut off. Were you there?

That was not enough for that poor boy. No, not nearly enough. The infection had spread because the doctors were too slow in their treatment I think. What do you think? Surely, they should have been able to take better care of such a brave soldier. It is not like they had so many to care for. Herr Beyerlein says that there were very few Germans wounded in Poland. It was a great victory against those stupid people that started this war. I fear Frau Stolz will not be the only mother whose heart is broken.

Please take care of yourself. I know that you are not in danger as a medic, but there are so many bad germs and you are around the sick and wounded all the time.

Please try to get a letter to your father. He worries so. Especially now.

Your friend
Lotte

Lotte's Diary
2 May 1940

Paul got a letter today. We were seated in the parlor resting after eating the noon meal Mama and I had prepared. Little Adolf was taking his nap, finally. Everything was quiet until there was a loud rapping at the door.

I leapt out of my chair to get the door. I knew it was news from Adolf. Finally, he would take me and Little Adolf to Berlin. It just had to be.

Opening the door I found Edgar Volk, a toothy grin marring his dull face.

"Yes?"

"I have a letter for the doctor. It is marked urgent."

"Give it to me."

"No! Herr Beyerlein said you are not to be trusted!"

Volk pushed his way through me, meeting Paul as he was coming to see what all the noise was about.

"Here, doctor! A letter for you from Vienna!"

Paul took the envelope, read the return address, and nearly collapsed. He backed to his chair and sat down heavily. Paul asked me to pay Volk. I gave him a 10 Reichspfennig coin. He pocketed it and left with a smirk. He must like giving people bad news. What a creep!

I moved to Paul's side. "What is it?"

He did not answer, only stared at the envelope as if it might bite him. Of course, Young Adolf picked that moment to tell me he was done with his nap. When I returned with him in my arms, Paul was reading the single page. Again, I asked him what it was about. Again, I got no answer. The look on his face told me most of what I needed to know at the moment. Waves of arctic fury, moist sadness, and a depressed acceptance washed over Paul's face.

He stormed out the back door, forgetting his coat and hat but leaving the letter. Naturally, I had to look. It was from his brother, Peter, back in Vienna.

———

Paul,

You must help!

Marta's family—her dad and mother, both sisters and her brother, aunts, uncles, cousins—everybody was taken into custody yesterday. The authorities would only say they were being "relocated."

I am so afraid. Every day there are trains, their cattle cars crammed full of people being "relocated."

My friend, Heinrich, the cop, is now one of them, a Nazi. I got him alone at the Winterbiergarten yesterday afternoon. A few steins of beer and he told me the Jews were all going to Mauthausen. I had heard of the place, but knew nothing of it. Heinrich was very pleased to tell me *that there "they would get what they deserve."*

I fear the worst. You must go and see what can be done! Heinrich said that it would be a few days before they leave Vienna. The trains leave Monday, Wednesday and Friday mornings. They arrive in the late afternoon the same day. He suspects they will leave on Friday.

Peter

I collapsed in Paul's chair. I did not know these people, these Jews, but I knew of them. Marta's family. Paul, Erich and Marta went to visit them once or twice a year. Her family never came here. Guess we were a little too backward for them. I could see the doctor getting a little upset but people are uprooted by war all the time. Why, it was the last war that got him here. Well, whatever he was going to do sure did not involve me or my son!

Lotte's Diary
4 May 1940

Guess I was wrong.

I had just about given up on seeing Paul again. When I went to look out the back window he was gone. Me and Little Adolf had a quiet supper and went to bed.

A gentle knock and Paul came in.

"Are you asleep?"

"Not anymore. Where have you been Paul?"

"I see you read my letter."

"I'm sorry. You left in such a hurry. I was worried. Where did you go?"

"You know what the Nazis are doing to Marta's family." More of a statement than a question.

"They are being relocated. Perhaps to Mauthausen, near Linz."

"Do you have any idea what that means?"

"You and Erich will be able to visit them often as they will only be

a few miles away?"

He said, "You know nothing!" and stormed out. Again.

What was with this man and his running away rather than talking? I looked to make sure Little Adolf still slept and fell into a restful slumber of my own.

The next morning as we sat down to breakfast he pulled the letter from his vest pocket. He cleared his throat. "I must go to Mauthausen tomorrow. I owe it to Marta to try to help them." Then much quieter, "I'd like you to come with me."

I could not refuse the man who had been like a father to me my whole life. I had to make arrangements. My Mutter would take care of Little Adolf. My Vater prepared the car. I made sandwiches.

We left before daylight yesterday, my Vater at the wheel,

———

A yellow haze engulfed us as we left Linz. We were still a few kilometers away from Mauthausen when the haze took on the stink of burning garbage. Sick and sweet at the same time. We glanced at each other.

Mauthausen was huge! And noisy! Steam engines huffed their black smoke into the air. Lines of people spilled from the rail cars clutching their children and few belongings. The fence must have been three or four meters high and topped with barbed wire. The outer fence was festooned with friendly signs and mottoes like "Arbeit Macht Frei" (Work sets you free). About three meters further in was another fence with angry signs saying the wire was electrified.

Behind these fences we saw clusters of people surrounded by guards and dogs, yelling and barking. The guards used their rifles to poke and shove them around.

I recognized one of the guards, Hans Schuler, from Oberschwarzenberg. He was only a few years older than me. I was sure he would help us.

Father approached Hans in a jovial manner, reaching out to shake the young soldier's hand. Hans replied with a swift motion of his rifle butt to my father's chest, sending father backward, landing on his rump! Paul and I helped my father regain his feet. Hans glared at us. He yelled, "Go away! Do not cause trouble! Whoever you are here for, you are too late!" Spittle foamed his lips transforming his face into a grotesque mask. Certainly, this was not the Hans Schuler I had grown up with.

He looked around trying to see who was watching him. He must have felt safe because he softened his gaze and spoke in a half-whisper, "Forgive me, Herr Schoener. I didn't mean to hurt you. It is just these Jews bring out the worst in me." Turning to Paul, "Sir, no one gets out of Mauthausen. The people you seek are gone! It is best for you to leave and forget them."

From behind the fence. "Hans, anything wrong?" Hans shoved us away from the fences, saying, "Go now! Before I arrest you!"

We backed away. We had no weapons, just words. Two old men and a young woman. What could we do?

Paul stopped in mid-backward-stride. He excitedly pointed to a small group off to the side. "There they are! There's Marta's family!" He waved, we all waved. Paul shouted, we all shouted. No one noticed us until Katrina, Marta's youngest sister saw us. Before she could tell her family, the guards began moving them into a large stark shed with a large sign on it, "Arbeitskraft, die Gebäude Verarbeitet" (Worker Processing Building).

For the few seconds that Katrina saw us, we could read the fear in her gaze. It still haunts me. I am so thankful Little Adolf was not here. Who knows how it might have scarred him?

———

Letter from Paul to Erich
10 May 1940

My Dear Son,

Much has happened since last we spoke, none of it good. I pray you can stay safe and return home.

Your friend, Lotte and her son, remain with me and they are part of my troubles. I have not known how to tell you and I am not sure this is the fair way, but it is the best I can do right now.

Your mother's entire family—your grandparents, Samuel and Elizabeth, your Aunts Tasha and Katrina, your Uncle Saul, your cousins—Marcus, Julius, Annie and Paulette were all removed from Vienna in May. They were sent to the concentration camp at Mauthausen, near Linz.

I traveled there as soon as I'd heard and was told I was too late. I fear the worst. If you could have seen the look of despair in her eyes as Katrina and her family were herded into a building—the last I saw of them—you would think as I do. They have done nothing to deserve such a fate. I do not know whether to blame the Nazis or the Army— or are they the same thing?

Which brings me to Lotte and her son. That woman continues to believe her baby is Hitler's son! There lives under my very roof perhaps the son of the most evil man ever. How can I deal with this spawn when he calls me Grossvater? He curls up in my lap and asks me to read him a story every night. Am I to hate this child as I hate his father? Unless you are really his father. Might you be? It would so ease my mind if you were to tell me it is so. Then I could love him as my own grandson, the son of my son. And it would make his life easier and Lotte's too. So long as she has everyone believing her lies she paints herself into a tighter and tighter corner. I'm afraid for her and her son. Acknowledge her and Adolf. Tell the truth, son. It is not too late!

I am sorry to share only bad news with you, my son. The times here are hard already. I fear there are many years of war yet to come. In my time, our war was to last only a few weeks, maybe a few months. You know how long it dragged on, how many men were needlessly slaughtered and hurt, how much was destroyed. Your war can only be worse!

Keep safe, Erich. Do what you can to help us back here. Do come home again as soon as you can. Your last leave was much too short.

Love,

Papa

———◆———

3 June 1940

Papa

I was shocked to get your letter!

Mother's family relocated! How is this possible? What did they tell you? Have you been back to Mauthausen? What are you going to do about it? I have asked my comrades about such a place. Two said they had been there. They would say no more. Just that they had been there. I am thinking they looked a little ashamed to be admitting even that much.

But, as you asked, I have thought about the matter of Lotte and Little Adolf. As you know, she refuses all my efforts at romantic love. I thought for sure we would be married once she was of age. Instead, she gets pregnant.

I saw how much you loved Mama and wanted the same for myself. I do not believe I shall ever have it now. I do not think I can go through the pain you must have felt when you lost Mama.

As to Little Adolf. I categorically state that I am not the child's father. Were that I was. Whether Hitler is, I do not know. There is no way to determine his paternity. Even a blood test, were it possible, would not be conclusive.

He is a fine child. And I know you are attached to him. I can see that. So, in the interest of making everyone's life a little easier, you may tell the village that I am the father. As to marrying his mother, I cannot do so now being in the army. Should I survive we will see.

Your loving son,

Erich

Lotte's Diary
7 July 1940

Paul got a letter from Erich today. It was mostly about me and Little Adolf so he let me read it. Erich continues to deny he is the father which is the truth. However, he is willing to become Little Adolf's official father just to make things easier for us. What a great guy!

I could see the relief painted all over Paul's face. He can finally confirm what it seems everyone has known—Erich is Little Adolf's father! Of course I know the truth and so does Erich. Little Adolf will know it also. But for now, he has taken the pressure off us both and for that I am grateful.

Erich made it sound like all of his mother's people are doomed. I sure hope not. They were not bad people, just Jews. I know Erich enjoyed his visits to Vienna. He always brought something back for me. Sometimes chocolate, other times a scarf or lace handkerchief. Once he even got me a ceramic Dachshund.

Paul went right over to Beyerlein's to read everybody the letter. Of course, he only shared the part about Erich being Little Adolf's father. The rest of it was too sad.

———

7 July 1940

Dearest,

How wonderful it was to see the newsreel about your triumphant trip to Paris. By God, you put those French in their place! It'll be a long time before they ever think they can beat the German people.

Here in Oberschwarzenberg there was a great deal of celebrating your big victory. A few malcontents have been asking what we gained from this battle. But I tell them to trust in you. When it is necessary for them to know you will tell them.

I don't want to upset you but Erich will offer to be Little Adolf's father. Before you get angry, let me explain. You are his father and he will always know that. But, things have been so hard for me here. And you never write back or come to visit. The whole town has been so mean to me because I say you are Little Adolf's father. It is not that they do not love you, my Fuhrer. Quite the opposite. You will find no hamlet that so solidly supports you.

You see, they think I made up the story about us to take the pressure off Erich. How funny! Now Erich is stepping up to take the pressure off me and Little Adolf. How gallant he is. But, he is as a snowflake in your blizzard, so do not worry. I will always be yours and Little Adolf will always be your son.

I went with Dr. Schwimmer in May to visit his family at Mauthausen, but we were too late.

Little Adolf is talking up a storm! All day long. He talks to all the patients, everyone at Beyerlein's store. On Sunday, he matches that old sourpuss, Father Sohn, word for word.

Everybody is so friendly now that Erich has acknowledged your son. All my friends are back. People are actually happy to see me now. Little Adolf has a house full of playmates now. Poor child. He was so lonely.

Erich, by the way, is a doctor in your army. Do you have some sort of special award or medal for him now that he is taking responsibility for your son? I'll never marry him, of course, so if you could do something nice for him I'd appreciate it.

Little Adolf and I walk all over town and into the country. Your boy literally struts. He is so funny to watch. So confident. The whole town loves him!

At night he looks up at your picture on the wall above his bed and salutes and says "Heil, Vater."

I was wondering if you could have one of your soldiers go to a store and buy Little Adolf a special gift. Nothing big, maybe one of those

Russian dolls where there is another smaller doll and then another one as you take them apart. I know he is a boy, but he really enjoys figuring out how things work.

I hope to hold you in my arms soon.

Lotte

————————

My Brother Erich
14 July 1940

We have just seen the newsreel! My Adolf in Paris! Signing the treaty that finally redeems the German people from the injustices of 1918. It only took our leader a little more than a month to undo what all those weakling politicians failed to do.

You must be so proud to be a part, no matter how small, of this great crusade.

Jurgens Bender is looking much better. Being home has helped him heal so much faster than your hospital ever could. His papa says he will be returning to his unit next week. But, why? Surely this war is now over. Who is there left to fight?

The farmers continue to complain. As soon as you boys come home everything will be back to normal.

I thank you from the bottom of my heart for the perfume. I am certain that Der Fuhrer thanks you also.

Little Adolf sends his love.

Lotte

————————

Lotte's Diary
20 July 1940

Amazing! Guess who showed up this morning? Heidi and Sofia! And they had gifts for Adolf that he should have gotten a long time ago. Better late than never.

I found out they are both engaged. Amazing all the stuff that happened since they started shunning me. Heidi is hooked up with Reinhard Schuler—a farmer in the high meadows. Sofia is promised to Ludwig Rodammer. He is the son of the town's only mechanic. He joined the army just after they got engaged.

Tomorrow I'm taking Little Adolf to Beyerlein's to see how we are treated.

—————

The home of Dr. Erich Schwimmer
Oberschwarzenberg, Austria
16 September 1991

"That day at Mauthausen is when my father became a resistance fighter. Mostly by himself, except for Friedrich Schoener.

"Can you imagine just the two of them taking on the whole Nazi organization? Can you imagine what would have happened if they had been captured? How that would have affected Lotte and Little Adolf and myself? I probably would have been shot, too, or sent to a concentration camp.

"There was not too much to resist up here. The Burgermeister pretty much was the government. Occasionally a Gauleiter Spiekerman came up from Linz to check things out. I guess he knew about Lotte saying Little Adolf was Hitler's child. I think he wrote her off as a provincial eccentric. We had a town full of them."

Erich and I are seated once again in his parlor. I have extended my stay here. There is so much more I want to know. And, of course, there is Hilde. That woman can cook! She bakes, too. I fear I am in love. She just smiles like a Buddha as she plies me with strudel, schnitzel, and schnapps.

I wanted to know how Erich's father handled the deaths of his in-laws. For, indeed, following the end of the war none of them emerged from Mauthausen or any other camp.

"Paul listened to his shortwave radio. He had just about the only one in town. He kept it tuned to local stations when patients were around. In the evening he and Friedrich would gather round it here in the parlor to listen to the BBC. They took notes to help them remember the news. Then during the day they would work bits of it into their everyday conversations with the townspeople. I guess they were hoping to find kindred spirits to join their brigade."

"Did they blow up any bridges or trains?"

Erich laughed convulsively for a minute. "Hardly! A couple of middle-aged army vets? Herr Schoener had been a horse handler, then my father's assistant. My father was a doctor. They each had a hunting rifle, but that was about all.

"Their resistance fighting was talk, but at least they tried. That is more than the rest of them can say. The whole town went along with the Nazis. Lotte was the worst! She was raising Hitler's son right in this house."

Research Notes

Mauthausen was located near Linz, Austria. Altogether, some 123,000 to 320,000 inmates found their deaths there. The Nazis destroyed so many of the records that only 40,000 victims could be identified.

First established in 1938 to exploit a granite quarry, it grew. By the end of the war there were over 100 sub-camps manufacturing Mauser machine pistols, ME 262 jet fighters, and consumer goods.

In May, 1940, the first mass deportations of Viennese Jews began. Most were members of the intellectual and cultural elite. Many ended up in Mauthausen. They left Vienna in cattle cars open to the weather, with little water or food, only a bucket for a toilet, crammed so tightly that they had to sleep standing up.

When their train arrived at the camp they were herded out of the cars then sorted by age and gender. Families separated here rarely saw each other again.

Marta's uncles, Marcus and Saul, and her brother, Samuel were likely sent to work in the quarry. There they carried rocks weighing up to 110 pounds up 186 steps for twelve hours a day every day until they were murdered. They were fed poorly and treated worse. Death was never easy. Besides death from exhaustion, there were beatings, lethal injections and "parachute training" with the guards lining up the prisoners on the lip of the quarry giving them the choice of pushing the man in front of them over the edge or being shot.

The women were probably assigned work in one of the sub-camps sewing army uniforms. They lived in unheated barracks sustaining themselves on sub-par rations until they perished from typhus or tuberculosis, were beaten to death, starved, shot or gassed.

The children too young for work were disposed of quickly. Like Marta's parents, who were too old to work, the children were loaded into a mobile gas chamber along with twenty others. This vehicle's exhaust was vented directly into the passenger compartment so that by the time it arrived at Gusen (another concentration camp) all would be dead. Their corpses were unloaded by Sonderkommandos and taken to the crematorium. Another group was loaded into the mobile gas chamber and it began its return trip to Mauthausen, This truck made several trips daily.

19

"I just know it is going to be a great year for us!"

3 January 1941

My Darling,

I just know it is going to be a great year for us!

Your son turned two, in case you forgot. (Hint. Hint.) I'm so sorry you missed his party. Mutter und Vater and Paul attended, and a few of his playmates—now that he has friends. In fact, we both do.

We gathered in Paul's parlor in the afternoon. I decided to not light the candles on the tree in case the kids got rambunctious. Lucky thing because Gerta's son, Egan, crawled right up to it, then tried to climb it. The tree toppled over, candles and ornaments spilled all over the floor.

I hope it was alright for us to have a Christmas tree. Little Adolf spent hours just staring at the tree, candles glowing like fat angels with halos.

Vater made Little Adolf a wooden horse, black with white spots, with a little leather saddle. It looked real pretty. Your son was ecstatic. Mutter made him some clothes—pajamas and two shirts. Very cute. Paul gave him several new books they can read together.

I gave him a big set of wooden building blocks from the both of us. I knew you would not have time to shop.

My friend, Erich, the man pretending to be Little Adolf's father, could not make it home. He sent a mechanical monkey that beats on a drum. Noisy, but fun.

Gauleiter Spiekerman comes up from Linz once in a while. Might you send me a message through him? It would mean so much. I sure hope we can be together for Adolf's birthday next year. Don't you?

Missing you,

Your Lotte

Lotte's Diary
5 January 1941

Christmas was not as happy as I wanted. There was no word or gifts from Herr Hitler. Not even a pfennig! Doesn't he know how much we need him? Will Little Adolf ever see his Papa?

Ludwig, Sofia's betrothed, returned home from his battle in Yugoslavia to recover from his wound. How he can recover from losing an arm, I'm not sure. And after the war—of what use is a one-handed mechanic?

Erich survived his battles. He hopes to come home on leave in a few weeks.

———

The Home of Dr. Erich Schwimmer
Oberschwarzenberg, Austria
17 September 1991

The leaden sky continued raining on the worst week of my life. The encounters with Erich, Heidi and Sofia; Hilde's chastising tongue; the distancing by everyone at Beyerlein's; all conspired to force me to examine not just this trip to honor Tante Lotte, but my whole life.

Perhaps it is more of a function of my age. After all, my race is half-run. And what have I accomplished? Sure, I am a professor at Heidelberg University in my chosen field. Few other men can claim as much. Yet, when I look around at the residents of this tiny, insignificant village I find myself jealous, yes jealous, of these simple people.

Who am I to interpret their behavior over the last half-century? If I lived in Oberschwarzenberg, this little town in the northeastern wedge of Austria, might I have done the same? How can I say I would have done better?

I am almost the same age as Little Adolf. He was born in 1938 on Christmas, me following him by less than a year in November 1939. We lived through the same decades, had many of the same relatives, grew up a few hundred kilometers apart. How can one compare a youth spent in Vienna with this place?

But, first, I had to get some of my personal history down on paper.

Lorenz Meyer
Philipphof Apartments
Vienna, Austria
12 March 1945

Vienna was bombed fifty times. Luckily, most planes went to the industrial area and oil refineries. They made our life rough, but we still had our apartment, and I was protected by my mother's sacrifices from the worst. My father, like Erich, Hans and the others served in the German army. As an educated man, however, he never left Vienna, nor did he ever see real combat.

Until that night the war had kept its distance. That evening the bombers pulverized the Philipphof. Over two hundred civilians, mostly women and children and a few of the elderly had joined Mother and me in the building's cellar. We thought to pass a terrifying night, but one we would survive.

My five year-old mind throbbed with the banshee howl of the bombers. Mother tucked me under her as the roar increased. Women shrieked and children cried. Something was informing our souls that tonight would be different.

The whistle of the bombs overpowered our prayers, turning

our faith to dust. Huge chunks flooded down: doors, sofas, a piano. Clothing floated like goose down on the breeze. If I had not been buried under my mother, who herself was being crushed by rubble, I might have appreciated the symbolism. But, when you hear your own mother's praying turn to choking you are brought right back to reality. All night she moaned, though she got quieter as the dark lightened to dawn. To this day I wish I could see her one last time while she still breathed. To feel her holding me to her breast, comforting me.

I cried quiet tears for what no thing in my short life had ever prepared me; buried under tons of wood, brick and glass; hearing moans of pain and shock. Lulled to a sort of sleep by Mother's quieting gasps. Her broken body providing my only refuge.

I awoke, if ever I was asleep, to the rising sun flooding me with its frigid rays. I had not noticed the cold until I saw its feeble rays darting through Mother's long brown hair curtaining me. I should have felt colder, and would have, without her saving embrace and the warmth of her blood pooling on my chest.

Mother whispered with her final breath, "Lorenz, I love you."

I could not help myself. I yelled and screamed with a whisperer's volume. "Mama, do not leave me!"

I tried. I really tried. But I could not block out the silence. Was I all alone? Would Father find me? Would anyone dig through the rubble in hopes of finding some life yet flickering?

My skin chilled as Mother's blood froze into my clothing and soul. I was shivering, teeth chattering, legs and arms trying to jerk but compressed from above and wedged in below.

The Home of Dr. Erich Schwimmer
Oberschwarzenberg, Austria
19 September 1991

A soft knocking at the door, felt more than heard. Its volume increased as my conscious mind shook itself and regained control.

"Yes?"

"Lorenz, we need to talk," Hilde said.

I was not in the mood for any interactions with this dragon. Too often she had strafed me with her cutting wit and dark rebukes followed by flirty entreaties. I had declared myself free of her despotism only a few hours ago. Now here she was. On the other side of Lotte's door. Am I doomed by a weakness for a soft voice, long hair and good cooking?

"Can it wait?" Playing for time, hoping to muster enough manly bravery to survive another encounter.

"This is important."

Was nothing Hilde wanted ever not important? She trivialized my feelings for her, trampling them freely as an invading army. Not a bad analogy given my history of strength when facing angry women. She was one of many, but she was the one I was really starting to care about.

"Coming." Like a flame to its moth, I arose from Lotte's desk, the very one she had used to write her love letters to Hitler, and oozed to the portal girding my loins with nothing more than a smile.

"Are you sure this cannot wait? I was right in the middle of writing a chapter."

"I have strudel," she said with a lilt. There are reasons men have been reluctant to let women fight wars: they are unrelenting, do not follow orders, take no prisoners, and always win.

I grasped the doorknob like a life ring seeing my resolve pool at my feet. With a twist of the knob she was in.

Hours later, though only eighteen minutes by the mantle clock, I emerged from beneath the duvet.

"I knew you were the one." Between gasping breaths and grunts, she had kept up this wondrous litany. Is any man strong enough to believe differently?

Surfacing like a porpoising U-boat, she brought me to port.

Oohs and aahs, the occasional "O, God" punctuated our storm. Her tidal waves matched my tremor.

What could the creator have been thinking? Making us like each other so much yet not *be* like each other. I wanted to doze in the afterglow, but Hilde wanted to talk. We talked. Actually, I mostly listened, but that is what she seemed to want. Whatever, it kept me out of the doghouse, at least for a while.

"Lorenz, I am beginning to develop some feelings for you."

I mumbled something that must have sounded to her like 'me, too.'

"We have to talk about the future." I've known of her for barely two weeks, liked her for most of those days, but had not thought beyond the next minute. Thus I was always a step or a mile behind her.

"The future," I queried?

"Yes, my love." Now I knew I was in trouble. In my experience, limited though it was, the next phrase would be how she wanted to change me without actually saying it and maybe scaring me off. "I'd like you to move to Oberschwarzenberg and live with me."

Okay. I have to admit that I had contemplated asking her to move in with me, to become a professor's wife and have a professor's children. Contemplated, not decided. Just thought about. Nothing serious. We hardly knew each other. Well, we did now. But I was not ready for this little chat.

Always the problem solver, however, I cut to the main issue. "When?"

"You are on sabbatical?"

"Yes."

"Then right now."

Things were going much too fast. Just a few hours ago she had yelled at me for snitching a few cookies. Called me a fraud for upsetting the locals. Said she regretted ever meeting me. Said Erich should have never answered the door, letting me into their lives.

"Okay."

She sprang out of bed, shrugged on her clothes leaving me gasping like a gaffed carp. "Move your things into my room while I fix supper." Something was fishy here. She didn't bring any strudel!

Closing Lotte's door, she blew me a kiss.

I determined to be strong much too late. But, I didn't have to do everything she wanted. I could write a bit more before I had to move my stuff. Missing one of Hilde's meals was not a prospect I wished to contemplate.

——

Lorenz Meyer
Philipphof Apartments
Vienna, Austria
12 March 1945

I must have dozed for hours because when I awoke it was getting warm. No breeze to cool me, lying beneath my dead mother.

From far away I heard shouts. I was not alone! There were others. Whether the living or the rescuers mattered not. I might live!

From above came the sound of shovels digging, pry bars levering, and orders being given. A voice louder than the others, full of authority, called all to be quiet so he could listen for survivors. It was Papa. He was here to save me.

My sandpaper-dry throat produced only a hint of "help." I gave it as much energy as my body could and produced a low whisper shielded by Mother's cascading hair. All I knew was that I wanted to be found. Over and over, I mouthed help. I could barely hear myself. Could Father ever find me if he could not hear me?

My tummy groaned with the beast of hunger, my bowels were cramped. Hours had passed since my voice shut down. Every once in a while the digging would stop and the listening start, but it did me no good. No one knew I was alive.

It was getting dark, hope escaping like Mother's last breath.

I awoke to shouts of "over here." Had they found me or some other unfortunate? Dust was drifting down. Only Mother's hair protected my lungs. Shoveling noises were closer. I heard Father's strong baritone. "I don't know how, but I know my family is right here. Dig slowly so they are not hurt."

Saved! I was going to be saved. Then the noise trailed off to my left. "Don't forget me, Father. I'm alive." How could I expect him to hear what I could not say?

———◆———

The Home of Dr. Erich Schwimmer
Oberschwarzenberg, Austria
19 September 1991

"Lorenz. Supper is ready."

Damn. I had not moved any of my stuff. Too involved in my writing. I grabbed a handful of clothing and quiet as a chirping bat I slunk across to Hilde's bedroom door. I could not remember if it squeaked. I opened it slowly. It squeaked, of course, but as soft as a cat's purr.

I put my load on her bed and went to get another. Two more trips and everything was there except my manuscript. I was hoping Erich would still allow me to use Lotte's room for my writing.

"Coming, dear." And indeed I was. Galumphing down the narrow, worn steps into the living room like a hound into the kitchen.

There spread before me was a roast of beef, baked potatoes, a nice red wine and just two place settings. Candles graced the table wreathing Hilde in their aura.

"Where's Erich," I asked?

"He's having dinner with some of his old army buddies."

"Just the two of us?"

"Are you worried," Hilde asked?

"Should I be?"

"More than you will ever know. I will give you just thirty minutes to finish your chapter. Then I want you in my bed."

I left the table with the grace and speed of a gazelle, ballooned up the stairs, hurled myself through Lotte's door and landed in the chair at her desk.

20

"He looks so much like you!"

11 November 1941

My Dearest Adolf

You will never believe dear how big Little Adolf has grown. He looks so much like you! You must be so proud to have fathered such a wonderful son. If only you could come see him I know you would be totally in love with him just as I am with you.

Every morning he awakens to your handsome face looking down on him. You are the last person he sees before he sleeps and when he awakes. I have even taught him to say "Seig Heil" every morning and evening as he gazes upon your picture. If you have the time, and I know you are very busy with those nasty Russians, could you send Little Adolf an autographed photo of you? All I have for him now is a picture I cut out of the Linz newspaper from when we first met. Since Little Adolf is the fruit of that meeting the picture is most appropriate but does not do you justice.

Not a day goes by that I don't relive that wonderful afternoon. To have been in your presence was so wonderful, but to have shared our love holds me in awe. I've told Little Adolf about that glorious time so often he knows it by heart.

You will forgive me, please. My teardrops are staining these pages. After my last letter I promised myself to not get too emotional when I write you. It is hard because I love you so much, but I'll try.

I cannot stop myself from telling you how much I miss your gentle touch, your bright eyes and your worldly manners. The people of Oberschwarzenberg, the peasants, even Erich and his father, the doctor, are so plain and simple. They know so little of what is really happening. They only see how your great struggle for the German people impacts their little lives.

I often wonder, is it good to raise Little Adolf in such a place? As your son and heir, he is destined for greatness!

I keep a bag packed by the front door if you should ever want us to come to Berlin to be near you.

I'll have Herr Morgen, the pharmacist, take a picture of Little Adolf to send you for Christmas. We are allowed to observe it, aren't we?

Mein Adolf, please keep remembering us and how much the two of us love you.

For now and forever, Mein Fuhrer!

Lotte

———

A Letter from Erich
12 November 1941
Mein Liebling, Lotte

You will never know how much I miss you. Could you ever learn to love me the way you do him? After all, I am real and he is so far way, almost a dream.

Thank you so much for the scarf. Knowing you made it just for me means so much.

To answer your concerns about my service. I suspect my aptitude prompted me to become a doctor. Though, I fear my heritage has earned me the honor of being assigned to the front. Every day, I am confronted with wounds that are far beyond my expertise and training. Having Dr. Schmidt at my side is the only blessing I can see.

I know you do not see any valor or honor serving the brave

soldiers, but I am most confident that I am really helping the effort. Should I survive, I will have valuable skills to use at home. Perhaps enough to support a family.

As the Russian winter comes closer the lack of warm clothing becomes more apparent. I can only hope that things improve for us.

Yours,

Erich

Dr. Paul Schwimmer
14 November 1941

Dear Erich,

Lotte showed me your letter. I am appalled at your lack of winter clothing. I am sending you a box of your old winter clothes. I only hope it reaches you in time!

At least in my war we had warm clothing. Though we lived in filth and mud, we were warm. Even the men at the front were given winter uniforms. I cannot understand how the Army can so fail its men.

I shudder at the thought of you trying to doctor your comrades in the cold. Everything hurts more, gets infected more. Medicines are not as effective.

And to think of those broken boys riding like cattle back to the rear area breaks my heart. How God can let this happen I'll never know.

I pray you never get wounded. I don't know what I would do if I lost you. You are all I have!

Lotte still has her Little Adolf to keep her company. She takes him everywhere. Every day they stroll through the village, visiting with anyone who has the time for idle talk. More and more, people, and I must admit to be leaning that way, are thinking she is a little unbalanced.

They say to me, "Treat her! Make her better." But, I cannot

heal her mind. I do not have the training. Perhaps, your grandfather could but he is in Mauthausen and vowed to never set foot in Ober-schwarzenberg after your mother's death.

Maybe, my son, when you return from this war you can help her. You two were like twins playing together, talking together. I always thought you two would marry and give me grandchildren for my old age. Ironically, I guess I have one if you count her Little Adolf.

Enough of these ramblings. Take very good care of yourself. I am saving a spot in my practice for you. What do you think of Dr. Schwimmer and Son? Nice ring to it.

Papa

Lotte's Diary
14 November 1941

Erich should be ashamed! Complaining like that! It's a big war. I am sure my dear Fuhrer is doing all he can to help his brave men defeat Russia. If he did not provide winter clothing, it must mean they are behind schedule. He depended on them taking Russia fast. They have let him down. Their failure is not his!

17 December 1941
Mein Liebchen

Isn't that a perfect picture of Little Adolf? I told you he looks just like you, especially those dark compelling eyes. He even walks with authority, ordering around the others. They don't all obey but they will someday!

We are going to have ourselves just a little Christmas since you cannot be with us. Herr Wallenberg brought in a load of trees. I could only afford a small one, barely more than a branch. But, I thought it is important for our son to enjoy Christmas just as generations of proud Aryans before him had—and as generations to come shall. He and I both yearn for you, especially around the holidays. Might you surprise us with a visit? We don't need presents—just you.

Dr. Schwimmer sent his son, Erich, some winter clothing so he can stop crying about the conditions in Russia. He should be happy just to serve you! At least, if he is warm he can concentrate on being a good doctor taking care of the brave Aryans you have entrusted to him.

Little Adolf and I will say a special prayer for you at Mass. I know you do not need His help but it cannot hurt, can it?

Erich writes that a friend of ours, Marcus Hoening, is returning home because of his wounds. Erich believes Marcus will not have to return to Russia. Certainly that cannot be true! Even with the loss of his leg, I'm sure he wants to fight for you. Couldn't he drive one of those big tanks or at least run the radio? I would if I could, but I have our son to care for. That is more important than any old radio!

I'll bet Berlin is beautiful. All the streets lit up for shoppers, wreaths on every door, stores full of toys. Here it is pretty drab. My family was never able to afford much beyond a tree and a few presents even in the best of times. Not that these times are not good. But, you know what I mean. The war and all dampens people's spirits. Surely next year will be better.

My dear, it's Little Adolf's bedtime so I must end now. Your son demands that I stick to his schedule.

Good-bye my love.

Lotte

———

Lorenz Meyer
Philipphof Apartments
Vienna, Austria
12 March 1945

I knew I was going to die. At my age I had died several times playing soldier with my friends. Death then only lasted a few minutes and was much more dramatic. We would recoil from the bullet's impact, spin around, fall to the grass, reach up for our comrades, cough, and speak some final words like "they got me."

The cold became my friend, numbing my pain, my senses. Mother's loving embrace was starting to become bothersome as her body sagged in death.

I sensed the scurrying of rats. I heard them gnawing on my mother. I would be next. I only hoped they would wait until I was really dead.

My life did not flash in front of my eyes. There had been too little to make the effort. My final thoughts, I determined, would be of last Christmas.

Gathered 'round the tree with me were my parents. No lights or candles this year. Father had just brought in one gift and it was meant for me. It was big, square and brown. No ribbon this year. No wrapping paper either. But still it was Christmas.

It was not that we were poor, just that there was so little to purchase beyond the necessities, which do not make good gifts. Father asked me to guess what was in the box

"Is it a train?'

"No"

"Is it a gun?"

Father answered "No" as Mother gasped. She was not a friend of firearms, even toy ones. I was running out of patience. I wanted my gift.

"Is it a pony?"

"Actually, you are pretty close."

Come on! I was supposed to believe there was anything close to a horse in a foot square box. It had to be a puppy. I leaped up to hug both my parents, gushing my thanks.

"It's a puppy! Thank you so much! That's the bestest gift ever."

I should have known something was wrong the way they looked at each other. But, what did I care? I had a puppy!

In a somber, most un-Christmas-like voice, Father suggested I might want to open the gift before I thanked them anymore.

I ran to the box, undid the flaps, opened and looked inside and darned near got blinded as a streak of orange leapt out and ran behind the couch. I could not help it. I started to cry. Not because of hurt, but fright. What sort of monster had they gotten for me?

Mother crouched down and took me in her arms. Papa tried to keep a face to match his tone, but finally broke out in deep, rolling laughs. Soon, Mother joined in, leaving me the only tearful one. Talk about mean parents. Getting me a gift that almost kills me, then laughing.

In between guffaws she was telling me it would be all right. Father, still on the couch, slowed his laughing as I kept sobbing. His face transformed to that look he had for me whenever I acted like a baby.

"If I'd known you were going to cry like this I would not have gotten you anything," he stormed.

A movement under the sofa caught my attention. A small paw was followed by another until the head of a kitten was framed. I stopped my sobbing and crawled over to get a closer look. The kitten pulled more of itself out until there was a whole cat looking at me. Slowly it came to me and rubbed its head against mine.

———◆———

"Meow."

I must have been dreaming.

"Meow." A little louder.

Were the ever-present rats disguising themselves as cats, trying to be friendly before they chewed?

"Meow". Almost a scream. I opened my eyes fearing the horror of feasting rats. Looking me directly in the eye was my cat, Butter. The last I had seen she was refusing to let Mama pick her up and carry her to the safety of the cellar. So we left her.

From above I heard Papa's voice.

"That's my boy's cat. Hurry and dig."

Strong hands pulled me from 'neath Mother, pulled me up on the rubble, and laid me down. Butter sat on my chest warming my heart. Papa held my hands as he cried. I lived!

———

The Home of Dr. Erich Schwimmer
Oberschwarzenberg, Austria
19 September 1991

Lotte's door opened.

"Time's up."

"I just finished."

"Lorenz, you have only started."

21

"The rest you know."

Erich Schwimmer
2 February 1942

My Darling Lotte,

Well, dear, we must still be behind his schedule as the winter clothing has yet to appear. Please tell Papa that his package has not arrived either. Perhaps he can send another. I fear we have much more winter yet to come.

How is Little Adolf doing? Are you two getting enough food? We hear from the replacements coming up from the Fatherland that there are shortages there. A few replacements I am told came from Austria but not to us.

I have so much to say to you, yet my tongue fails me. Talking about the past takes up much of our day when I am not treating these boys for frostbite, wounds or dysentery. Especially Old Merz. He was a baker's apprentice before the war. Every day he regales us with recipes and descriptions of the most delicious pastries, cakes and strudel. In our mind we see stores bulging with food but it does not fill our bellies.

I have re-lived our childhood so many times that I sometimes think it is real and this whole adventure is just a dream. Were that so!

There is a commotion outside. Old Merz just shouted that a supply truck has arrived. I must go dear Lotte. Let us hope it is full of warm clothes, medical supplies and food.

All my best,

Erich

P.S. The supply truck only carried ammunition!

———•———

Dr. Paul Schwimmer
6 February 1942

Son,

I think it high time that I share my past with you. While your mother lived she forbade me telling about my years in the army and the disputes with your maternal grandparents. Regrettably, she is no longer with me and it is long overdue. You may not learn much from this discourse except to persevere in your dreams.

When I was about your age I only knew a few things: I wanted to heal and give life and Vienna had an excellent medical school. So I applied and was accepted. By far I was not the brightest or best but I was sufficient.

We dated, Marta and me. Her parents were aware of me but they did not see how much we meant to each other. When the time came for me to ask her father for her hand I was already a doctor and I was terrified. If he refused I thought my life would be over, so much I loved her. And, he did say NO. Her mother said maybe but could not defy him.

Luckily for us your two aunts, Anya and Tasha, knew that their chances for marriage depended on your mother getting married first. Your grandfather was a strong man but he could not hold out against those four women. Reluctantly, he finally agreed.

We married in 1912 and moved into a nice apartment. Though, eventually I was successful in Vienna I longed for the peace and serenity of a settled life. But, then came June 28, 1914.

Idealistic fools thought killing one duke would change their lot in life. How right they were. Over nine million soldiers were sacrificed to avenge the death of one second rate duke of a backward empire. As a young doctor it was expected that I would volunteer.

Austria began to mobilize not knowing in exactly what direction we would be going. Over the next few weeks the alliances became clearer. On July 28, we invaded Serbia. We were going to teach them a lesson. Then Russia attacked us and we were truly in it. I regret to tell you that our brave troops fought well but could never claim victory over anybody. First the Serbs, then Italy. They all fought us to a standstill or defeat. Finally in 1917 we fought Russia and I was wounded.

Many of my friends and comrades never came home. Many more left parts of them forever on the battlefield. I was lucky to survive with only one wound.

I returned to Vienna only to find doom and desolation. Then the letter from Lotte's father arrived. Your mother's parents were adamant that we were making a big mistake. They could not imagine me taking their daughter, a sophisticated and worldly young mother and plopping her into the hinterlands. But, I persisted and Marta loved me. So off we went.

The rest you know. I hope in the knowing you can see that there is a life, often a very good one, after war.

Be careful, my son.

Papa

—•—

8 June 1942

Father

Thank you for telling me about your past. I regret having to wait so long to really know you. After all you wrote I guess I do not know all the rest. I still do not understand why Mother died so young. Even now I miss her!

Here we have survived the winter with its three meters deep snow followed by spring's meter deep mud until now it is warm and dry and once again we are in the fight.

The parade of casualties seems endless. Every day for twelve hours I am on duty helping those I can and blessing those I cannot. Whatever good a blessing does from one like me. I hope to God, whichever one they believe in, hears me and grants them eternal peace.

Guess what? The winter clothes you sent me arrived—yesterday. Now I'll have to hide them until the snow flies as I fear we will still be here. Our advance has been stalemated. These Russians know no fear. They charge us without weapons! How can a country throw away its youth like that? I guess only that they think they are protecting their homes.

Don't they know we are here to rid them of Communist tyranny? I, for one, still believe. Could I be wrong? An awful lot of Austrian boys are dying for—I'm no longer sure what. I guess the Fatherland.

Please say Hi to Lotte for me

Erich

22

"He looks just like you, of course."

25 December 1942

My Dear,

A very Merry Christmas from me and Little Adolf. I know you do not really believe anymore, but we do. Your son is four years old. He looks just like you, of course.

I pray every night that Erich and his comrades will all return safely. How cold it must be there! I just know they will give you that city before your birthday. Won't that be a great gift?

Speaking of gifts. Again, I had to get gifts for Little Adolf on my own, even though I said they were from the both of us. All the other fathers gave their sons presents. Why not you? I know you are busy, but not once in four long years have you sent us even a note to show you care. The mail does go both ways, you know.

Forgive me for speaking so frank, my love. But it is so hard on me having you for a lover and never have you come to visit.

Paul's house gets so cold we can see our breath in the morning. By the time I'm cooking breakfast the kitchen is at least a little warm. I am not complaining, not really. I have it no harder than anyone else here. It just seems that if you really cared you could send us some coal or even a little firewood.

Excuse my penmanship but I am shivering so much. Little Adolf and Paul are hungry for lunch so I need to say good-bye my love.

Your Lotte

Lotte's Diary
26 December 1942

The news is not good—at least according to Paul. All I really know is what I hear on the German stations. They say all is fine. I trust them more than the English!

I have not heard from Erich for the longest time. Neither has Paul. Perhaps that is why he is so concerned about his son. I tell him that I heard that everything is alright. He just stares at me and shakes his head.

On the other hand, Little Adolf had a great Christmas and birthday even if neither of his dads sent him even a note let alone a gift. We made the best of it.

I'm going to have to give Little Adolf a different name. He is four years old and not so little as before. Already he weighs twenty kilos. No wonder—the way he eats!

And active! Always climbing trees, getting all muddy and wet down at the river, or covered in snow like a midget snowman. I wonder what his daddy was like at this age?

Little Adolf is sure a kind and caring child. Every night he brushes my hair 100 strokes. I wish it was Herr Hitler wielding the brush!

I'm sure he is going to grow up to be the guy who takes good care of his mama in her old age. My Mutter und Vater are getting old. Already they are in their fifties. I suppose I'll have to take care of them when they get older. Paul, too, maybe.

I've got to get Little Adolf to stop making fun of Vater's missing teeth. Mutter tells him that he had been very bad and the tooth fairy took back his front teeth. She hopes she can scare my son into being good.

23

"I fear we will never see him again."

Lotte's Diary
19 January 1943

I am truly concerned that Erich is not well. I pray that he was not frozen to death like so many others. Yet, people who did not lose a loved one in Russia say that freezing is almost a painless death. A soldier just lays down to sleep and never rises again. Somehow, I do not think it can be that gentle. I know that we spend a large part of every day just sitting around our poor little fires, shivering. I do not find it enjoyable, let me tell you.

Lotte's Diary
8 February 1943

Great News! Erich is alive. He made it back to Germany! Paul is smiling all the time now.

I do not understand why he was returned when the Army needs doctors. Erich said he might be allowed to come back home for a few days. I sure hope so. Little Adolf misses his "father." Every night after he salutes his real dad I have him pray for Erich. I guess prayer works.

Lotte's Diary
5 March 1943

Erich is home! As soon as he walked through the door I ran and leaped into his arms. Oops. I forgot I do not love him that way. But the hug felt so good! I'm sure Herr Hitler would understand. Best I don't tell him though.

I listened to Erich and Paul talk after supper. Most disturbing! Erich telling how the army had no winter clothing, not enough food, not even enough bullets. Their horses froze to death and their tanks would not start.

Bunch of cry-babies. Things are rough here too but do you see us surrendering? No! Little Adolf comes in to the house his face as red as a lollipop from the cold. Does he complain? No! Paul is having trouble getting medicine for some of his patients. Does he complain? No! We Germans are stronger than that!

I am sure Erich is making it sound worse than it really was. He has to. How else to explain him being here and everybody else still in Russia. Herr Hitler would not let his soldiers put up with so much hardship.

——•——

The home of Erich Schwimmer
Oberschwarzenberg, Austria
20 September 1991

Having read Lotte's three brief diary entries from early 1943 I've decided to spend the next two days reading from Erich's journal, Lotte's diary and their letters. I want to place them in chronological order, thus giving me a better sense of their lives during this period. I begin with Erich's story as written by Hilde.

The home of Dr. Paul Schwimmer
Oberschwarzenberg, Austria
5 March 1943, Morning

"You are so thin!"

That is how my father, Paul, greeted me when I knocked on his front door. It had taken me almost a week to travel here, much of it on foot. I'm sure I looked worse than I was.

"Come in. Come in, my son." I followed the old man into his

house, my house, though it felt very foreign to me. I stood looking at him, hardly believing, barely remembering a time without cold, mud and death. He turned from me and called, "Lotte! Adolf! Look who is here."

Flooding from the kitchen came Lotte, as beautiful as I had remembered. Her blond hair was pulled back and piled into a severe bun, her blue eyes sparkled in the dim, her footsteps soft as her approach. I did not know whether to hug her or just take her hand.

Little Adolf made the decision for us. He surged to me, short legs pumping away, cheeks bright and eyes gray and somber, and leapt into my arms, holding me like a boa constrictor. I had not expected such warmness from a child I only begrudgingly acknowledged as my own.

Lotte joined in the hug while Dad looked on and smiled. His little family was now complete. I loosened the boy's grip and his mother's embrace. I was not used to such closeness. The homey smells cloyed, the room squeezed me until I was gasping. Turning, I raced to the door and threw myself through.

Threatened rain, now real, exploded on my face, washing away the stench of home. Would I never be civilized again? For those cold miserable months I had dreamed of coming home. Lotte cooking, Dad sitting by the fire, Little Adolf writing or drawing at the table. Now, here I was. Home. And scared.

Dad found me a few minutes later sitting on the front stoop, face buried in my hands, sobbing. He sat in the wet, putting his arm on my shoulder and holding me like the confused child I had become.

I felt the old man shudder, then shiver, realizing that he was not used to such weather. I turned into his arms, trying to speak. He patted my head and held me all the tighter. His shivers matching my sobs. "What a pair we are, my son."

A snort and a cough brought back my voice. "Papa."

Through the door, I heard Lotte ask, "Are you OK?" Was she

asking me or Dad? Did it matter? I would never again be OK.

"We'll be in soon," Dad answered for us.

To me he said, "Son, we will talk later. For right now, we must be brave for Lotte and the boy. They have been waiting for my heroic son to return and you must not disappoint. Besides, this weather is hard on my old bones."

He lurched up, pushing off my shoulder, lending his hand to me. I grasped it in mine and let him lift me, light as a leaf. Together, father and son, doctors and soldiers both, we stepped through to my new life, if only for a while.

True to her word, Lotte made no attempt at intimacy. Cordial, but correct, she served lunch, then dinner. Little Adolf, became a growth, a fungus firmly attached to my right leg. All during the day he never left my side for more than a minute. He was a remarkable child, impossible to not like. Paul just looked on and smiled. He knew I was losing the battle. The boy was becoming my son.

He glanced at Paul to see his Grossvater's approval. Barely four, he was a real talker, telling me all about the town as if I had not lived there most of my life. Between Lotte and her friends, and being my father's constant companion, he was party to it all. He finally wound down a few hours after supper, not complaining when Lotte took him to their room, my old bedroom. Guess I was destined for the couch.

Paul and I were left sitting in arm chairs facing the fire, drinking wine. I think he was waiting for me to start but I outlasted him. Finally, he spoke, "Erich, I never spoke to you of my war. You were never old enough and then you were gone. Your mother, well, she knew a little, but some things are too hard to share. So, I'll understand if you wish to not talk."

"Then you know the guilt of dying boys I cannot help," I answered. "You know of the cold, the mud, the blankness of men pushed too far too young. I felt more of a butcher than a doctor. Legs and arms stacked like cordwood, corpses in stiff, still rows laying at attention. Their young souls fleeing this hell, yearning for peace. Is this what your war was like?"

"Yes."

I demanded, "Why didn't you ever tell me? You could have warned me. You stood by while I entered this inferno! Nothing! You told me nothing!"

"Where could I have found the words to tell you? How could I describe the horror? Even now, thirty years later, it seems a dream."

"You never tried."

"The next generation never listens to the old. If it did, that would be the end of war."

After a lapse, he continued, "I wanted you to be a doctor, but I never encouraged you to join the army. I never made you join the SS."

"I had no choice in being in the SS. They took us over just like they did the Poles and the French."

"And you never tried to get a transfer?"

"You know why," I answered. "Gnadde is my protector. Without him I could be arrested or shot."

"Even after they killed your mother's family!"

"You made me a half-Jew, a Mischling. I was a good Catholic until she died."

"I am too old to fight a battle that cannot be won," Dad said. "We both are what we are. We both have responsibility for Lotte and the boy. How we got here matters little. The future must be our focus."

"I fear this war cannot be won. Hitler has declared war on America. We are surrounded by enemies who get stronger as we bleed."

"My war ended when the Americans joined. I fear you may not be as lucky. My leaders were only stupid, not crazy."

———◆———

The next day, Paul and the boy went out on rounds. Lotte and I strolled to Beyerlein's. Walking side by side like any married couple. Villagers greeted me when they recognized me, but Lotte was clearly the center of their attention. Small towns might eventually accept almost any indiscretion, but rarely do they forget. In their eyes I was the man who abandoned Young Adolf and his mother. I got a few points for claiming the child was mine, a fiction Papa forced me into. Still, I had not married Lotte so the boy was technically a bastard and as such not quite as good as everyone else.

Lotte marched into Beyerlein's facing them straight on. She was a brave one. I followed her lead. Johann was barely civil, Gerta and her cackling flock less so. We bought our few purchases to the counter, some flour and coffee, a few sausages, sugar. The total was at least double what I remembered. I paid using some of my back pay.

Upon our return, Lotte went to prepare lunch while I went for a stroll. The spring flowers were starting their reach for the sun, bees buzzing the buds, birds building nests. It all seemed so normal it was unreal. I crossed the bridge over the Weissbach River, beyond St. Polycarp's.

I hiked up a small hill, and just sat. So much and so little had changed. If I survived the war, if we survived what would our lives be? Would Oberschwarzenberg be subjected to the destruction we had visited on Poland, France, Greece, Yugoslavia and Russia?

The war had changed me. Of that there was no doubt. If Lotte's story about Hitler fathering her son were true how would I raise this boy to not follow in his father's footsteps? If I failed to return, how would he turn out?

———

The sun was setting, cooling the hill where I had slept. I awoke hungry. I awoke aware that I must make the time I had left valuable. Little Adolf seemed to like me, and I was certainly starting to love him, despite his mother. If any good could come from this war it would be to never have another Adolf Hitler. I resolved to become the boy's father. For his good and for the world.

———

"I don't want to."

Who the hell does, I thought to myself. To Little Adolf, I replied, "Your mother and grandfather want us to go to church with them."

"But, Papa Erich, I'm tired."

Not nearly as tired as myself, but I am going to do all I can to see that this boy gets a good moral compass.

"How about we go fishing this afternoon?"

"For real?"

I nodded. "But, you must go to Mass first."

"Oh, alright."

From the bottom of the stairs. "Hurry up you two! Breakfast is ready."

"We are on our way, Lotte." To Little Adolf, "I'll race you to the table." Like a tornado, the little guy jumped into his clothes, tucking in his shirt as he galloped down the steps right into Paul's hug giving me a chance to sneak by and win the race.

First the whine, "Grossvater not fair," followed by the usual from Paul, "Life isn't fair, my boy," with Lotte providing the punchline, "It's a circus."

To which I could only shrug. I would not be there long enough to become a real part of the family. In just two weeks, I had to leave.

We men took our places as Lotte served us. Coffee for the men, cocoa for the boy, tea for Lotte. Eggs and sausages for all. Besides her looks, this woman could cook.

The kitchen was exactly as my mother, Marta, had kept it. For the ten years between her passing and Lotte's arrival, Frau Schoener had seen to it. She and my mother had been so close, almost sisters, which cemented my relationship with Lotte, though I was eight years older. Now, she was taking Marta's and Hannah's kitchen, making it her own, yet theirs, too. Well, it made me glad I could use the excuse of the hot coffee to camouflage my tears.

From the day Lotte was born I had loved her. At first, I know, it was brother and sister love, but by the time she blossomed at thirteen it was much more, at least for me. I never seemed to find the words to tell her how I really felt.

When I went away to medical school in Vienna. I dated. But, I never loved.

Two or three times a year I would leave Vienna to return for a few days or even a week. Lotte and her two buddies, Sofia and Heidi, were always together giggling. Later years, they would be talking about boys. Though Lotte never seemed too serious, Hans was always hanging around, trying to touch her. I suppose that is when I first came to dislike him.

I came back for two weeks following my graduation and before I was to report for duty in the Austrian army. This was the Spring of 1938 just before Lotte went to sing for Hitler. I suppose the timing and my going off to serve conspired to start the rumor about my fathering her child. I swear now as I did then that I never touched her. Nor have I since.

Little Adolf was eating so seriously that we adults could talk with little fear of corrupting him.

Paul led off on his usual rant. "Wonder what that old fraud is going to talk about this time?"

Lotte, shocked as usual, looked around. Seeing no one, she admonished him, "Not in front of the boy."

"Erich and I know all about Sohn's Christian beliefs, don't we?"

"Then why do you go," she challenged.

"Somebody's got to keep track of the old bastard."

"Paul, you must no...."

"Look how he has treated you and Little Adolf."

"He baptized him."

"And kicked you out of the choir."

"Paul, I am trying to forget all that."

"I'll never forget how he treated my Marta. In fact, him and this whole town can go to hell!"

At this, Little Adolf startled. I grabbed him up and took him to the living room. Shutting the door, I sat him on my lap. Their words were reduced to rumbles and did not interrupt the story I was reading to Adolf about the Prodigal Son.

Paul and Lotte said little on our walk to church. Little Adolf wanted to talk about that afternoon's fishing trip, especially as we crossed the river.

Lotte's Diary
7 March 1943

After breakfast when Erich and I were alone at the kitchen table I asked him why he left the battle. After all, it seems his men will need good medical care even as prisoners! Do you know what he said?

He said his commanding officer, a Captain Gnabbe, said Erich will be needed by the living, that he and his men were as good as dead. Another quitter! He sent Erich out on one of the last planes on January 24 with a load of wounded to care for. Lucky him. Having Gnabbe looking out for him like that!

The home of Dr. Paul Schwimmer
Oberschwarzenberg, Austria
8 March 1943, Evening

With a wink to me, Paul shoved himself up from his chair and said, "Think I'll go upstairs and read Little Adolf a story."

Paul had been getting less subtle about what he felt was my need to talk with Lotte. Apparently, he intended for me to cross my Rubicon tonight and so I did. Lotte, I'm pretty sure, knew what must be coming. She had tried successfully to avoid us spending time together. Every night she had gone up to read Adolf a story and never returned.

Tonight she would not be so lucky.

I know Lotte had stated quite clearly in her letters to me that I was not the boy's father, that she could only love Adolf Hitler. However, unlike der Fuhrer, I had claimed Adolf as mine. I had even offered to marry Lotte to still the wagging tongues but she had refused. Thanking me for giving the boy my name was the extent of our relationship.

I was returning to my unit in a few days and I needed to try one more time.

Turning to her, I said, "Lotte. . ."

"Please do not start. I have made my feelings clear dear Erich. There is nothing more to say."

"Lotte, I have always loved you."

"Erich, I have told you that I love Herr Hitler. There never will be anyone else."

"I took responsibility for Little Adolf!"

"For that I am grateful. But that cannot change the fact that you are not his real father."

"Can you ever learn to love me?"

"But, Erich, I do love you. Just not in the way you want me to. Can't we just stay friends?" She patted my hand like I was a little boy. "Remember all the good times we had. All the times I relied on my big brother to fight the bullies, to help with my homework. Why, Erich, there will never be anyone closer to me than you."

Another pat and she was gone. I stayed a while staring at the dying flames before lying down to a troubled sleep, thankful that my time here was almost over.

———

Rau's Hofbrauhaus
Oberschwarzenberg, Austria
9 March 1943, Evening

After last night's fiasco, I resolved to spend my evenings here, drinking. One advantage of being in the army—my drinks were free—as long as I was willing to listen to the old men brag about their war or answer questions about mine. Only one comrade, Luther Hoppe, was there to share my duties. He was serving on the U68, a sub formerly commanded by Captain Karl-Friedrich Merten, currently being refitted at Wilhelmshaven. As he had seen combat firsthand I was comfortable letting him handle our side of the discussions. I had little desire to share the terror and destruction I had witnessed. Returning to my unit sounded better all the time.

———

Lotte's Diary
10 March 1943

A courier came with orders for Erich. His unit is being reformed and they need him. He has to leave soon. Little Adolf is really going to miss him. They have been together every day, all day. They are so much like each other you would think they are really father and son. But, I know better!

I am making him promise to write to Little Adolf every week. And me, too. It was great to have a man my own age around. I'd started feeling like an old crone! Now, I feel young, again!

The home of Dr. Paul Schwimmer
Oberschwarzenberg, Austria
12 March 1943, Morning

Friedrich Schoener and Dad gave me a ride to the crossroads for the start of my return trip to France. Paul's tired old mare had a colt late this winter so it tagged along. Little Adolf wanted to go, but Lotte said that would be too hard on the nag. I think she just wanted an excuse to not have to go along, afraid she might start crying or something.

Following one of her best breakfasts of my stay, we hitched up Dolly and started south on the Schwarzenberg am Bohnwald towards

Linz.

——

Lotte's Diary
12 March 1943

Erich left. I fear we will never see him again.

24

"J am going to miss Mama and Papa."

1 March 1944

Mein Dearest Liebchen

You will never believe the beautiful flights of bombers that filled our skies last week. There must've been hundreds. I took young Adolf out into the street to see them. Their roar had awakened our whole village. Everybody was standing outside, looking up.

All those silver airplanes! You must be so proud! Neighbors said those bombers belonged to the Americans! How can that be? I remember the speech where you described these Americans as weak and mongrelized. Surely they are not capable of building such machines.

Dr. Schwimmer asked me that if they were German then why did they have big stars painted on them instead of swastikas. I told him that it was your brilliant idea to make our planes look American so the Allies would not shoot them down. Any fool could understand your strategy, dearest. So few people are aware of your intelligence. Little Adolf was so angry he wanted to kick Paul right in his old leg!

After all the excitement died down, we went to the market. The Burgomeister was holding forth on the latest war news. I did not listen! I know all is going well for you and the Reich. How could it not?

Later, I ran into Frau Zollner the old rumormonger. She wanted to tell me the same drivel but I cared not. One thing she did mention, however, seemed to be important. She said there is a new shipment of granite coming in from Mauthausen where Paul's wife's family is staying. She said they were going to use it alongside the street for sidewalks. Apparently grass and dirt are not good enough for her.

> *Your Lotte*

14 April 1944

> *Mein Liebchen,*
>
> *I hope you had a fun time during your visit to the Berghof. It is about time you took a break from all this war stuff. People just do not appreciate the great task you have undertaken, not just for Germany, but for the whole world.*
>
> *Little Adolf and I saw a newsreel of your time there in March. Blondi is such a handsome dog. I'll bet she cannot wait for you to come home every night. I know you must be tired at the end of your day, but taking a dog like that out for a walk around the block is just what you need. How lucky you are!*
>
> *Here, at our home in Oberschwarzenberg, you are missed. When are you coming to see me again? It's been six long years. Little Adolf will be starting school next fall. He looks just like you, and is he smart? Just like his Poppa! He knows all his letters and numbers.*
>
> *We both know you are busy. But it is hard for Little Adolf to be the son of the greatest person alive and yet never to have met you. I'm afraid some of his classmates will be mean to him. If they could see you two together, then they'd understand.*
>
> *I had a most unsettling experience yesterday, Little Adolf and I were out in the forest gathering firewood. Some day, Liebchen, when you have time, you will have to do something about these long cold winters. We came across a large gathering of rough looking, unshaven men all wearing the most ragged and shabby of clothing. They were cutting down our beautiful trees!*
>
> *I asked them why? Everybody knows we are only supposed to take fallen wood and dead trees. Not these beautiful, live ones.*

They acted like they could not, or more likely, chose to not under-stand what I was saying. Even Little Adolf tried to explain to them that these forests have supplied our village with firewood for generations. Well if looks could kill, you would be a widower mourning the loss of your family!

Finally, a German soldier came over. He told me and Little Adolf that these are what are called Russian POWs. I couldn't believe these are the sort of soldiers who are giving you so much trouble on the Eastern Front! They looked pathetic! Take it from me, Liebchen, you have nothing to fear from the Russians.

I turned back to these Russian POWs, and looked for the smartest one of the bunch. I walked over to him and began explaining to him that he should be happy he was captured. He should get down on his knees and thank God you, Liebchen, saved him from communism! Now he can work for us Germans, who know how to show our appreciation for hard work.

But, all he gave me in return was a blank stare. The guard told me they do not speak German, only their Slavish grunts and moans. I could see I was wasting my time, and Little Adolf's patience, trying to educate these, I hesitate to use the word, men.

We just turned around, picked up our wood and went back home. I hope that guard really punishes those Russian POWs for their igno-rance. Some people you just cannot help!

Little Adolf just told me he wishes to go for a walk, so I'll end this letter here, and mail it today. As always, all my love Liebchen. Do not forget the only woman who really loves you, and your wonderful son, Little Adolf.

Yours,

Lotte

25 August 1944

    Mein Liebchen,

    I am going to miss Mama and Papa.

    My God, I do not know where to start! Young Adolf saved my life. Thank God he was here. I must tell you what occurred just last Friday afternoon.

    As usual this time of year it was cloudy, very cloudy. In fact, the rain had just stopped. It had boomed thunder and flashed lightning all morning. We were with Paul in his parlor. I worked at understanding **Mein Kampf** *while Little Adolf played with his toy army men.*

    Just before I started lunch, I was at the part where you wrote, "Suddenly a voice seemed to be saying to me, 'Get up and go over there.' It was so clear and insistent that I obeyed automatically, as if it had been a military order. I rose at once to my feet and walked twenty yards along the trench, carrying my dinner in its tin can with me. Then I sat down to go on eating, my mind being once more at rest. Hardly had I done so when a flash and deafening report came from the part of the trench I had just left. A stray shell had burst over the group in which I had been sitting, and every member of it was killed."

    Little Adolf got very anxious after lunch. He has a great vocabulary usually, but all he could say now was "We must go!" over and over. I tried to calm him. I tried telling him that the weather was not so good for an outing. The boy was possessed. He would not stop. Finally I decided to humor him and got ready to go. Paul offered to take us in his car, but Little Adolf only screamed "No time! No time!" For what I wondered. But, I followed Little Adolf's orders.

    I suggested we go to Mutter und Vater's house just across the road. Little Adolf shouted "NO!" about eighty times. Then where should we go, I screamed. He pointed down the road towards the town's center and ran off. Paul and I followed warily not understanding at all why we were following a five-year-old. We attracted other people like iron to a magnet.

Suddenly we heard the strangest droning coming from the sky. The noise grew in intensity. We were frozen in place! Surely, this must be what a Valkyrie sounds like. Shrieking and droning. Getting louder, almost hurting our ears. Poor Little Adolf was beside himself. He wanted to run. He tugged at my hand, pulling me away from that hellish sound.

You would have been so proud of your son! He led that parade of innocents in a headlong rush! He never faltered, pulling me with him. How smart he is!

We ran and stumbled like leaves in the Fall. The screaming Valkyrie was getting closer! Running as fast as old people can, we reached the school steps where Little Adolf was beating on the door. Of course, it was locked. School was out. He took off again leading a large group of us around the side of the building. He saved my life! There were many who did not follow his fine example, who were not so blessed as I.

The Valkyrie came plummeting, wailing in its death throes right into our town. The explosion as it crashed was as loud as a thousand thundering clouds. And the fire. Like the inferno of Hell that awaits those who oppose you, my lover! Light as bright as the sun! The ground shook like Frau Vollmer's hands.

Little Adolf was eager to get me up on my feet to see what had happened. Little Adolf tugged fiercely at my hand, trying to lead me towards the inferno. Forgive me, but I had to tell him in my most angry voice that it was not safe.

He squirmed out of my grip and ran straight to the fire, anyway. Such a good little leader! Showing the survivors how to rescue the injured. I struggled behind him, calling his name, encouraging him to slow down, to be careful! How like you! He plunged on just the faster until we were so close we could see the markings on the craft. It was one of yours, Dear Liebchen. You must really speak to Herr Goering about this. So many hurt and injured, so many dead.

After a little, the fire died down and we could see that several parts of the plane, mostly the tail, were only charred. Little Adolf demanded that we get closer. I could not refuse him! We edged closer until we could look inside the plane. There was strange writing on everything! I was puzzled by this. Certainly, I thought, if our brave German boys were flying such a wondrous craft, then the words would be in German.

Then it came to me. Those words must be English. If this plane had come down in England imagine how confused the people would be? Bombed by their own Allies! It would demoralize them, bringing the peace you always wanted. How clever you are, my dear!

My parent's house was gone. So were two houses on one side and one on the other. In their stead was a smoldering pile of rubble and the sweet stench of burning flesh. My parent's flesh. The ones who abandoned me. We found enough parts of Mutter und Vater to bury. Nothing else survived, only memories.

Paul's house, my home, had all its windows blown out. We would have been pin-cushioned had we not left.

The funerals start in a few minutes. We are mostly burying memories for there was little left of them. If only they had followed Young Adolf! They would be happy and alive, helping us rebuild.

Take care, my dear. Please write, or even better, visit. Young Adolf misses you so much, as do I.

Forever yours,

Lotte and Young Adolf

Lotte's Diary
30 August 1944

I hate seeing my parent's house every time I look outside. There is so little left and that old bomber is laying on everything.

Their funeral was a farce. Two caskets when their remains would have fit in a coffee can if we had any. The church took care of the arrangements so that was a blessing.

1 September 1944

My dearest husband (dare I call you that?)

I am so happy you were not hurt too bad. Those men should have known better. You are too strong to perish. You and your Reich will last forever!

I'm really missing Mutter right now. I wish with all my heart that your bomber could have crashed somewhere else. Even after all they did to me I shall miss them. Poor Adolf blames himself for not saving them. But he did all he could in keeping me and Paul safe. How much more could a five year-old do? Even your son?

School starts next week. His teacher, Frau Langfelter is so old she taught me! Adolf will give her a challenge. He is a bright and inquisitive child. Always wondering why or asking how. It will be nice to have a break.

Little Adolf wants to meet his real daddy. He likes Erich well enough, but he is your child. I'll never let him forget that!

Lotte and Little Adolf

———

4 September 1944

Dear Erich

A German or an American bomber, I am so confused, crashed down on my parents' house. Your son and I and your father were saved because Little Adolf made us leave the house and take refuge by the school just as the fireball erupted. How brave he is. Just like his father!

Little Adolf started school yesterday. Already, Frau Langfelter wants to talk with me. I wish you were here to help me raise him.

Paul just told me that Paris has fallen to the Allies. This silly war cannot end soon enough for me.

Your son says he misses you and wants you home, too.

Be safe!

Lotte and Adolf

25

"These people are the biggest fools around."

Berlin, Germany
8 September 1944

Dear Lotte,

The most unbelievable thing has happened. After giving the Germans over five years of faithful service I am being dismissed because my mother was Jewish! Can you believe it? The bastards are even taking away my pension. They gave me the few Marks I'd saved so I can try to make it back to you and Oberschwarzenberg.

These people are the biggest fools around. They are losing this war and now they are sacrificing several of my comrades to their silly prejudices. Well, I have had enough. They don't want me and I am certainly tired of them.

When I think of all their soldiers I have patched up so they could fight for these Nazis again it makes me sick. And all the boys I couldn't save who died for these idiots.

I am leaving for home today. It is many kilometers but I have enough money to take the trains if they let me ride. Some stationmasters will not care they are transporting a Jew, but some will so I expect I'll be walking most of the time.

Wish me luck,

Erich

2 January 1945

Dearest Husband

What a Christmas we had! Once again I had to buy your son's gift on my own and tell him it came from you. This year you got him a drawing book and some pencils. He just might become the artist you wanted to be. Let's hope!

Paul's practice has continued to suffer. We barely had money enough for food for the three of us.

I'm not sure I understand, my dear, why you discharged Erich right when you need doctors most, but I am glad you did. I only wish you'd given him more money or even some food. He is still not home and I fear he has been hurt.

Soon, if God wills, we will have two doctors and not enough work for even one. Do not worry about us, dear, we will do okay until your final victory. Just do not take too long.

Paul's radio reports your last offensive failed. I'm sure that is not true, is it? I cannot believe that the Russians or the English will invade. Surely, you can stop them!

You should see how big your son is. He is a whole meter tall and weighs twenty-eight kilos. He is doing well in school, but talks too much, draws too much, and does not take direction well. Sounds like his daddy so I do not get on him about it.

His teacher gave him an assignment to do a project over the holidays that shows how patriotic he is. Well, of course he is. He is doing a history of the war comparing your victories with the others. So far you are looking good.

We are buried under a half meter of snow. Since we have nowhere to go it is not too much of a problem. How we are looking forward to the spring!

Little Adolf asked me to ask you when you might have time to visit. Though he has not met you I know he misses you.

Your, Lotte

The Home of Dr. Erich Schwimmer
Oberschwarzenberg, Austria
20 September 1991, early afternoon

"I am wondering, Erich, why you joined the SS given that your mother was a Jew."

"A question I have asked myself many times, Lorenz. Like many people in that era I was not thinking clearly. We just wanted to see and hear what fit into our lives. Hitler provided that. I knew that the Jews were not the problem that he made them out to be. But, he was right about the Bolsheviks, wasn't he? He was right about World War I and the Versailles Treaty, he was right about …

"Erich, please. You and I both know that is bullshit and well in the past. What is current is a world still recovering from the horror of the Holocaust."

"I had nothing to do with the Holocaust!"

Guess I'd hit a nerve there. "Erich! You were in the SS. They ran the death camps, including Mauthausen! Does that not make you complicit in the deaths of your mother's family? Your grandparents, aunts, uncles, cousins! All murdered by the SS! Your SS!"

We were both breathing hard by now, red-faced, leaning into each other. Only the fact we were seated kept us from coming to blows. As if on cue, Hilde rushed in, knelt between us facing Erich, but talking, actually more like yelling, at me.

"You are a bastard and an idiot! All you do is get people upset and angry. Oberschwarzenberg was a nice quiet town before you showed up. Get out! Leave us alone!"

Then she turned her focus on Erich, leaving me to stew or leave.

"Uncle Erich, it's OK. I'll protect you. He's leaving right now!"

She raised up to enfold him in her embrace. As he calmed, the tears started to flow. He snuffled out a few words that sounded like, "I'm sorry." At least that is what I chose to hear.

In a calmer tone, she said to me. "Please leave us now, but come back in a few hours."

This was all new to me, too. I was not use to being so aggressive. I had always tried to get along. But coming here had slowly raised my anger level. I had not expected this many hypocrites in such a small hamlet. Her thinking she had to protect her uncle from me? I was not a violent man!

I left knowing this conversation was far from being concluded.

———•———

This time the three of us were seated in the kitchen at the table on those hard kitchen chairs endemic to this area. The setting sun sprinkled off the flocking dust motes. Erich was sipping whiskey from a water tumbler. A half-empty bottle stood near.

"Herr Professor, you are entirely correct. I was in the SS and it ran the camps. But, and this is very important, I did not know about the Holocaust until I left the Army. By then it was far too late. I, like most everyone in the world, could not believe that such a thing was happening in civilized countries like Germany and Austria.

"Please recall," he continued, "that Hitler was seen as a savior. Many, many people were caught up in his web of lies."

I studied him for a moment, then spoke.

"As a matter of fact, you are correct. *TIME* magazine had named Hitler "Man of the Year" in 1939. The world gave him the Olympics in 1936 when Dachau had been already in operation for three years. The British and French forgave the Versailles Treaty's demand for repayment, gave back German territory, and gave him Czechoslovakia without a fight in 1938. Henry Ford applauded Hitler's anti-Semitism.

"Erich, please accept my apology. I know you were not responsible. I just went off on a tangent and got emotional. I usually am so circumspect."

"Lorenz, I accept. Let us have a drink to peace and understanding."

Hilde jumped up to get glasses. Erich filled them. And we toasted. Then we continued our talk.

"So, if I understand you correctly, Erich, your commanding officer, this Lt. Gnabbe, knew of your Jewish background?"

"As you know, I was a mischlinge."*

"And he protected you until his death in 1944?"

"I was a doctor and therefore valuable. As far as the other men knew I was as German and Christian as any of them. Which, of course, I was. Nevertheless, I felt that I always had to be exceedingly careful when talking about my family and life back in Oberschwarzenberg.

"I knew that my past could catch up to me at anytime but I thought they would make an allowance for me, a doctor. I had been with the 2nd SS Panzers, my God! And now that same SS was telling me I could not practice medicine in their country or their army! Whoever heard of such silliness.

"The rules that Hitler imposed on the Germans were first announced at a party gathering in Nuremberg. They mostly were concerned with marriage and citizenship. I was already in the Austrian Army in 1938 when the Anschluss, the annexation of Austria to Germany, took place. The Germans knew they would need trained doctors so no one looked too closely at us Austrians. I was amazed to find myself serving in an SS unit. But I had little choice. To ask for a transfer would be to expose my past and put my father at risk. So I kept quiet and did my job. From Poland, through Belgium and into France, and the years of war in Russia only to be treated as an animal which has outlived its usefulness! Put out to pasture with only the few Reichmarks I had saved, barely enough to get me home!

"I left Berlin and headed south. I ended up having to walk most of those kilometers. I witnessed things I never wanted to see then and never want to see again. Often as I waited for a stationmaster to decide if I was to ride the train or walk I would see a whole train of cattle cars hauling people!

"What have they done to merit such treatment," I asked anybody near me.

"They are just Jews," they answered.

"Where are they going," I asked.

·"Depending on where I was the answer could be Auschwitz or Mauthausen or Treblinka. Always they were going, always they were moaning and crying out. Most Germans refused to look, to see how their friends and neighbors, their fellow human beings, were being treated.

"And me a doctor. What could I do? I could hardly take care of myself! Often I joined in not looking, not seeing because I did not have the power to change anything.

I asked him, "When did you learn that these trains, these camps meant death to your fellow Jews?"

"I learned the hard way. I was at the train station in Passau, Germany right on the Austrian border. It was a busy day, a Sunday, October 1st. The station was clogged with families and soldiers, the SS and Polizei. I still wore my uniform though it was dusty and a little frayed after so long on the road. I had recently made a sling for my right arm that helped me blend in with the other wounded on their way home for recuperation.

"In a crowd of over a dozen soldiers, I was waiting for the ticket agent. As I neared I saw the delay was caused by an SS man in his long black coat and black uniform checking papers. Already there were two soldiers being held at gunpoint by a dozen of the local Polizei. Thus far, I had been quite lucky.

"Back in Nuremburg, a similar screening resulted in my temporary capture. Three Polizei, a driver and two guards accompanied me to SS headquarters. There, I was ushered into the office of Sturmbannfuhrer Mosel. He was one of those Aryan super men with blond hair and deathly blue eyes. Luckily, he had a wife who was pregnant. Her call was put through just before I feared he might get violent. He ordered me to go to his home to birth his child. Since I had no choice other than being shot, I went.

"It was a breech delivery. I had never delivered a baby before, but I remembered enough from helping my father that I was able to save the baby, a three and a half kilogram boy, and the mother. We delivered both to the hospital and he took me to the depot. He offered no thanks but I had my freedom.

"I doubted I would be so lucky this time. I saw no way out. The exits were all covered by the Polizei and I was not a violent man ready to take hostages, so I just waited my turn and my fate.

"I handed him my papers. He did not introduce himself, just focused his mole-like features on my ID. Either he read poorly or wanted some drama. He kept me waiting for what seemed half a day but was only two minutes on the large clock above his head.

"So, you are a doctor," he began. I saw no need to respond to the obvious. "A wounded doctor? Going home to recuperate?"

Getting no response, he finally looked up at me comparing me to my photo. In 1938, I stood just under two meters, weighed eighty-three kilos. Now, I felt shorter, the war and tension eating away at both dimensions. I was down to barely seventy kilos. I noted his rank.

"Lieutenant. You are of course, correct."

"Don't pander to me!"

"I only meant to compliment your deductive powers."

His scowl softened into something far from a smile. "Let me see here …"

Erich paused is his monologue, breathed deeply, then looked at me with exhausted eyes.

"You have my journal there. May I see it, please."

I handed it to him. He flipped through some pages, stopped and studied an entry, then passed it back to me.

"My memory of what followed had been robbing me of sleep for years. I recorded it here thanks to Hilde and found some peace."

He then bid me goodnight. Even Hilde soon tired of watching me read and ponder and said goodnight. I could not stop until I was done.

Dr. Erich Schwimmer
Railroad Station in Passau, Germany, 1944

Time slowed. It was hours between every click of the second hand. The clock looked down on me wherever I moved in that little room. An old chair tipped up to a chipped wooden table, its top scarred by carvings of initials and dates, only a few still readable: "Heinz Wassermann—6/12/42," "Sukie Schwartz—8/11/41," "Johann Hildner—2/2/43."

Were these others Jews? Gypsies? Mischlinge? Where had they been going? Where did their journeys end?

I tried standing, pacing, sitting. Nothing made the clock go faster: 9:43. I had been in here over eight hours. Had they forgotten about me? Was there another SS wife in labor? Might I get another free pass?

Thoughts of Lotte and Paul swirled my consciousness. The inviting warmth of Little Adolf's hugs. Despite all, I loved him dearly. Even the decrepitude of Oberschwarzenberg was looking better to me the longer I languished.

The clock hit 10:18. For the hundredth time, I tried the brass door knob, willing it to turn, to let me free. This try was no different. I sat and wept. After all that happened in the few weeks since my discharge this had to be the worst. I had been on the road, scarcely spending more than a few hours in any one place. Now, I was penned in this windowless cage, no more than a few meters square, walls painted a vomitous shade of green, dusty white ceiling and paint splotched, splintery wood floor. In time, I would look back and think this was the finest hotel suite in the world.

I must have dozed. I looked up and it was now 3:43. Afternoon or early morning. I had no way of knowing. The rest gave me the energy to assess my situation. I was a doctor, a member, perhaps no longer in good standing, of the 2nd SS Panzers. I was a citizen of the Reich, though now considered a Jew. I still had my knife but no gun. I was locked in this pen in the railroad station of Passau, Germany. My bladder was ready to explode. I rose and paced, working the sleep out of my joints. Two steps up, turn, and two steps back. After twenty-three laps, what else did I have to do besides count them, my bladder could take no more. The only receptacle was a small metal wastebasket. I moved it into the corner farthest from the door as if that could provide me some privacy should the door open as I knew it world as soon as my stream began.

Wads of paper, very official-looking paper, full of swastikas absorbed my urine, but did nothing for the stench. I was beyond shame after seeing so much death. Every one of them it seemed had chosen the moment of death to let loose their last evacuations. I only hoped this would not be my last.

The door slammed open as I finished. I buttoned my trousers as I turned to see who had invaded my space.

"Jew bastard! What are you doing?"

"I thought it must be quite clear," I assessed his rank, "Lieutenant."

"Do not get impertinent with me!" He slapped me! Right down to the floor! I started to rise, getting to my knees and hands. He kicked me in the gut, dropping me like a sack of potatoes. I was blubbering, not used to brutality. I'd seen plenty but never been on the receiving end. I found it immediately demoralizing. I stayed down. He kicked me in the ribs. I heard them break, at least three on my left side. Then a kick to the head.

I awoke trussed in the back of a truck. Canvas sides and metal floor did little to protect me from the cold. Two guards, barely sixteen-years old, armed with outdated rifles, were slouched on the bench seats on either side of my prone figure. I was faced forward looking only at canvas and wood and steel. I thought it better to remain still. Listening to their conversation, though enlightening, was far from reassuring.

"What the hell did we do to get this duty? Guarding a damned Jew!"

"Why didn't they shoot this bastard back in Passau?"

"Or better yet, hang him."

"How does he rate?"

"Look at his shoulder. He is SS."

So, they at least knew a little about me. And I had to agree with them. Why was I still alive? Consciousness faded to gray as they each put their booted feet on my back. Never wounded the whole time I was in the war, finally out and now tortured by the army I helped to heal. I knew I had broken ribs, an injured jaw, and maybe a concussion.

I could see the sun angling in and deduced we were heading east-northeast. Not the safest direction for me. It held death in the east from the Russians and the north held death from the Nazis. There is little worse than feeling your life spiraling out of control. Yet, there seemed nothing I could do to arrest my descent. So, I slept.

———

A harsh kick roused me from my dreamless sleep. Nothing had changed except that we were no longer moving. Boots still rested on my back and my body hurt even more. The cold had entered my guts, replacing the numbing fear.

"Where are we," I managed to ask.

"We are in Oberschwarzenberg, for what good it will do you, Jew dog, on your way to Auschwitz."

Oberschwarzenberg? Auschwitz! This was quickly becoming a nightmare. If only I could wake before I died.

"Why?"

"Because that is where dirty traitorous Jews like you are sent."

"It does seem a lot of effort to send him all the way there when we could kill him right here."

"We have our orders, Helmut. And we will obey!"

"Of course, Siegfried, I was only wondering."

The tailgate creaked down and the strong hands of the driver dragged me back. My trussed hands provided no protection as my head hit the bumper, bounced off the step, and plopped onto the muddy ground. I was home. This had to be a dream. My goal of the past months accomplished. My guards jumped down and released my hands, stood me up.

"I live here!" I pointed back up the street to my father's house.

That earned me a rifle butt to the kidney. I doubled over.

Only the driver spoke. "You may relieve yourself. Sorry we do not have a wastebasket." The guards chuckled and kept their guns aimed at me. Despite the stress, I was able to urinate.

"You do not understand. My father lives just up the hill."

The driver kicked me, sending me sprawling. My face just missed the puddle of my own urine. My chest was not so lucky. I was again tied and tossed into the back as the three took care of their own needs: bathroom, cigarettes, and schnapps.

———

My memory of the trip south to Linz is clouded by my injuries. These Nazis did not waste any sympathy or medical supplies on me. Why should they? I would be dead soon.

We arrived in Linz a few hours later. It was dark, blackout. The truck moved through the streets to the city center and the freight yards. With a shudder it stopped. The truck's racket was replaced by a low moaning that seemed to surround me.

Again I was pulled out of the truck with less concern than for a bag of rye. The drop to the harsh concrete knocked me out.

Shivering awoke me, but it was not my own. Several bodies surrounding me were quaking. The open slats of the cattle car increased the already frigid conditions. Only the Nazis could treat one in such a way that he would welcome death.

I rose, my bladder overcoming my pain, to search for whatever passed for a latrine. A fellow, whom I later learned was named Bader, pointed to a bucket already overflowing. He shrugged, saying, "Sorry, mein Herr." I ached the few meters, trying to hold my breath, and failing. The pail's stench overcame all the other smells: filthy clothes on louse-ridden bodies stewing in loose bowel movements and vomit right where they laid, in old excrement odors from previous occupants.

I aimed for the bucket but was guilty of spraying all around it—joining the crowd and adding to the problem.

"Where are we," I queried Bader.

"Linz, on our way to Auschwitz."

"Why are we not moving? How long have I been here?"

"Mein Herr," he responded, "I do not know, and a few hours."

I was at a loss to decipher his response until I realized he had answered both questions.

"Who are all these people?"

Bader looked round the dirty car, then answered. "I have been on this train now three days. We have made many stops picking up these wretches, a few at a time. They are all, of course, innocent and so have been charged with no crimes. So it hardly seems to matter."

"Why are we here, then?"

"By the look of your uniform, I'm guessing, you are a mischlinge like me. Most of these wretches are also. We have over a dozen military men, a few government workers, a Catholic priest, and a Lutheran minister. The women are wives, sisters and mothers, girlfriends—all guilty of being Jews or their friends."

"I was never a Jew, though my mother was. I was raised Austrian and Catholic. I am a doctor in the SS. I do not belong here."

"Your father's sin, marrying a Jew, is reason enough. I fear that a few days from now none of this will matter."

"Because …"

"Because Auschwitz is not a prison sentence, it is death."

The steam engine's whistle preceded the jerky start of my final journey. To have been home for those few minutes only deepened my agony. I never expected to see it again. From up ahead I could see a glow in the sky. A certain stench, that of decaying and burning flesh, human beings, sliced the air sneaking between the slats. It brought no warmth, only doom. A kilometer later, bright lights shut out the dawn. My companions began to stir, the few that lived. I noted, clinically, that some twenty looked dead: lips blue, frosty icicles on their eye brows. I had learned all the signs of frozen death in Russia. A few more, perhaps a dozen stirred as the train slowed, losing its rhythm. An equal number of us stood.

"We must help them to stand lest they be shot where they lay."

Bader responded. "It will only drag out their suffering. Let them lay in peace."

"But, I am a doctor. I must help them. I took an oath."

"Is that one stronger than the one you swore to Hitler?"

Shamed, I said no more.

Hardly had the train stopped when the door was flung open. We stood frozen, blinded by the lights and awed by the noise: steam engine huffing, dogs barking, guards shouting. Bader herded us to the door, pushing the timid to leap to the platform, falling en masse. Rifle butts and truncheons rained down on us. The hounds snarled, nipped at our hands and feet.

A loud speaker squealed, then boomed. "You will stand at attention!"

The guards and dogs backed away, maybe a meter, allowing us to stand. Bader kicked and shoved, getting us into two ranks. An overly tall Neanderthal watched over Bader, then stepped forward.

"I am Sgt. Bliel. You will follow orders or be shot. Turn right and march to the doctors."

Off to the side I saw a table with two officers seated. The doctors, I presumed.

Behind Bliel was a cluster of straggly men, dressed in gray-and-black-striped uniforms, dirty and unshaven. Some were pushing carts, others held long curved hooks, one or two had shovels. A half dozen guards surrounded them.

We marched, leaving our car full of the dead and weak. We had not gone more than ten or fifteen meters when we heard a barrage of gunfire. I turned round to see the guards standing on ladders spraying the car with their submachine guns.

Bader, next to me, said, "Now they will have peace." I could not argue.

The denizens of the eight other cars were bunched in front of the doctors awaiting their fates. Another look back nearly caused me to vomit. Those men in the striped uniforms were at our car. The ones with hooks gaffed the dead bodies pulling them to the platform where others loaded them onto carts. A few muffled groans told me the guards had not been successful. But, no matter. They were all beyond my help.

"Next!" I moved to stand at the table.

"Who are you?"

An interesting question. Many answers, though most did not matter.

"Major Erich Schwimmer, 2nd SS Panzers, 186589012."

He glanced up at me, assessing with a hawkish nose. His cap shaded his eyes making him all the more sinister.

"You are a doctor?"

"I was."

From out of the dark a man stepped forward. Dressed in the

standard SS uniform, sharp creases, bright buttons, black as the night. It took my red-rimmed eyes a second or two to focus, but he looked familiar.

He spoke to the doctor. "I know this man and his skills. We will want him to live."

The doctor nodded. To me, he said, "Over there." He pointed to a small group of prisoners being held by three guards and their dogs. Bader saluted me. He was not so lucky.

My arrival at the group prompted the guards to order us to attention and march us off. We passed through tall, electrified gates in two fences, past numerous guards and their ever-present dogs. Low, long buildings we passed were just starting to disgorge their contents. Even in Russia, I had not seen such a feeble looking group; sunken faces and stooped bodies. The barest of shoes hardly protected them from the stones and cold. Threadbare gray costumes—I could not then call them uniforms—hung on withered frames. Even on our quick march I could diagnose them: malnutrition, beriberi, broken limbs, missing fingers, exhaustion. Was I to look like this? How long would it take?

Sooner or later my own number would come up. My only hope was to stay alive long enough for the Russians or Americans to overrun this place.

———

Every day started with a roll call and ended with one. The guards were dressed in woolen uniforms, long great coats, and leather gloves. We literally died for such during those Russian winters. But here they stand, fat and warm, while we shiver in our ranks.

The longest roll call took over two hours in forty-degree cold. We stood at attention the whole time. They said it was because a few Russian POWs had tried to escape yesterday. So today we were required to observe their punishment. First they were tied to a post and whipped, fifty strokes each. Then the Alsatian hounds were loosed, tearing men's flayed flesh from their frames. After a few minutes, the dogs were called off. The Sonderkommandos had to carry the bodies to the scaffold where they were hung—slowly. Their feet jerked for several minutes as they strangled.

I saw Hans Schuler every day at roll call. Would talking with him help me? Would it even be allowed? Helsinger, a short stout Bavarian, standing with two U-boat listings noticed my interest. He sidled up to me after roll call this morning, eyeing me with his sly face and peasant manners. I guess he wanted to show off to his buddies.

"You are SS! You should be embarrassed!"

"What do you mean," I asked him.

"I see how you are looking at that guard."

Jesus! Bad enough being caged in filth waiting to die. Now I was being accused of being a homosexual! I remembered my Hippocratic Oath and decided it had no place here. Instead I looked at the odds. Three to one, except they had never seen me take action. Always I had tried to get along. That mostly worked for me in my civilian and military lives. My experience here, however, showed that going with the flow only resulted in death and degradation. Quickly, I punched Helsinger's red, bulbous nose. I heard the satisfying sound of bone fracturing and cartilage tearing. Nose gushing red, he backed away before falling to the floor. The sailors stepped up, looked at their leader, and stepped back, then picked Helsinger up by the armpits and dragged him away.

Hans observed this altercation. A day later, a group of us were removed.

We were stopped at a corrugated steel structure. The sign over the door declared "Shower Building." The guards ordered us to strip right there on the frozen ground. The cold wind shattered what calm we might have had. We leapt around trying to keep warm until the last man had finished. A guard opened the door, light flooded out. The warmth hit us like a tidal wave. I just might live. Surely, the Nazis would not waste heat and light on the doomed.

We marched in to our little bit of heaven. Heat washed over us. The walls were lined with shower spouts, at least a dozen on each side. Little shelves held slivers of hard, yellow, stinking soap. Very grainy. Harsh on our cold bodies. The warmth caused us considerable pain as we recovered.

"Quick! Into the showers. We do not have all day."

Worn, but clean, gray clothes waited for us on a table near the exit. Without needing orders we dressed quickly, finding the clothes that fit each of us the best. How I missed my wool great coat, my comfortable boots, starched shirts and pressed uniform! Warm and dressed, we were marched outside. The wind had warmed a little, but after a few hundred meters we were all shivering again. Our next stop was a barracks—although that is a generous term. No windows, and narrow, perhaps six meters wide and twenty deep. Up the two steps we marched single-file. One pathetic light bulb lit the whole room.

A guard snapped at us. "Find a bunk. Rest while we process the others." He slammed the door, threw the bolt and we heard the padlock close. I chose a lower bunk near the bulb. This was to prove a mistake later, but for now the light, though dim, mirrored the hope in my soul. My closeness to the earth gave me a little strength. I tried to sleep through the constant chatter from my fellow prisoners. They clustered around the light like moths, circling my roost. I had no choice but to listen.

I was able to put together a picture of who we were. There were scientists and engineers, a few welders and mechanics, and me—the doctor. Most were from France and Spain, a few from the Netherlands, and a smattering from Germany and Austria. The babel of languages devolved into variations of German and French. Some were educated and worldly enough to translate. No one talked about religion. If any were Jews, they kept quiet. The clot drifted apart after it was clear that none of us had the slightest idea what was happening.

The door flung open, bleeding in the early dawn's wan sun. Guards rushed in, each accompanied by a snarling Alsatian. Shouts, unintelligible to our frozen ears, were followed by strikes from heavy wood truncheons. It seemed that we were to get out of bed and stand at attention. At least, that is what we did and the violence stopped.

Though starved, I had finally slept for a few hours.

The guards gave us a minute to dress, then herded us out of the building into freezing cold. They marched us to another building several hundred meters distant. It was like a beacon with its bright lights. As we got closer the warming scent of fresh-baked bread drew us. We approached the door, a guard opened it and we limped in. They indicated we should be seated at a trestle table halfway down the room. That proved to be close enough to wallow in amazing odors, but too far away to actually eat.

Hans Schuler approached, quieting our whispers and questions.

"You will enjoy your breakfast, then the commandant will talk with you."

With that, a troop of women streamed out of the kitchen carrying pitchers of coffee, bowls of potatoes and ham, platters of bread and bowls of butter. They were led by two matronly figures with trays of plates and cutlery, cups and napkins. Each of us was served and the extras were left on the table for us to enjoy. There was little chatter as we all dug in. Many had not seen food in several days, including myself.

"Attention!"

We scrambled to our feet, throwing down napkins, grabbing a last bite of food or sip of coffee. A short man marched in flanked by two equally diminutive uniformed men. Their insignia was not familiar to me, a triangle lined in black on a circular red background. A dove stood in the middle, olive branch clutched in its mouth.

The trio marched up the aisle, stopping when they were abreast of our table. Turning as one, they stood at ease. The leader, in the middle, refused to look up to see our eyes and his were hidden under his cap's visor. He nodded, and the man on his right, said "You may be seated." Now we were below his eye level, so we had to look up at him.

The one on the left said, "Herr Doktor Professor Wein," nodding to the man in the middle.

I glanced to Schuler. He glared at me making it clear I was not welcome to look at him again.

Wein began. "Our great leader, Adolf Hitler, has given you men the greatest honor any true German could ever enjoy. His struggle, our struggle, has been and will be the cleansing of this planet of all its undesirable elements and enemies of the Fatherland. No doubt this is not news to a group of distinguished men such as yourselves."

Was this guy for real? We had been losing this war ever since we invaded Russia. The Americans and British invasions of Italy and France assured that it will end sooner rather than later.

"We have, many of us, long known the why of our great struggle. Even the how has been evident, at least in part, between our great victories in the East and our holding actions against the English invaders. Some traitors have tried and failed, might I say, to remove our Fuhrer. Those few malcontents have been treated to Aryan justice. Other defeatists are running for cover like the despicable vermin they are. They too will benefit from our justice."

Since when was death a benefit? I answered my own question realizing I was already in a death camp. That most of my railcar mates were already ashes.

"Our leader recognizes that camps such as Auschwitz are the source, the key to our salvation, our victory."

Wein was near shouting now, imitating Hitler's style and bombast. He took a minute to calm.

"He is allowing you to build the salvation of the German people."

Wein turned, marching out followed by his men. At the table and afterward in our barracks we gabbled among ourselves asking what we were to do and why us?

The next morning was a repeat, except breakfast was a glutenous lump laced with sawdust, coffee the color of muddy water, and we had to serve ourselves. Following our fifteen-minute repast, Hans Schuler ordered us out to the yard. Three trucks awaited us there. We were broken up into three groups and boarded our assigned truck under the watchful eyes of several guards on the ground and some already ensconced in the trucks. Our convoy trundled out of the camp past a phalanx of guards on ladders spraying new carloads of unfortunates.

———— ✦ ————

Several days later, we lumbered up to another barbed-wire-enclosed camp, Dora-Birkenau. We were marched through the guarded gates to a long, low building.

The interior was painted a bright yellow, even the floor. To the right stood a rudimentary kitchen, straight ahead lay a curtained area for sleeping. By far the bulk of the space was given over to several workbenches lining the walls with scattered tools, rickety shelving, and a few feeble lights. In the middle was a trundle cart, bright in the dimly-lit space. The cart was empty.

We were called to attention by a Lt. Pfalzgraf, as a tall, gaunt, cadaver of a white-coated man entered behind us, slamming the door shut. This, we were to learn, was Herr Doktor von Schluckebier. He ghosted up to Pfalzgraf, nodded once and addressed us.

"No doubt you have already met my leader, Herr Wein." We nodded. "You have not been chosen by der Fuhrer or anyone else very important. You just happen to have the skills we need right now and you survived your trip from Auschwitz. Therefore, you are now mine. Any deviation, any slacking, any sabotage will be dealt with summarily.

"Lieutenant?"

"Yes, sir!"

"You will please demonstrate what I mean."

Pfalzgraf nodded to one of his men who nodded to another by the door. A pair of Sonderkommando struggled to pull in a bony object, hardly recognizable as human. Dragging him in front of us, they shoved him to his knees in front of Schluckebier.

"This is what happens to anyone who disobeys," Schluckebier roared. He stared at us as Pfalzgraf took out his Luger, clicked off the safety and shot the dreg in the back of his neck. Even for a man reduced to maybe forty kilos, ribs sticking out through his thin shirt, head shaved to defeat the lice, the shot was not immediately fatal. It, however, was bloody. The poor wretch wallowed in his own widening pool of blood, his legs twitching, eyes locked on Schluckebier before finding his release.

The Sonderkommandos each grabbed a foot and dragged him out leaving a long bloody streak.

Schluckebier continued. "You will be building the V-1, our best hope for winning the war. On the workbenches you will find blueprints and tools and on the shelves all the components. You will build three units every day without fail, even if you have to work without food or sleep."

Some groaned.

"You have observed the price one pays for failure." Then, turning to Pfalzgraf, he said, "Organize them and begin production. No food or sleep until the third has passed inspection."

With that he marched out, leaving us.

"I will give you ten minutes to organize yourselves." Pfalzgraf and his men turned to the kitchen from where we soon smelled coffee and frying sausages. Two of the engineers, LaChance and Rodriguez, took the lead dividing the rest into teams based on skill level and experience. The Frenchman's group would assemble components and the Spaniard's would assemble them into a finished weapon. Maurer, a history professor from Munich, was made spokesman because he spoke French, Spanish and German.

I stood alone. I was the oddball. No skills or knowledge or aptitude for weaponry, its design or use. Quite the contrary. My whole life had been dedicated to fighting death, not causing it.

Pfalzgraf returned and Maurer gave him the report on the two teams.

The lieutenant looked at me. "Your job is to keep the rest of them alive long enough for us to win. After the war you will all be set free, unless you fail, then ..." he trailed off looking at the blood stain.

We worked until early 1945, when the Allies overran the last of the V-1 launch sites in the west. We made several variants of the V-1, buzz bomb, Feisler 103: the regular with 850 kg of Amatol-39 high explosive payload, a kamikaze version, and the Fi-103D-1 that was designed to carry a warhead of nerve gas.

A moral quandary surrounded our work and our lives. The Christians among us regretted making weapons for Hitler to kill more people, especially British and Dutch civilians. On the other hand, staying alive seemed more important. Pfalzgraf and Schluckebier made it clear that any failure on our part would be met with summary execution and there would be a hundred, a thousand others who would literally kill to work and live in our comparative comfort.

We soon worked out a strategy, thanks to Maurer, with a little input from me. Watching everyone else work offered me the opportunity to see the bigger picture. Day after day, LaChance's crew out-produced the Spaniards. I suggested to Maurer that instead of numerical equality we needed to look at output. Thus, we moved two men to the Spaniard's team, slowed LaChance's workers a little and still built three V-1s a day—but with less effort. One thing I can say, we never missed a meal or a night's sleep. This arrangement made my job essential. Any sickness that struck one man could be quickly spread to the others. I set up a quarantine section, then filled in the best I could for the sick worker. The only time we came close to failing was in February. 1945, when a wave of dysentery swept through the work camp.

26

"Have we really lost the war?"

13 May 1945

My Dear,

Can it really be true? Have we really lost the war?

Everyone says the Americans won! That the Communists are in Berlin! Some even say you are dead. I know that cannot be true. You would never abandon us!

I shall continue writing you. I'll never give up on my son's real father! Surely you must have left a forwarding address.

Little Adolf spent a whole day in his room crying when they said you had died. He was sad, losing his father. He never met you, but I told him all about you. I told him to stop crying, you were not dead. We both look forward to having you stay with us until you can again re-build Germany. It is crowded here, but we will make room. I probably can even find a room for Eva, if you must bring her.

Write us, come to us. Let us know you are safe. We all love you.

Your Lotte

17 May 1945

My Dear

Paul's radio said you committed suicide. How can that be when I know you are alive—somewhere. Paul believes the BBC, but I believe in you. Maybe somebody died but it sure was not you, my love. You are far too wise.

Little Adolf has made friends with a few American soldiers who came to town. They said they are occupying Austria! Why? We do not need them. We can take care of ourselves!

Those soldiers were so nice, giving candy bars to the children. They promised that there would be trucks coming with food in a day or two and they were right. Finally, we have enough to eat.

I sure wish I knew where you are. I'd come to you even if I had to walk! And I'd bring your son. You two need to get to know each other. Some days I read my old diary from the day we first met. So long ago, yet it seems like just yesterday. Come to me, my lover. I'll take care of you. I love you.

Lotte

5 July 5 1945
Lotte's Diary

That little worm, Hans Schuler, is back. He's trying to make nice after the way he treated us at Mauthausen. What an idiot I was to ever care for him!

You should see him trying to be friends with Little Adolf. Giving him chocolate he probably steals from the Americans. Trying to play with him like he was six years old himself. This war sure made men act unusual.

Erich returned in early June. He talked with Schuler once and wants nothing more to do with him. I do not know what was said, but Hans ended up with a broken nose that Paul had to treat.

He must have done something really bad for people to treat him so. Only his brother helps him, giving him an old herder's hut up in the mountain. Heidi cooks for him sometimes but will not talk about him.

Lotte's Diary
15 July 1945

This town is so funny. As soon as they heard the war was over and we had lost, all the Nazi stuff disappeared. No more swastikas in

Beyerlein's window. The Burgomeister burned his uniform, and just before the Americans got here, he called a town meeting. He ordered us to remove anything that was Nazi. We were to act like common folk. He said it was important that we all forget what happened during the war. Pretty hard to do with Hans the Hater back in town.

Paul is totally upset. He blames Hans for what happened to Marta's family. Though he does not really know, he assumes they all died. Erich beat Hans up and Paul had to patch him up, even though he hated the man.

I say Hans is not responsible. He was just following orders. But I do not tell Paul what I think.

Lotte's diary
23 August 1945

Paul's radio keeps talking about trials. The English want to punish us for fighting the Communists. The Americans came to town yesterday asking a lot of questions. They are looking for anybody who was a Nazi, in the SS or Gestapo.

Only Herr Beyer was a Nazi and the whole town agreed to say he was not. Erich, though, cannot deny his time in the 2nd SS Panzers. They are having a hard time figuring out why a half-Jew would join the very SS that was killing the Jews.

They should talk to Hans the Hater, but Heidi told the town it would be better for them to just forget her brother-in-law ever lived.

————

The home of Erich Schwimmer
Oberschwarzenberg, Austria
22 September 1991

After lunch we took ourselves back to the sitting room.

"Lorenz, I promised you a story. Are you still interested?" This with a wink.

Two can play this sly little game. "I sure am, Uncle Erich."

With a chuckle, he began.

"What you said about the SS, me, and Hans the other night was all true. It is something I must live with. There was much turmoil after the war. Refugees, returning soldiers, the American 'invaders ...'"

I raised both hands, but he continued.

"That is how we saw things. You need not agree.

"The fighting had ended but the feelings continued. People could not go from Jew-hating Nazis to calm country folk that quickly. Oberschwarzenberg was far out of the way, yet we had to deal with Hans and his crimes, Lotte, and Little Adolf, and rebuilding the town after the bomber crash. On a more personal level, I had to find a way to make sense of my life. I was living with my father, with Lotte and her son, with no money. Food was short. That first winter we were on the brink.

"Some people wanted to continue the fight. Some wanted to wipe out every trace of the Nazis and start the forgetting. Others wanted to leave. Go to America.

"We had to organize or we would all perish. The only structure that would work was to re-assemble the vets. They alone knew the horror of the war and had the skills and training, nay the discipline, to start our lives anew. There were six of us. There was Hans and myself, Rodammer the one-armed mechanic, Egan the grocer, and the Hoppe boys, both farmers. I had the highest rank so took charge. We called a meeting at the church so there'd be room for everybody. And we laid out our plan."

"The people just gave you control?"

"These people had been subservient for the past decade. They made it easy for us. We got Father Jung and the Burgomeister on board. That was all it took."

"You wrote about this in your journal?" I asked

"Yes, I did."

I handed him his journal, asking, "Would you do me a great

favor, Erich? I'd like the experience of hearing you read your own words. Would you do that for me?"

He stared at me for long seconds, then softly replied, "Very well."

He took the book and began.

———

Chapel of St. Polycarp
Oberschwarzenberg, Austria
17 October 1945

Like a hive of angry, hungry wasps, the bedraggled crowd filled the old church to bulging. Father Jung sat at the altar flanked by the Burgomaster. The priest was attired in his finest robes. The burgomaster was in a brown suit, yellowed shirt and gray tie. The six veterans, we thought of ourselves as the Onkels (Uncles), sat behind them.

Father Jung approached the podium. The audience slowly quieted.

"My children. We must thank the Almighty that we have survived his terrible judgment. We must trust in his grace to deliver us from our despair. We must give Him thanks that he has brought back to our community this group of men," he spread out his arms indicating the men behind him. "to help lead us through this time, to help us rebuild our community, to make us great once again."

The Burgomaster elbowed his way up to Jung and jostled him aside. "I am sorry," he said, "to interrupt the good father but we all know where the church has taken us in the last few years. As a politician, I can take no comfort in our current situation and must share with him some responsibility for these straits. We are both old, too old to give you the leadership you deserve. This group of men behind me are the capable leaders now. They have the skills and the energy to get us through.

"Their leader, our very own Dr. Schwimmer, will tell you what they have planned. I suggest and implore every one of you to support their efforts."

He turned to me as he passed on the way back to his seat.

I nodded to my father, Paul, who was flanked by Lotte and Little Adolf. The wind whistled through the north side of the chapel, whooshing around the windows, snow blowing through the ceiling cracks. The sparse lighting kept the congregation in the dark, their attention focused on the podium. As the ranking officer, I had taken charge of this group, the Stadtsteuergruppe (city control group), and therefore, the town.

I looked out at the people remembering all we had been through, all the evil done in their name. I did not seek forgiveness, nor offer it. Things are as they are and must be dealt with.

"In this time of trouble, the few have gathered to save and serve the many," I told them. "We humbly seek your support for the actions we must take in our time and your name. Only decisive, strong action now can stave off a future of want and hunger. If not for ourselves, then for our children we must come together. There is no room for individuality. Our community must do what is right for the majority.

"The Stadtsteuergruppe has been established to assure the means to guarantee our future. Past divisions and differences must be forgotten. Only a strong group can survive these times.

"We did not fight for you only to see you dissolve into a mindless mass obsessed with easing your own suffering with scant concern for others. Over two dozen of us served you. Only we few have returned. We will not stand for anything less than complete commitment.

"From this day forward we few will be guiding you to a greater future than any could dream. You know us. We are your sons, brothers, husbands and cousins. We wish nothing for ourselves but pledge our very lives to saving our community.

"We have assessed our needs and the resources we have available. Each of us will be issuing bulletins which have the full support of the Burgomaster and the church, and therefore, are the law. Egan Beyerlein will coordinate food and hard goods distribution. Hans Schuler will handle public works: sanitation, replacing housing, etc. Ludwig Rodammer will be in charge of transportation. Heinz Hoppe will be gathering food from the farms and gardens, orchards and woods. Luther will be gathering together every drop of fuel, stick and lump of coal. I will be handling the medical and housing needs. You," I spread my hands out to the congregation, "are charged with doing what needs to be done whenever you are told.

"For tonight, I implore you to read our first bulletin and be prepared to comply with it by 8:00 a.m. tomorrow."

With that I sat down. The audience did absolutely nothing. They did not know what to do. No one had told them to stand and leave or sit for more. Inertia demanded they sit so they did. The Burgomaster arose to address them.

"Please come forward to receive your copy. Henceforth they will be posted at Beyerlein's and here at St. Polycarp's."

A slow rustling, like a turkey vulture mustering enough momentum to rise from his carrion, coursed through them, causing them to rise in waves until they were all on their feet. Some shouted support for the Onkels, others heaped abuse on us for our audacity. Many just stood, waiting their turn to get their orders for the day.

———•———

"And you made the railroads run on time," I quipped.

"I resent your inference," Erich sparked in anger. "The people needed leadership," he roared, "that only we could offer. We only did what needed done. We saved this town!"

"You became Oberschwarzenberg's Fuhrer," I asserted.

"You cannot know all the challenges we faced."

"And all the people went along with you and your cabal?"

"These people had been led by dictators, emperors and

demagogues for generations. We tapped into that natural bent to save them."

"Your approach was so perverse it interests me."

"We just allowed the natural urge these peasants had for sharing and communal action to surface. For instance, we closed up about half of the homes so we could heat the others. I gathered together all the medicines, bandages, and herbal remedies into my clinic. Egan gathered all the food, spare clothing, firewood, coal, and tools into his store as a central depot. All the farms were assessed by Heinz Hoppe for their spare grain, animals that could be butchered, and fuel was drained from their equipment to heat homes. The school was converted into a feeding station using the gathered grains and meat. People gathered there thrice daily for meals.

"Hans organized crews to rebuild homes, install plumbing and central heating. He drew up plans for the water and sewer systems. He wired the town for electricity. Rodammer demanded that no one drive without his permission. All vehicles were drained of their fuel which was stored at his garage."

"Somewhat ironic wasn't it?"

"What do you mean?"

"The man raising Hitler's son and a member of Hitler's SS, becomes Oberschwarzenberg's fuhrer. A nice symmetry I would say."

"Say what you will, Professor. I am comfortable with what I had to do. As to the irony, the Stadtsteuergruppe, as a political force was disbanded the next summer. We, however, remained committed to each other, helping out when we could. In fact, those few heroes, helped me put the addition onto this very home later that year."

"I am mystified, Erich, how you, especially, given your parentage and your training as a doctor, could ever make peace with Hans, let alone incorporate him into your cabal. His presence had to sicken and disgust people."

"Professor, I, that is we, had to do as Churchill so famously ordered, not just our best but what was necessary to survive. The war changed us all, most especially Hans. His skills were undeniable and essential. And as you have discovered, most of the people here supported Hitler and benefited from the Nazis. I was the only one, besides my father, to have suffered persecution. I have put all that behind me."

"Hans seems to be still strong in his anti-Semitic beliefs. Did no one challenge him?"

"He did not tell you about the time the Jüdische Rachesucher came to town?"

"What did they want?"

"As you might presume from their name, the Jewish Revenge Seekers, were looking for the SS men who ran the camps. Everyone knew that the bulk of them came from Austria. They started in the big cities right away in 1945. By 1950, they were looking in the country-side. Oberschwarzenberg is about as far in the country as you can get so we were near the bottom of their list."

"Who besides Hans were they looking for?"

"He was the only one."

"He should not have been hard to find. What did they do to him?"

"They did not find him. By then he had improved the town. We had sewers, electricity, all the homes were repaired or rebuilt. He was a local hero. He told everyone that he had secret sources of money that would disappear if he was ever captured. We liked the money and what it did for the town, so we conspired to protect him.

"We erected a headstone in the cemetery showing that he had died in 1946. Everyone told the Jews the same story so they came to the same conclusion. After a week they left."

"You of all people," I challenged, "joined in this charade!"

"I was already raising Hitler's son. Being deceitful comes easier the longer one does it."

27

"I had a hard time calling him by that damned name."

Lotte's Diary
15 November 1945

Paul has finally agreed with me. We are going to have to add onto this house or Erich and I must get our own place. We cannot go to my parents. The bomber got them and their house. There are no empty houses in town, and we cannot afford to buy one anyway.

Lotte's Diary
17 November 1945

Erich is gathering together some of his old buddies to help build the addition. Paul is adding two bedrooms, one for Adolf and one for us. Ours needs to be large enough to fit our single beds. No hanky-panky!

The home of Erich Schwimmer
Oberschwarzenberg, Austria
22 September 1991

The interview with Erich continued.

"After I returned from the war and began to rebuild the town, I started to get closer to Little Adolf. After what I went through, I had a hard time calling him by that damned name. It was all right for Lotte and the rest of the town. Even my dad called him that—after losing all of Marta's family to Mauthausen's killers.

Hell, he even forgave Hans Schuler! I only accepted Hans

because he brought much to the town upon his return that helped balance all the evil he had perpetrated.

"Paul and Little Adolf were very close, the ideal grandfather doting on his handsome grandson. Most of the town conveniently forgot the child's parentage when the war ended and Lotte's threats began. I became his father, though not Lotte's husband."

———

20 April 1946

My Dear Husband

Happy Birthday!

You should see how well your son is doing in school! He is the absolute smartest of all the seven-year-olds. How could he not be, with you as his Papa?

Of course, Dr. Erich Schwimmer, with whom I live, has claimed Little Adolf as his own to quiet the local tongues. He is very good with your son. You should see them working on the homework. I have to caution Erich to not give him too much help. After all, Little Adolf has to learn to be independent just like his daddy.

Father Sohn says it is time for his First Communion. Though Paul and Erich are not big on the church, I guess I still am, at least a little. So, if you do not mind, I am going to let him do it. All of his friends are taking the communion, so it would seem strange if he did not. He wants to fit in so badly. Having you as his father has not made it easy for either of us.

The weather has been dismal. It matches the tone of the whole village now that the war is over. We are worried about how the Allies will treat us. Johann Beyerlein and the others tell them we were forced into Germany in 1938 but they do not seem to buy this. So far, only a few jeeps have come through. Victors handing out chocolate to our children. You may be sure that Little Adolf has never eaten even one morsel. He and I will never give in as long as you live.

Paul gets the Vienna paper once a week. They are always telling us how the war is over and you are dead. I have to believe about the war but I shall never believe you were so weak that you took your own life. Surely you would have discovered a far more glorious way. Stay strong, mein Fuhrer. There are two people who continue to love you and miss you.

I know you must be very busy rebuilding your forces, but if you could send even a postcard, I would appreciate it.

The Mother of Your Son, Lotte

8 June 1946

My Dear Husband,

What a glorious spring. Truly the world is awash in hope. I pray the bad days are behind us and hope that you will once again rise to the power so rightfully yours.

Little Adolf stands a full meter and is putting some meat on his bones now that the rationing is less severe. He had some rough times in school earlier—like the fights—but he settled down. Uncle Erich helped a lot as did Grossvater Paul. When those two are around nobody picks on either of us. They will deserve a medal when you get back on your feet, my dear.

Your son has been very naughty. I caught him yesterday drawing on the walls of our room. I never thought paint could splatter so much. What a mess! At first I was very angry. Then I thought, of course, he is an artist just like you. Then I calmed down.

After all, we are still visitors in Paul's home and have to be careful. Since my parents died in the bomber crash, I have no choice but to stay here. A woman with no skills and a growing child has few options. Unless you want to help?

Flowers are blooming and the farmers are planting. Erich and a few of his comrades are rebuilding the town. We barely survived this winter. Food and fuel were in short supply, but it was worse in the bigger *cities. We are more self-reliant here.*

Your son is without shoes he is growing so fast. Erich said he can buy him a pair when school starts. But for the summer, he is barefoot. Most of his friends are, too, so it is not as shameful as it could be. Still, der Fuhrer's child should not look so ragged, don't you think?

By the way, there is a Russian prowling around asking a lot of questions. He thinks he is being so sneaky but we all know. Nobody is telling him anything. Your son and your secret are safe with us.

Your Lotte

———

Phone call with Sergei
25 September 1991

"Professor, finally you ask about Hans Schuler. He is most interesting.

"I first met him in 1946 in Oberschwarzenberg. Of course, I'd known about him since we took over Auschwitz and Mauthausen. We knew the Jews wanted him for war crimes, but he would serve a higher purpose for us.

"I thought he could be shown the benefits of watching over Little Adolf. I could make Schuler 'disappear' from the official records. Lots of records got lost then. One more hardly mattered. Let the Jews do their own dirty work.

"Hans accepted my offer, agreeing to report on Lotte's son monthly. In return, we paid him fifty dollars per month cash, as he was living in the American sector. The money did not seem to be as a great motivator as disappearing.

"Most of his reports had little value. Nothing much happened there. But, every once in a while, he sent us a nugget.

"Please come back. Moscow is so boring."

28

"I was never jealous of that Braun woman."

18 October 1946

Dearest Adolf

Oberschwarzenberg has been saved! You trained your soldiers well, mein Fuhrer. I don't know where they get the strength to carry on. All I can say is I am glad they were on your side.

Erich and his friends built an addition onto his house so Little Adolf and Erich can have their own rooms. I will remain in Erich's old room where I have lived for so many years. I hope to never have to move from here. Unless it is to be with you, my dear.

You have become quite the world traveler. People see you in Argentina, Canada, Spain, Africa and Egypt. So many sightings can only mean one thing. You are alive! I never doubted it, but it was hard convincing others when those Russians showed pictures of what they said was you and that woman. I knew they were fakes.

I was never jealous of that Braun woman. You needed a woman for the public to see. But I knew I was the only woman to bear your child. No one can take that away from me. Ever!

Erich did buy shoes for your son so he could start school like the rest of the kids. He took Little Adolf right over to Beyerlein's and bought him the best pair they had. You should have heard the gossips. Some saying Erich is not the real father and shouldn't the great Hitler be paying for them? Others saying they should be quiet because Herr Hitler was paying for them. I do not know where Erich got the money. My only concern was that Little Adolf should not have to suffer just because his father is unavailable, should he?

Frau Lotte Hitler

———————

27 December 1946

Merry Christmas, Mein Fuhrer,

I hope you had a merry Christmas. You do celebrate, don't you?

Little Adolf is not so little any more. He is eight years old! I swear he looks more like you every day. Handsome and tall.

All I could afford was to buy him a sleigh. Actually, Erich and Paul had to help and we had to buy an old one and fix it up before anybody turned it into stove-wood. He was not the only child to get a used toy this year. So much of our money has to go for food and fuel, even with Erich's committee running things. I'm sure things will be better next year.

Frau Lotte Hitler

20 April 1947

Happy Birthday, my dear

I sure hope it is warmer where you are. This has been one of the coldest winters I can remember. Lucky for us, Erich's committee once again saved us. I sure hope we do not need him and his cronies much more. They are so bossy. Always saying all this is for our own good. Don't they know we just survived six years of war?

Your son continues to grow. He has become such a young man! Always courteous and the smartest in his class. He sure takes after you.

Many of the people here seem real old when they get to be your age. I'm sure, though, you are still vigorous. Fifty-eight isn't that old, is it? But, before you get much older you might want to visit your only son and heir. I know he misses you. He tells me every night as I tuck him in. It is nice that he has his own room, now. Still, nothing and nobody can replace you.

    Your Lotte

4 July 1947

    My Dearest Leader

    Another school year ended for your son. Again, the top of the class. What can I say? The walnut doesn't fall far from the tree. Ha!

    Little Adolf and Erich went fishing yesterday down at the river. Your boy sure can fish. Together those two caught over twenty. I had to help clean them, otherwise they would not have been edible. Those two! They made such a mess in my kitchen. I had to shoo them out to the garden to pick a salad. That they could do!

    Erich never says too much about you. I think he was very disappointed to lose the war. There have been many times he has said, "I wish Hitler would come here. I have some things to talk to him about!" I think he wants a medal or some such. You men and your war reminders!

    I had a disturbing conversation with Hans Schuler last month. There I was shopping at Beyerlein's, when he comes up behind me, taps me on the shoulder, and scares me half crazy. I was afraid the SS or SD was back again.

    He said he just wanted to talk. You know we were pretty good friends before the war. But, the war changed him. He attacked my father when he went along with Paul to Matthausden to check on Paul's relatives. I guess they were already gone. Still, Hans did not have to hit my Papa.

    He accompanied me to the steps where we could sit in public. I no longer trust this man! All he wanted to talk about was Little Adolf. And here I thought he was interested in me! Well, I can tell you that conversation did not last more than a few minutes. I will not be interrogated. Especially by him!

You should see Plockenstein. High up there is still snow! Erich and I walk the meadows at its base after supper. He tries to hold my hand but then I remind him of you and he just sulks. Poor boy. He still loves me, but I cannot return the feeling.

The Allies continue their persecution of your followers all over Germany and Austria. Jurgens Freihof says the Allies are lucky we did not win or it would be them in the docket, getting hanged or thrown into prison for just following your orders. Every time the paper arrives, I check to make sure you are still free. It is always a relief!

Keep safe, my love.

Lotte

12 October 1947

My Dearest Adolf,

I am getting a little worried. I never hear from you. Not even a penny postcard! Your son asks after you just about every day. What am I supposed to tell him when he asks me why his father has never visited? All he has is your picture. Actually, that is all I have—and Little Adolf. And the memory of that day we first made love.

Paul took Little Adolf all the way to Vienna in August. At first I thought it was not such a good idea. But Paul convinced me that they would be safe. He has not seen his family for ever so long. And Little Adolf is his only grandchild. So, I said yes.

Those were the two longest weeks in my whole life. I had never been away from your son before, not even a day. They returned with piles of presents and several albums of photos. What a haul! Christmas is assured this year. The only thing to make it better is for you to visit.

There was a Russian in town again. Sniffing around. Asking Sofia and Heidi and everyone else about me and your son. Nobody told him anything. They all worry what you would do to them if they blabbed. But he did spend quite some time talking with Hans, according to Heidi.

Though Hans is annoying, the way he creeps around like an old dog looking for shade, he is the richest man in town. He never says where his money comes from and none of us can figure it out. Without Hans, Oberschwarzenberg would still be a nothing. Now we have a water plant and a sewer system, a paved road, and all the homes damaged by the bomber crash have been repaired or replaced. I guess every cloud does have a silver lining.

    Your Lotte

28 December 1947

    Mein Herr

    Talk about snow. I'll bet we got a half-meter of it already, and we still have over three more months to go. Every day Erich sends us out to shovel. We have been putting the snow in the Weissbach and over the ridge. It is hard, cold work, but it must be done.

    It is such a blessing to have enough food for once. It has been years!

    The tree this year was spectacular. We were swamped with the gifts Paul and Little Adolf brought back from Vienna. Your son bought you a gift, too. I asked him what it is, but he said it was your gift and only you can open it. I promised to mail it to you as soon as I have enough money. I sure hope your people will send it on. Little Adolf loves you so much.

    Can you believe it? Our son is nine years old! It seems just yesterday that we were together after the concert. I have to admit, these have been lonely years without you. My heart cries out to you to come visit us or at least send us a letter. Even a postcard would mean the world to us. I know most of the world has despised you, but you are the man I love and I'll never betray you. Never!

    I never thought I would appreciate indoor plumbing as much as I do. To think of all the years I had to trudge out into the cold! I even had to potty-train Little Adolf outside. It all seems so barbaric now. I'm sure you would have gotten around to it if the war had not been started

by the French and Jews. Too late now. Like you, we must forge ahead,
rebuilding what we can.

Your Lotte

20 April 1949

Mein Fuhrer,

I guess you are stronger than me.

Please forgive me for trying to challenge you. I should have known
you would do what was best for you and Germany, not me and Little
Adolf.

I cannot and do not want to live without you so I am going to
write to you, but only once a year on your birthday. If you ever find the
time to write back, I'll write more often.

Christmas went well. Not as many presents as last year, but still
good. Your son again bought you a gift and again I will try to get it to
you, though you never buy him anything in return. The newspapers say
you and your friends amassed fortunes from the war. Surely you can
spare a few Marks to help us, can't you?

Your son turned ten. You were not here to ask and Erich and Paul
did not care too much either. But everyone in town made it clear that he
needed religion. So I sort of insisted and went ahead and let him get his
confirmation. Since the war, church has become more important here
in Austria. Guess everybody is trying to prove they weren't Nazis. The
fools! Following you was the greatest thing in my life next to loving you
and having your son. That you do not acknowledge our love matters
not. I know what is right!

Paul died. Up to the end he rarely attended church. Many years
before the priest would not bury Marta, Paul's wife, in the cemetery just
because she was a Jew. So they buried her in the back yard and that is
where we put Paul. They are together again. Will we ever be?

Your Lotte

20 April 1950

Happy Birthday, Adolf

I am still determined to see your silence as a sign that you are working too hard to respond to me. Thus, I bide my time here, raising your son and loving you.

Our son, "Little Adolf," is growing so tall! He is almost up to my shoulder. Erich gives him a physical every year and he continues to be healthy. I feed him the best food I can afford. Erich helps, of course.

Christmas was cold and wet. Many days before and after were near zero with a cold wind rushing down Plockenstein. Some of the younger children were almost blown away, were it not for the efforts of our boy. He walked as many as six of the littler ones to and from school each day.

I am considering taking Erich up on his offer of marriage. All my friends think me a fool for waiting for you. Heidi and Sofia both have husbands, their own homes and children. One cannot but feel mis-used.

I know I promised to be yours for life, but even the most stalwart can lose their faith. I am only thinking, but I have to admit Erich looks better all the time.

Your Lotte

20 April 1951

My Husband

Are you in contact with Hans Schuler? The reason I ask is he tracked me down a few weeks after my letter to you last year. In fact, it was early June. I was walking out of Beyerlein's, when he was walking in. He grabbed me by my arm and told me he has some important news to tell me. I told him there was nothing he could say that would be the least importance to me. Boy, was I wrong!

Hans said that you did not want me marrying Erich or anyone else. He said you wanted me to concentrate all my efforts on raising our son. I was stupefied! How did he know? I had told no one, not even

Erich.

He said all I needed to know was he was representing you and that I was to follow orders. Of course, I will do whatever you want.

After all this time without a peep, you finally say something. I was overwhelmed. You do care about me and Little Adolf. You do love me. My darling, I am yours forever.

Your son, our son, is becoming such a man. Though he is only twelve, Erich and his comrades have started including him in their meetings and activities. I don't know all they do, but I know they saved Oberschwarzenberg after the war. So whatever they are doing now is fine with me.

Erich, of course, has taken over for his dad so we still have a doctor in town—and I still live in his house. Just like with Paul, Erich takes Little Adolf out on rounds. Sometimes I have to wonder if Erich really is his dad, but then I remember us and there is no question.

I'm still only going to write you one letter a year until I actually hear from you. I do not trust Hans most of the time but will this time. He told me what I have longed to hear. My life is complete.

Your Lotte

25 December 1956

Mein Herr,

The most joyous time of the year finds me despairing of ever hearing from you. Your only son and heir is planning to finish school in June and then try to find you. Some of the village men have been counseling him, especially that despicable Hans Schuler. That terrible little Russian, Sergei, has been sniffing around, too. I am at a loss about what to do.

How I wish you were here to help me. But, why should now be any different? I have had to raise our son all on my own, except for the help and support of Erich. I owe him so much and so do you.

I have faithfully written to you on your birthday for the last eighteen years. Never once did you acknowledge my letters. You do not even know my birth date, do you?

Here I am, almost thirty-seven years old. No husband. No home. Hardly anything to my name. And now your son says he is leaving me. How am I to survive without you two? I swore to you a long time ago I would never have another man in my life. I have never wavered. Nor have I ever been rewarded. Much the opposite. Many people still consider me crazy. Few are my friends, except Sofia and Heidi. A few of Erich's friends tolerate me. Paul has joined his wife in the back yard, so I am mostly alone.

I find myself trying to convince Little Adolf to not search for you. He needs to get on with his life, not stop at eighteen as I did. Besides, if he found you imagine how I'd feel. Would you accept your son but not his mother?

Your Lotte

The home of Dr. Erich Schwimmer
Oberschwarzenberg, Austria
17 October 1991

Erich is dead.

What can I say about this most extraordinary, gentle man? He was a great and dear friend of mine, as well as Tante Lotte. I am grateful that I was able to meet him and learn their stories. If Little Adolf is still among the living, then I must also thank Erich for being his father and role model.

He had a tough job being the sane one, with Lotte and her delusions and trying to raise Little Adolf to be a good and moral individual. For a good man such as he, it had to be a struggle.

Though I only knew him for a short while, I feel that I lived with him for decades. He was the embodiment of all the decent people trying to make this world a better place.

I chose, with Hilde's permission, to dig Erich's grave myself. He had left a space between his parent's graves for his own. The ground, rocky and hard from the cold, challenged me for every shovelful.

When I think back on those warm September days only a month ago, though they seem to be years ago, I know a part of him hoped someone would be interested enough in Lotte and her son to visit with him. I am thankful it was me that fate chose.

Two hours and two feet deep into my work, Hilde brought me a cup of her strong coffee. I was beginning to appreciate whoever invented the backhoe, and wishing I had one. Teaching history did not prepare me for heavy manual labor, even though it was a labor of deep respect.

After two more hours and two more feet Hilde called out from the back door that she had prepared lunch. I climbed the ladder out of the grave, resting my shovel against Erich's coffin.

When I returned an hour later, the gaping earth called to me. Only two more feet. Where did this six feet deep for a grave ever come from? Certainly not from those who did the digging.

Finally! After six of the longest hours I can remember, the grave was complete. I called to Hilde and she came out all bundled in a long red woolen sweater pilled with age. Together, we lowered the coffin.

As we finished, Hilde started to cry. Her Uncle Erich was her last relative on the Rosenberg limb of her family tree. Turning from my gaze, she spoke to his grave. "Dear Uncle, thank you for all you have done for me and for allowing me to do for you. Rest in heaven with your parents and Lotte."

She reached into her pocket and handed me a folded piece of paper.

Opening it, I read.

————

Lorenz,

Hilde is not responsible for what I am telling you. It all happened before her arrival. Please forgive me for being less than truthful.

I believe Little Adolf did find his father, Adolf Hitler. He returned to Oberschwarzenberg in 1964 with a wife and baby, claiming he was becoming an artist. He said he was living with the man and his wife in Braunau am Inn and had changed his last name to Braun.

I challenged him several times to tell Lotte and myself the truth. He claimed he was. He was a good kid, but not a great artist so his story was suspect. They visited us every summer until Lotte's death.

Their son is married and has a daughter. I am not sure I would recommend tracking them down. Little Adolf always denied our every effort to visit them. He never said why, but always implied much—none of it good.

Lotte chose to believe the best. The Onkels and I forced the town to keep the visits a secret. That is why no one you interviewed ever mentioned them.

From what little I know, I expect your Russian friend might be able to tell you more.

Erich

29

"Why Didn't You Tell Me?"

The apartment of Sergei Androvsky
191 Kerensky Prospekt
Moscow
30 October 1991

"You knew Lotte's son was Hitler's!" I yelled through the splintery door. Not much of a greeting. Sorry. I could not keep the hurt and accusation out of my voice. Here I was, back in Moscow, standing in the hallway of a rattrap apartment block. My belabored breath clouded my view of the drabness—carpet, ceiling, walls, and lives. Pounding on the door of 6L, after a long flight, and an even longer taxi ride into town then climbing six flights of old stairs smelling of urine and old garbage, I wanted some service.

Sergei Androvsky, my archivist "friend" from the summer, had since retired, though how one could tell escaped me. His job in the archives was to not be seen, get too drunk, or shower too often.

Sergei opened the door.

"I knew you'd come back."

"Why didn't you tell me?" I hoped the anger in my voice came through.

"In Russia, volunteering information is not safe. Had you asked, I would have told you."

"Well, now, I'm asking!"

"Come in before someone sees you."

At few decades ago, this might have been a pretty nice apartment building when it was built back in Stalin's time. Now, after forty years of spotty maintenance and general abuse it had lost its splendor.

Sergei's unit consisted of a living/dining room/kitchen space—what many in the West would call a great room—here more of a so-so room. The walls were freshly painted and plastered with pictures of the war, framed medals, and a portrait of Stalin. Through an open door a small bed and dresser sagged opposite the toilet.

"Here! Here! Have a seat." Sergei brushed magazines and food scraps from a wooden kitchen chair and offered it to me. "Let me get you some tea. Maybe something to eat."

I am seated once again in the apartment of Sergei Androvsky, former Red Army Sergeant, former KBG underling and my only source into the Kremlin archives and much of my family's history. Only a few months have passed since my last visit, but much has changed—except Sergei. Still hyper as an ant at a picnic he sees to my every need and want except for more information. He extracted this visit by saying what he had to share was far too important to risk sending in the mail or over the phone.

"I'll have what you are having."

Turned out he was only having tea and so was I. He parked the other kitchen chair, faced me and waited. We sipped, taking each others' measure. Finally, realizing he was getting no younger, I broke the silence.

"Sergei, my friend, please tell me about Lotte's son, Adolf. We both know that much of what I need is not in any official record. What I want is what you have up here," pointing to his head.

He sipped more tea, then spoke. "You are correct. We did much more than gather and inventory her letters to the monster. We sent agents there several times to observe Lotte and her child. They appeared to be as normal as anyone else there. No one would tell us anything of value. We hired that Nazi, Hans Schuler, to watch and report. This went on for several years until June 1957 when the boy turned eighteen and left Oberschwarzenberg.

"I assumed that at some point the boy would seek out his father. Eighteen is a transition time from boy to man, after all."

"Even though Hitler was dead? Lotte was the only person in the world who still thought he survived the war!"

"She was not the only one, Professor. Many in my own government had suspicions, including me. You have to remember the Cold War was in full bloom, the Korean War had recently concluded, and Hungary's revolt had been put down. If there was any possibility that the old bastard still lived we needed to pursue it.

"I went myself to Oberschwarzenberg to observe Lotte and Adolf. Still they lived with the doctor and his son, also a doctor. I posed as a businessman looking for a site for a new factory. This assured the cooperation of the Burgomeister and most of the people. I opted to stay with the priest as he had the only spare room in the whole area. And where better for a Communist to hide?

"Young Adolf certainly looked like his father. The same weak chin and dark hair. But it was his eyes. They took you in if you were with him for long. In just the few minutes I spent with him I could feel the magnetism his father had. This boy could go far if we didn't control him."

"You are telling me you set up his whole trip?"

He stood up. "A minute, please." He shuffled to the bedroom door and went inside out of my sight. I heard what sounded like a door open, then close. Sergei returned holding a red-bordered folder. Holding it out to me, he said, "This is a copy of the KGB's file on your cousin."

I had not thought much of Little Adolf, who was now in his fifties, as a relative. It was not until the past three months that I'd even thought of his mother in that context. I was related to Adolf Hitler's only known child!

With sacramental grace he handed me the folder bound by a thin piece of leather. The top sheet was written in Cyrillic and therefore unreadable. I looked at him.

"I forget how limited your education has been, my friend," he drawled.

He reached again into his bag and produced a bound volume, motioned that we trade, and replaced his Cyrillic version with another in German. The cover sheet read, "Inventory Lists of Germanic Field Kitchen Manifests." I glanced at him.

"You dragged me all the way from Oberschwarzenberg for this!"

"Open it," he said with a smug smile creasing his lips, showing his yellowed teeth. His eyes, though, sparkled. Sergei was enjoying my responses.

The next page was entitled:

Observation, June 18, 1957:

"Subject is crossing the border into Germany. Hektor has been alerted."

"Hektor?" I asked.

"One of ours," Sergei explained. "It was no mistake that Hektor picked him up and passed him onto Gottlieb in Berlin. Both worked for me. Crazy old coots—but who knew?"

"Wasn't it hard to cross the border back then?"

"Of course it was. But Young Adolf had a guardian angel watching over him—me. I approved his visa immediately. I wanted nothing to interfere with his search."

"You wanted him to find Hitler?"

"Actually, that was secondary. We had infiltrated a couple groups of old Nazis. But not all. We wanted Little Adolf to lead us to the rest. Then we could liquidate the whole damned bunch!

"I arranged with the border patrol to let him through with only minimal hassle. Too easy and he might get suspicious.

"Hektor got him to Gottlieb who initiated the boy into his group, Die Alten Weisen (the Old Way). This was my last chance to direct him to where we wanted him to go. We sent him to the British Occupation Zone because we knew Hitler liked England. Unfortunately, there was a traitor among the traitors who sent the kid to Berchtesgaden in the American Zone where he disappeared into the Nazi underworld. We lost all contact with him except for his sporadic letters to Lotte."

Author's Note:

The following pages are written from Young Adolf's perspective based on Sergei's documents and a meeting in 2014 with a man known as Adolf Braun II who convinced me he was my cousin, Young Adolf—Lotte's son.

Braun made it very clear that he was giving me his time and knowledge only because of his love and respect for his parents. However, he warned, it would be much to my benefit to never publish my book.

3 July 1957

Dear Mom and Papa Erich

Congratulate me! I made it to Berlin!

What a mess! Streets choked with rubble. The people are so poor. It is hard to believe Germany could be so defeated. Dad would not be pleased.

I had to walk some of the way, but lucked out getting a ride. It was raining hard, the storm had been building for a few days. A rumble, a flash, and the heavens opened.

Just outside of Passau I got the ride. Guy said he was a vet. Certainly was old enough. All he did was complain, yet it beat walking. He said there was no work in the Soviet sector but he had enough money to travel. Said he had a good pension. Apparently better than yours, Papa Erich.

This guy, Hektor, was too old for the war but said he served in the last days in the Volksturmm. He had some stories to tell! Fighting the Russians, then having to live under them. He was not happy. Hektor was coy, but apparently belonged to a whole group of unhappy people.

I stayed at his house a few days. He introduced me to a few of his comrades. A great group of guys! They still believed in the old days, the old ways. I mean I was tempted to tell them who I was, but decided not too.

I'm staying at the youth hostel on Chausseestrasse. Hektor gave me the name of a guy, Herr Gottleib, he said I should meet. I'm going to look him up tomorrow. I'll tell you all about it.

Your Son,

Adolf

8 August 1957

Dear Mom and Papa Erich,

Amazing! Gottlieb was in Dad's bunker before the end. He was only an aide, but he actually got to meet Dad.

He agrees with you. Says Dad did not die. I'm sorry I ever doubted you, Mom. It just seemed too good to be true.

There is some sort of association that I am going to be initiated into. I cannot tell you anymore.

I'll be on the road again for a while, so might not write soon.

Adolf

<hr />

When I left home in June 1957 my mother was not happy as I'd been her life for almost two decades. Taking care of me had always been her highest priority. I promised to write her often.

Erich, I think, understood. He, of course, knew he was not my biological father, but he also doubted, or refused to believe, that Hitler was. Erich had been a good father and I would miss him.

Nobody else in Oberschwarzenberg was unhappy for me to

leave. They had covered for me all those years out of fear that I really was Hitler's heir. Lotte had them convinced that my safety was very important to some powerful people.

Then there was that old Nazi, Hans Schuler, always nosing around. He spent a lot of money rebuilding the town after the war. I wondered where the money came from. He hinted to everyone that my safety was important to him. Money talks!

My first stop would be Berlin. I would have to go through the Russian zone to get there so I applied for a visa. It was approved quickly, though I'd been warned that it could take six months. This being the Russian zone, I had to approach carefully. Invaders on every corner, their flags on our public buildings, their fat officer corps stealing food, fuel and anything not nailed down—all implied that speaking freely would not be tolerated. Then there were the secret police and informers.

I crossed the border at Passau. I hiked and hitched rides wanting to know about Germany from the people living there. I rarely heard good talk about Dad, but when I did I gravitated to its source, usually an old soldier. Funny, they all knew Dad. In fact, they were his drinking buddies before the war even though he rarely drank.

The home of Herr Paschaltz
Forno di Zoldo, Italy
11 November 1963—18 June 1964

Maria, mi bella femina was the daughter of middle-aged Herr Paschaltz and his Fascist frau, Francesca. Like my mother, Lotte, they were true believers left over from the early, still optimistic, years of the war. Their daughter, twenty year old, Maria—of the well-rounded figure and high intellect—had absorbed much of their dreams but was more aware of the horrors, much like myself. Perhaps that was our bond. Less love, more politics.

"Breakfast is served," Francesca barely whispered against

Maria's door. She knew we were sleeping together, had been since my second night in their home.

"We must get up, mi bello," Maria murmured like a faint sea breeze into my ears.

I recoiled at the very thought of leaving her warmth for the chill of northern Italy.

"Couldn't we just once eat breakfast after the sun has risen?" I reached out to enfold her in my arms doing my best to convince her to stay with me.

Like a lithe, dark-haired snake Maria wriggled out of my grasp. She stood at the side of the bed glancing at my reluctant body. Slowly, so slowly, she pulled the blankets from the bed exposing my skin to the dark and cold.

I mock-yelled at her, "You are a terrible little person."

She responded by filling our water glass half-full and then tossed it on me. I leapt out of bed and chased her for a step before she turned with a finger across her lips telling me to be quiet.

"But, she knows," I whispered. Then I heard the harsh, heavy plodding of her father coming up the stairs.

Francesca yelled down at him, "Maria is getting up now. I will wake up Adolf. Sit down. Your family will be at breakfast in just a few minutes."

Maria and I quickly dressed. No need to get Francesca in trouble. I was sure her discretion was all that stood between Maria and the door for me.

I did wonder, however, just how dense Herr Paschaltz could be. I came to believe that he chose to not see. He held very little interest for me as I had met and dealt with his kind all over Germany and Europe in my effort to find out if Hitler, my father according to my mother, really lived as so many of his followers believed, or had he perished in April 1945 by his own hand?

Paschaltz waited for us at the table. A good country-style

breakfast: potatoes, ham, pancakes and eggs prepared by Francesca were a real tradition in this family. Unlike their neighbors, all Italian, who started and survived much of the day with a few biscuits and dark coffee, this family knew how to eat.

I was seated to the right of Paschaltz, the patriarch, and across from my Maria. Francesca held down the end of the table closest to the kitchen, where she ruled. Paschaltz wore an open peasant-style canary yellow shirt with a loden green sweater buttoned over. His brown corduroy pants bloused his dark brown boots. In contrast, the women wore dresses, knee-length, and slippers. Maria's matched her blue eyes, while Francesca's was of a red intense enough to incite any bull. I matched the patriarch in every detail, except for his expansive girth and bushy white beard.

"Today, my friend, I wish to introduce you to a few of my friends from the old days."

I was finally maybe getting somewhere. While I gloried in Maria's love and her mother's cooking, I found the old man to be boring. For seven years I have listened to old men talk about and brag about the exploits of their youth. In the main they were Party members, many were soldiers, more than a few bureaucrats. They survived by living on the fringes of modernity in small villages far behind the times and far away from modern concerns and influences. Forno di Zoldo, a small dot on the Cellina River, some thirty miles south of Austria, was perfect in this regard.

"Who will I be meeting," I asked.

"Some men who knew your father."

How often had I heard this description, gotten my hopes up, and discovered more dead-ends. Seemed a lot of people knew of my father, but so far none actually had seen him after the war nor had any idea where he would be if he was alive.

With some reluctance, I asked, "Are you sure they know where my father is?"

"There is at least one who claims to have seen der Fuhrer in 1946."

"I guess it is worth a try."

"Good, I have some loose ends to take care of. We will go following supper. Is that acceptable to you, dear?"

Francesca just nodded. We finished our meal in quiet as the sun lightened the gloom and warmed the cold.

Maria asked her father, "Daddy, might we borrow the car to go into Belluno?"

"What do you need that justifies such a long trip?"

"Papa, it is only an hour away." She gave him a look that could melt the ice on the Lac di San Groce.

30

"You're kidding, right?"

I knocked on the door of what was supposed to be Adolf Hitler's home. I heard a dog bark and the shuffling steps of someone approaching from the other side..

"Who is it?"

"Depends on who you are," I replied.

"I was expecting no one."

"Herr Paschaltz sends his best."

The door swung open revealing an old man and his dog. "You have the proof," he demanded.

"It is a little embarrassing. Might I come in and show you?"

"Tell me what it is first."

"A birthmark, somewhat squarish, high on my right thigh.."

"Close the door and show me."

I entered the house, stood in front of the man who might be my father, Adolf Hitler. "I will need to see yours also," I demanded.

We both loosened our belts and shrugged our pants down to our knees and pointed at our matching birthmarks. We raised our pants. He led me to a soft chair and settled himself in opposite me.

"Why did you not come visit or even acknowledge me?" I demanded. "Why did you let me rot in that God-forsaken place? I searched for you for seven years."

"And now that you have found me," Hitler answered, "what will you do?"

I was stunned to the core. I had abandoned my home, my mother, survived as a pauper, risked my life more than once without ever asking myself that question. Blondi bounded over to protect the old man, though I was not interested in harming him. After all, he had done nothing to me, though not much for me either. Yet, now that I knew he existed as more than my mother's fantasy, I wanted to get to know him.

All his followers, new and old, that helped and hindered my journey had told me that they suspected that Der Fuhrer still lived. This despite piles of documentation to the contrary. Now, here he was. And here I was.

His face held an enigmatic smile while his dark old eyes crinkled with delight.

"My son, I have followed your life from the moment I met your mother. I never abandoned you though I could never acknowledge you. Better she should soldier on without relying on me."

"But not even a birthday gift? Never anything! I was your son!"

"Have a cup of tea." He turned around and ordered, "Eva, if you please? We will have tea on the patio."

Eva had aged well. Her golden hair had lightened a little. She was still slim, sort of. She was just beginning to get her hausfrau hips. She wore a flowered housedress, white lilies on a field of dark blue. Whereas, Hitler wore a casual white shirt and dark slacks. These two looked like any other retired couple living out their years in this historic village.

Blondi followed us out the French doors to a flagstone-covered backyard about ten meters square. A low-cut stone fence separated it from the sidewalk. We took our seats surrounding a round table, its umbrella already open.

A shadow muted the light in his eyes.

"You are my son. How I have waited to say that to you. How long I have waited for you to find me."

"Why didn't you let me know where you were? Why let me waste seven years?"

"There is one thing I have learned, my son, and that is that struggle is just as important, as valuable for a people, a country, and even-more-so for a man. Surviving leads to thriving. Such has been true for me, my Germany and such will be true for you—my son and my heir. Surely you read my book?"

"Read it? Mother read *Mein Kampf* to me from the day I was born until I was old enough to read it myself!"

"Then you know what I had to say about struggle?"

"Dad, I know your book like others know the *Bible* or *Koran* or *Torah*."

"Recite to me then the second paragraph of the book."

And so I did. *"German-Austria must be restored to the great German Motherland. And no ...* [all the way through to the end] *... and the tears of war will produce the daily bread for the generations to come."*

"Hearing you speak my words takes me back to the day I first penned them."

Eva bustled out with a tray of pastries.

"Mein Liebchen, for you and your son." She petted old Adolf on his shiny pate and ruffled Blondi's smooth coat, then returned inside.

My father raised a glass in a toast, so, of course, I joined him.

"To my son and my heir."

Our glasses clinked and I drank deeply. He sipped, his eyes never leaving my face. I began to blush. Only my mother had ever looked at me that intently.

"How can you be alive? You were born back in 1889. You would be seventy-five years old!"

"My son, I only ask you to believe your own eyes. As to my age I have always tried to take good care of myself and I have Eva to care for me. She makes sure I only eat what is healthy." He leaned into me and whispered, "She is quite a little dictator when it comes to me."

He guffawed, something no picture of him had ever shown me. I could not help myself. I joined in.

I genuinely was beginning to like der Fuhrer. But, I had to persevere for a minute.

"How about Blondi? How can she still be so young?"

"I would like to credit superior German medicine and scientists but the honest answer is this is my Blondi's great granddaughter." Again he laughed. My old man had some sense of humor.

"I saw pictures of your corpses!"

"My son, did you really think I would die for the German people? The very ones who let me down so often?"

"But, I saw the pictures!"

"You saw just what I wanted you and all the others to see and believe."

"But, I saw the pictures!"

"What you saw, my dear boy, was the corpse of one of my stand-ins; an unemployed actor who pretended to be me right up to the end."

"How could that be? They had your dental records. They had proof!"

"They had what I chose to give them! With the right doctors almost anyone could be made to look like me. Eva had a stand-in. Even my dog, Blondi, had one. Loyal to the end.

"Where better to hide than right out in the open? The last place anyone would look is my hometown. Eva and I got here before the American invaders."

Not only was he my father, but one of the most powerful men in the world! His eyes, those eyes that mesmerized millions were still bright as lanterns and as dark as the night. Don't ask me how that can be. It just is.

I only knew about him from my mother—positive—and all that people said and wrote—mostly negative. I had spent the past seven years tracking him down to please my mother.

We ate and drank the afternoon away. He got me talking about Oberschwarzenberg and all the people living there. Almost made me homesick. Just before dusk Eva again came out to the patio to announce supper was ready.

At the table with my father to my right and Eva to my left, I basked in the glow of their love and affection for me and for each other. For too long I had been on my own unable to trust anyone. Now I felt like I was finally home.

"You must tell us of your travels," Eva said.

I pushed back from the table filled with sauerbraten, dumplings and a rich torte.

"My struggle to find you began in 1957 when I left Ober-schwarzenberg. My first challenge was crossing the border into Germany. I chose Passau and prepared for a struggle. However, things went surprisingly easily …"

———•———

A night spent in a comfortable bed! What a blessing! No bugs or rats, well ventilated. Clean sheets, sky-blue walls without cracks or mold. Green carpet— no tatters, spills or terrible smells. And the final touch—the aromas of fried bacon and coffee wafting up the stairs to my room. My room!

I had followed a long meandering road to end up a few miles from where I started. For seven years I had been bounced from one group to another, one old soldier to another, and here I was. Finally, I had found my real father. No disrespect to Erich. But, you cannot beat the real thing.

For her whole life my mother believed I was Hitler's heir. But to what? All he seems to have is this modest house in a modest town in a forgotten part of Austria, itself a second-rate country. In the back of my mind I had hoped he would be a super-wealthy villain, someone out of James Bond. Instead, he was an old man painting postcards for tourists.

31

"My son, Adolf from Oberschwarzenberg."

The Home of Adolf and Eva Braun
Braunau am Inn, Austria
4 July 1964

I took a seat between my parents, Adolf and Eva Braun.

"My boy, what have you decided?"

"My father, I feel I have no choice but to follow my destiny."

Hitler nodded to me." We begin after breakfast."

Eva rose to bring in platters of eggs and ham, potatoes and coffee. My parents ate sparingly, especially Dad. When I commented, he only chuckled and nodded to his wife. I understood immediately. He may have been the Fuhrer, but Eva ruled the roost.

I ate a hearty meal feeling I had to prepare myself for a long tutoring session on the patio.

———

"The first thing you must know is that I have changed my mind about how to maintain and expand the greatness of the German people. War and conquest are not the solution I once thought them to be. The German people are superior in many things but they are not the most populous. Any war of attrition will be lost."

"You finally figured that out?"

He glared at me. Once a Fuhrer always a Fuhrer. Hitler took a few deep calming breaths.

"My son, you must understand that we are of different generations. Mine was at the cusp where open war became much less effective than the undeclared kind."

"You mean like the Cold War?"

"Exactly. I have accomplished much in the few years following the war."

"Germany is divided. Our economy is still struggling. The Communists and terrorist groups operate openly," I rejoined.

"All true. And all according to my plan."

"You planned for defeat? For occupation? For the Nuremburg trials? For the starvation and suffering? For the division of Germany?"

"Maybe planned is the wrong word. Let us say I learned my lesson and have learned how to have my ends be met by others. None of them aware that they are working towards my goal.

"My former enemies came to realize that myself, like many former Nazis, could be of great value. I live here safely because I have helped the Allies and they have helped me. I am a calming influence, never letting things get out of hand. "

"What is your goal?"

"A strong Germany, of course."

I started to speak, but before I could say another word he said, "I implore you to just listen to me for a few more minutes."

So, I did.

He told me about his money in Swiss accounts. Much of the gold the SS collected from the doomed Jews in the ghettos, at the screening stations in the concentration camps and from the teeth of the dead had been melted down and deposited in the Swiss banks during the war. Some funds were also hidden within Germany and the other conquered countries, including Austria. That was the source of Hans Schuler's money in Oberschwarzenberg. There were other men in other towns who had similar access. They helped the towns modernize and bankrolled much of Germany's industry in its growth and recovery.

Similarly, there were opportunities for his believers to contribute to Hitler's efforts through donations and fund-raisers. A few marks here, a few there building into a considerable war chest. Money sent from outside Germany was kept in its local currency so it could be sent back to terrorists and be harder to trace.

He sponsored terrorist groups throughout the world, but particularly in Europe and the West. "The Communists will destroy themselves trying to keep up with the West. I just make sure they do not get too far behind."

He supported the efforts of Palestine Liberation Front, African National Congress and a hundred others, whether real revolutionaries or mischief-makers because it all led to disruption of the ruling forces and reinforced Germany's role.

"Look at how the Americans botched their war in Korea. Look at how their French allies are lousing up in Indo-China. I predict, in fact I am sure, they will bleed themselves white over Vietnam. At home their children rebel."

Hours later he was bragging about his longevity.

"One of my greatest joys was attending the funeral of Stalin."

"How in the world did you do that?"

"The how I will get to. Perhaps," he slyly said, "the more important question is why."

"Okay. Why?"

Der Fuhrer began to chuckle, increasing in volume and tone to hysterical laughter. He suddenly began to gasp for breath. I feared he was going to check out. I leapt up and went over to him, but was not sure he needed me. While I pondered, Eva came running out. She glared at me.

She demanded, "What did you do?"

"I only asked him why he attended Stalin's funeral."

"Oh, that." She gave my old man a mighty shove to his back sending him sprawling onto the table. Then she left the room. He looked up at me, eyes ringed in red, saliva oozing from his mouth, his bald pate sweating.

Between gasps he said, "She still has no sense of humor."

I was quickly losing mine, too. "So, why?"

He started laughing again, recovered just enough to say, "Because I could!"

Adolf Hitler, Der Fuhrer, my father had been putting together a plan of personal survival should the war go against him. Early in 1944 following his defeats in Russia and Africa, the loss of Mussolini and Italy, and the increasingly poor showing by his Japanese allies, he got serious. By May everything was in place: fake IDs, the home where he now resided, the Swiss bank accounts and the help of a few trusted lieutenants like Herr Paschaltz. D-Day confirmed that all was lost. More and more he empowered his double to represent him. The July 20, 1944 bombing at his Prussian headquarters resulted in arm and leg injuries upon his double while Hitler remained safely at the Berchtesgaden with Eva and Blondi.

The world and history observed Germany's deterioration mirrored by his own. I had seen newsreels of a man far older than his years determined, some would say demented, to find victory long after defeat was certain. But, we were seeing the double, not my father, who played his role to the very end. His death that seemed such a release for Germany and the world was not.

He and Eva spent Christmas 1944 comfortably in Austria while his troops, the Soviets and Allies struggled on two fronts during one of the coldest winters in memory. I asked him why he did not order Germany to surrender then. So many thousands of lives could have been saved.

"My son, there is a time for everything, for peace and war, for killing and dying. None of the combatants had yet reached their nadir of defeat or acme of victory. As long as Eva and I were safe that was all that mattered. After the fighting stopped I could begin my struggle to

claim victory. Now, less than two decades later, I am far along on my
road to final victory."

"But you have no country, no army, nothing!"

"Quite so, it would seem to the unpracticed eye."

Eva came out to call us for lunch, a very late lunch.

"This afternoon I will begin teaching you, my son."

———————

Eva asked me about any girls I might be interested in. "You
know," she said, "you are old enough to start your own family."

"I was about your age when I first fell in love with Geli," Adolf
said.

Eva shot him a glance full of hate, her brown eyes immediately ringed with red. She threw her napkin to her plate as she shot
to her feet. Poor old Adolf looked like he had just stepped into a big
steaming pile of Blondi's poop and tracked the stink and stain into the
house. He pushed himself to his feet and grabbed her as she ran past.
Enfolding her in his arms, she cried on his shoulder. They spoke softly,
so softly I barely heard a word. All I heard for sure was his "I'm sorry."
After a minute, Eva quieted and they returned to the table. We ate for
a minute in silence before he spoke.

"What I meant to say was that I had heard about you and Maria."

Then Eva's voice as soft as a summer breeze on the patio. "She is
a wonderful girl. Did you know we are her godparents."

"Her parents have been very helpful to us," my father said.

"How?"

"Paschaltz secured this home for us. Francesca decorated it.
They lived here until we left Germany late in 1944. Eva wanted to be
in her own home for Christmas." Hitler winked at me, "She is such
a softie." This earned him a sock to his arm from Eva. "It is also true
that I wished to be at home. I was fifteen the year my mother died and
I moved to Vienna, My father had died two years before so I was all

alone.

"The years of struggle I spent in cheap hotels, the homes of friends, prison or army barracks. By the time I became politically active I was staying in better hotels, then at the Chancellery. Sure, I had Berchtesgaden, but it was so far from Berlin and the war that I barely spent any time there.

"November 1944, Eva said we should wed and settle down." He turned and gave her a goofy grin, "What choice did I have? I surrendered."

"We have been here ever since, except for his funeral trips," she concluded. "But, now you must tell us of you and Maria."

"Sounds like you know as much as I do."

Hitler stepped in, "All we know is you two spent much time together."

Eva asked, "Will Maria be joining you here?"

I was taken aback. Maria and I had been intimate for those months, but had never really spoken of a future. I was too focused on discovering the truth about my father. She was just twenty, young and playful. Her father never admitted our intimacy.

"I'm not sure Herr Paschaltz would permit that," I said.

"He will follow orders!"

"Then, Father, I would like to have her visit."

He nodded to Eva.

"But, only if it is her wish," I added.

"I already know she wants to come," my step-mother said.

"You have spoken to her?"

"Just about every day since you left her house," Eva answered.

"And her father?"

Dad said, "Again, he will do as I order."

I had to ask, "When will she arrive?"

"She left yesterday," Eva said. "She should be here tomorrow in time for lunch."

I could only look at my father and shrug. Obviously, der Fuhrer and his heir were no match for Eva.

My father picked up a large notebook as we adjourned to the patio. The summer sun had warmed the flagstones. They radiated a comforting heat as we resumed our seats.

Neighbors strolled by calling out greetings to Herr Braun, as they called him. "Not painting, today?" or "Finally retired, have you." or "Aren't you going to introduce me?"

By the end of the day I had met a dozen people who had absolutely no idea, or at least acted that way, who their neighbor really was. He proudly introduced one and all to, "my son, Adolf from Oberschwarzenberg." If any wondered why they had never heard of me they were too kind or circumspect to make an issue. He never mentioned my last name and I had to admit I was becoming unsure of it myself. Was I a Hitler, a Schoener, or a Schwimmer? Or was I now to become a Braun?

Between neighbors I pursued one topic. "Do you think you can talk about the funeral trips without choking."

Though the old guy smiled he managed to control himself. "Actually, it was pretty easy. Because Hitler had died in Berlin in 1945, and I had arrived here in 1944 as Herr Adolf Braun there was no real issue. I had already obtained all the documents necessary for Eva and I including passports. It was only a small matter to obtain new documents from the Allies and later the Austrian government in my new name. There was so much disruption after all. Anyone with proper papers was assumed to be that person.

"As to Stalin's funeral, well I just went as a regular citizen. No need for recognition or special honors. I just wanted to see the bastard dead and buried."

He ranted a while about Stalin until having to pause for breath, allowing me to turn the conversation.

"No one made an issue of Eva Braun keeping her name and

looking like herself?"

"Again, the proper forms carried the day. Changes in her birth-date, birthplace, occupation, and so forth were enough for her to start anew. Especially married. And with her double sticking with mine to the end there were no questions."

After hearing more about their idyllic life here, I abruptly asked for his personal view of how Germany had fallen into two world wars.

"That bastard Churchill and his country were responsible for both of Germany's wars."

"I thought Germany or the Jews or the Serbians were," I said.

"Let me tell you some history you'll not find in the textbook ..."

And he was off into another rant, though a quieter one, which allowed for no interruption..

"The first war, my war, was a commercial and industrial war. German bankers and businessmen did not want war. The German people did not want war. But, Britain wanted war as a means of blunting our efforts to become a world power. We would have paid a high price for British neutrality. For them it was a war of choice not necessity.

"All the thousands who died, my friends and countrymen, did so for nothing. Our front lines in 1918 were those of 1914. Though we were exhausted we were never bettered on the battlefield. Only the politicians defeated us and sadly it was our own, the Germans, who agreed to that treaty of shame, Versailles.

"Ironically, perhaps, its major provisions were financial. The French, in particular, stripped much of our industry, demanded millions of Marks in restitution, and stripped away German people from their homeland as a sop to the new mongrel countries invented by the winners and quickly abandoned by them a few years later."

From the notebook, he quoted Lloyd George who said in March 1919, "You may strip Germany of her colonies, reduce her armaments to a mere police force and her navy to that of a fifth-rate power; all the same, in the end she feels that she has been unjustly treated in the peace of 1919. She will find means of extracting retribution from her conqueror … Injustice, arrogance, displayed in the hour of triumph will never be forgotten or forgiven."

"Only a strong Germany," my father continued, "could take back its honor and right the wrongs. It became my fate to be their leader though I neither sought it nor planned for it. Indeed had I had my own way I would have become an artist, an architect perhaps, had I been accepted into art school as was my right and destiny. Instead I was thrown into poverty, living with the working class and lower in the cesspool of the Hapsburg capitol, Vienna."

"I'm not sure I am following you. I thought we were talking about the wars."

"You are quite right. My personal history can wait. As I was saying, or better let me quote Churchill himself. In 1935 he wrote, 'History is replete with examples of men who have risen to power by employing stern, grim, and even frightful methods but who, nevertheless, when their life is revealed as a whole, have been regarded as great figures whose lives have enriched the story of mankind, So may it be with Hitler.'"

I was astonished! Churchill actually had a kind word for Hitler!

My father continued, "In 1937 Churchill wrote, 'One may dislike Hitler's system and yet admire his patriotic achievements. If our country were defeated I hope we should find a champion as indomitable to restore our courage and lead us back to our place among nations.'"

Now he was calling my dad a hero!

"Yet Churchill saw fit to lay the entirety of the second war upon my shoulders. England had nothing to do, no responsibility for its own actions—or inactions. The ego of that fat, cigar-smoking, gin-swilling liar knew no bounds. And the world went along with him!"

"Well you did invade Austria, Czechoslovakia, and Poland.

Then Belgium, Norway, Sweden, France, Holland, Russia, Africa, Italy and how many others."

"That was later, you see. Austria and Czechoslovakia were less invasions than German people seeking their own kind, being reunited with the Fatherland. The Versailles Treaty and Wilson's twelve, sixteen or twenty-four points (the man never stopped, it seemed) enshrined the concept of self-determination. It was only a problem to the West when I used it.

"After Munich and the regaining of the Sudenten Germans I did little but encourage people to utilize the self-determination aspect of Versailles. You see Czechoslovakia was a mongrel state put together in 1919 to satisfy the British and French desire to hem in my people. The conglomeration they devised was weak and non-democratic from the beginning. By 1 January 1939 Poland and Hungary had taken large chunks. It was only left for Slovakia on March 14th to declare independence followed by the Ruthenians who joined Hungary.

"Listen to what Liddell Hart said of Neville Chamberlain declaring on March 31, 1939 that Britain would go to war with Germany if I attacked Poland. 'The Polish guarantee was 'foolish, futile, and provocative … an ill-considered gesture that placed Britain's destiny in the hands of Polish rulers, men of very dubious and unstable judgment. The Polish Guarantee was the surest way to produce an early explosion, and a world war. It combined the maximum temptation with manifest provocation. It incited Hitler to demonstrate the futility of such a guarantee to a country out of reach from the West, while making the stiff-necked Poles even less inclined to consider any concession to him, and at the same time making it impossible for him to draw back without losing face.'

"Sir Roy Denman wrote, '…the most reckless undertaking ever given by a British government. It placed the decision on peace or war in Europe in the hands of a reckless, intransigent, swashbuckling military dictatorship.'

"Paul Johnson wrote, 'The power to invoke it (the war guarantee) was placed in the hands of the Polish government, not a repository of good sense. Therein lay the foolishness of the pledge: Britain had no means of bringing effective aid to Poland yet it obliged Britain itself to declare war on Germany if Poland so requested.'

"All we asked of Poland was access to Danzig and self-determination for the Germans within its artificial borders. When Britain and France guaranteed its borders in contravention to the treaty, to Wilson and the League of Nations they blew a small localized problem into a world war. Never forget, my son, I never declared war on anybody. The RAF bombed Germany months before I ever attacked them."

I started to protest, but he continued. "I had no intention ever of going to war with Britain or France and especially the United States."

"But you did!"

"You will find, my boy, that it was they who declared war on me. Up to March 1939 we had all gotten along well. America was a strong isolationist so only was involved on the periphery. England and we Germans come from a common stock. Even the French and Germans have some far distant relatives. I had no fight with either. My focus was to the east. I had reclaimed the Sudetenland, Rhineland and Austria by then. I was focused on Poland wishing the return of Danzig, a city of 350,000 Germans, all wanting to return to my Reich. And access to Prussia across the Corridor. Chamberlain agreed, as did Daladier, that these were righteous claims. Poland had not existed until 1919 and was an agglomeration of Poles, Germans, Slovaks, Jews and others. None had any desire to be ruled by the Poles. They were forced to live in a dictatorship. But I was in no position to demand their freedom. I just wanted to accomplish my limited goals and avoid war.

"The British stepped in to guarantee the Poles that if I attacked they and the French would declare war on me. Me! I never did anything to them except treat them with the greatest deference and respect. I even treated the Poles with respect trying to save them from Russia.

But all I got was hostility and provocations. I had no choice but to attack. To not have done so would have brought my government and country down. That I could never have withstood, not after Versailles.

"At the end of the war, Churchill declared that the principles of the Atlantic Charter did not apply to Germany. This resulted in the forced relocation of eleven million Germans in which two million died, The territories of East Prussia, Pomerania, Eastern Branden-burg, Silesia, Danzig, Memel, and the Sudetenland were cleansed of Germans. Concurrently the Nuremberg trials of German war crimi-nals were being held.

"Other than a few relatives who I never got around to has anyone really missed all those Jews and other undesirables they say I eliminated? Would the people of the Mideast be happier if I had gotten them all or just the few I did? For a people who started a country at the expense of others, often called imperialists or worse, they are no more tolerant than I was. I had my Nuremburg laws, they have theirs. I had my Jews whom I discriminated against, they have their Arabs.

"So I learned. I read and I listened. I knew I had not been perfect but had not realized I had been so fatally flawed. Yet a few could see that much of what I had achieved had been worth the cost.

"I also had no territorial goals outside Europe. I only sought peace. But France and Britain made it clear that I would only know the peace of the beaten or the victor. Neither had any interest in an alliance of equals that included Germany."

He stopped, temporarily spent. I was exhausted.

32

"I would be different!"

I awoke early this morning to an absolutely glorious sunshiny morning. To tell the truth, it would have been a great day regardless of the weather. According to Eva, the manager of this whole affair, my Maria would arrive just after noon. Before our reunion I would have to spend a few hours being instructed by my dad. I hoped to move him beyond his musings about the world wars and his own history to the present and future. However, there was still one gap I wished to have filled.

Once again we three sat through a fine breakfast and then Adolf Hitler and I adjourned to the patio accompanied by the ever-faithful Blondi. Comfortably ensconced in our chairs, shaded by the umbrella, with a carafe of coffee and pastries on a sideboard, we began.

"Tell me, my son, what should we talk about today?"

"I think I understand your take on the wars and the general scope of your recent activities. Now I would like to better understand your early years in Vienna."

"As you might remember, I had to leave home following the death of your grandmother." His monologue took me from his home near here and through his formative years in Vienna. There he worked menial jobs, learned to hate autocrats, despise democratic parties, and to assess and, to an extent, discount the common man.

In Vienna he first came face to face with Jews. He accepted the common thinking that they caused much of the world's trouble and that they remained a race apart. The Christian churches, especially the Catholics, were still calling Jews "Christ killers."

His wholesale acceptance of this blather clouded his future. Luckily, after the war he began to see how badly the rich had manipulated him. It was a group that contained some Jews but was populated in large part by so-called Christians and pseudo-patriots. In his opinion, the bourgeois were little better; and the common man followed sensationalism which the government and media readily supplied.

He said he would never apologize for the Holocaust, but did allow he had been less than critical in his thinking of the matter.

"I have something to show you in the cellar," Dad said.

I followed him down the stairs, the middle of each tread worn shiny smooth. One weak overhead bulb lit our way. At the bottom he turned on a switch, bathing the room in bright light. He walked to a table as I stood in wonder.

The walls were shelved with steel and wood, floor to ceiling. The shelves, eight per wall were stacked with baskets and boxes, each marked with the name of a country. In alphabetical order. I turned to my left and found Uzbekistan at eye-level. I pulled out the heavy wood box, opened the lid to find stacks of colored paper. I removed one to better see it in the light. I was holding a *100-drachma* note. I reached in again to pull out about twenty pieces—all the same. I glanced at der Fuehrer but he only grinned.

I tried another box on another wall. Switzerland this time. The first piece was a 1000-*kroner*. I again pulled out more—all the same. I turned to him.

"What is this?"

"This is the means for us to realize our future, Germany's

future," he answered.

"There must be thousands of Marks here."

"Oh, far more than that, my boy. I'd venture to guess that there are about a billion Marks worth of currencies here."

The light was finally starting to burn a little brighter. "So, this is how you are financing all the revolution and subversion you told me about."

"Indeed it is. I control or influence virtually every group in the world from right here. I provide them with funds and advisers, technology, contacts, weapons—whatever they need to help me."

"Surely they do not know that it is Adolf Hitler who is behind all this."

"Of course not. Local couriers deliver the currency of each country to their indigenous group. The group assumes that someone local is supporting them."

"Where did you get the money in the first place?"

"You might remember reading about how the Reich amassed a tremendous stock of gold during the war?" I nodded. "We are converting it into currency through our Swiss bankers. Some of the couriers are bringing money here, some are taking it from here."

This was dizzying. I sat heavily in one of the hard wooden chairs surrounding his mid-room work area. My feet and thoughts reverberated off the rough cement floor. This crazy old bastard had really done it. He was winning the war. The twenty years since its conclusion he had built up an army, developed a nearly boundless treasury, and set up a network that did his bidding. Not with Panzers and concentration camps, but with AK47s, terrorist bombings, student and worker protests, revolutions and insurgencies, all to his greater glory. The man was brilliant!

"I will teach you how to do all this," he promised.

I never realized that some hours have more than the requisite sixty minutes. Eva promised, or maybe it was that she had only speculated, that Maria would arrive around one o'clock in the afternoon. Whatever, I was sure that the time was firm and that the clock hands were slowing down as they moved closer to that time. Then the damned things hurried their spinning as they passed one o'clock on their way to 2 p.m. They sped up just as my anticipation turned to worry. Before I knew it the clock chimed three o'clock and yet there was no sign. By then I had pretty much reverted to a child pestering Eva and Adolf why Maria was late, had she been hurt, was today the wrong day, on and on.

Eva smiled at my antics. "If one did not know better, I might think our son is in love with this girl," she said to Adolf.

He responded, "He reminds me of all the times you were late, my dear."

"I knew you would wait."

"The anguish always made my love deeper when you arrived."

"So, I noticed."

Hitler turned to me. "Beware my son, the wiles of women."

I could only nod.

Finally, at four thirty the doorbell rang. I ran for the door failing to see Blondi lying in my path. I sprawled face first on the hardwood floor as Eva opened the door. I looked up to see my dear Maria, burdened with sacks and bags, looking past Eva at me.

Hitler bustled up to greet and help Maria. A kiss on each cheek was followed by, "You must forgive my son."

"Too bad he lacks the manners of his father," Eva added with a shaking of her blond tresses.

These people were playing pretty hard with my distress. I failed to see the humor, especially lying on the ground.

"Son, why don't you get up and greet our guest?"

I struggled to regain my feet. Blondi licked my face forgiving my oafishness or maybe in thanks that I had not hurt her. As for myself, I had bumped my left knee pretty hard and both wrists had taken the shock from the fall. I limped to the door.

Maria stood her full five and a half feet of beauty. Her dark hair swirled to below the collar of her white blouse, cut just low enough to revive my spirits. Her pixie face, red-lipped and blue-eyed, cried out for a caress or kiss. All I could manage though in my best two-year-old voice was, "Where have you been?"

Maria said nothing, just breezed by me, trailing a wonderful perfume. Dad offered his arm, which she accepted. Eva led them into the parlor leaving me at the door, wallowing in my immaturity, wondering how I could recover my adulthood without seeming more the fool.

Eva came to my rescue. She called to me, "Would you be a dear and close the door?" Seemed easy enough but it took two tries as I closed it from the outside the first time.

I entered my parent's home again. Eva said, "Thanks. Would you like to bring in the tray of glasses and tea, son?"

I raced to the kitchen. I took a few minutes to regain my composure, got the tea out of the refrigerator, gathered up the glasses and entered the parlor all the time looking out for Blondi. I could not afford another embarrassment.

There they were seated, judge and jury, awaiting my next move. I decided to take a play out of my dad's playbook. "What I meant to say, my dear Maria, is that it is so good to see you."

She rose, took two steps towards me, jostled the tray and pitcher, slipped her hands round my waist pulled me in for a very welcome, very adult kiss. Eva bounced up to relieve my hands of their burdens so I could return Maria's caresses. After a few seconds by my reckoning, my father grunted just loud enough to bring us back to the awareness of others.

Maria's face was flushed the same color as her lipstick, which I found reassuring. She returned to her seat, sandwiched between Eva and Adolf, leaving me to fend for myself on the thoroughly misnamed, at least in my case, loveseat. Man, that girl looked good!

She caught them up on her parents, both fine; her travel here, some delays but not bad; her shopping trip before her departure, special chocolates for my father and perfume for Eva; her shopping upon her arrival, and buying wine for dinner. Meanwhile I was vacillating between exploding in frustration and reverting to my earlier childish persona.

Finally, I stood up. "Can I get tea for anyone?" All three nodded. I poured, then grabbed a chintz doily draping it over my arm like a waiter and delivered the tea to each, saving Maria for the last. Blondi darted between my legs just as I was bending over. Maria grabbed the glass before I could spill it and my father grabbed me before I fell on Maria. Was that dog jealous or just mean?

Soon Eva announced that it was dinnertime. Maria jumped up to help but Dad gave me a wink and told her to sit, that he would help Eva. Even Eva was shocked. Maria moved over to the now appropriately named loveseat with me. We fell into each others arms lost for a few minutes in passion. She broke off and whispered that we must talk.

I said, "OK, but can we kiss a little more?"

Maria shook her head, removed my hands from her shoulders and held them in her lap. This looked pretty serious. I began to fear she had traveled all this distance just to tell me to get lost. I really wear myself out jumping to conclusions. However, what she had to say did cause me to immediately reassess my whole life and future.

———

"I must say you two are more subdued in your reunion than Eva and I ever were."

Eva gave him one of *those* stares.

"I mean," he continued, obviously trying to recover, "that it is so nice to see you together. Might I be permitted to make a toast?" He uncorked the wine and poured all of us a generous glass and for himself barely a swallow.

He intoned, "For my son and his Maria, may they enjoy as much love and life as Eva and myself." We clinked glasses and sipped. Maria gave me a look, serious but friendly, as well as a kick to my sore knee. I almost dropped my glass. Eva and Dad looked at me. I feared I was becoming a total putz in their eyes. I was so close to sharing my father's power and trust I did not want to lose it now.

Adolf began to pass the potatoes around, but I interrupted him. "Sir, if I may?"

He placed the bowl back on the table and nodded to me.

"I would like to announce …" I glanced at Maria. Her face was apple red. Eva gazed at her while my father stared at me. "… that is … well … I mean to say …"

"Please hurry it up boy. I am hoping to outlive your news and I am hungry," he admonished.

I took a deep breath. "All right, here it is. Maria and I are going to have a baby."

For the first time in his life, I think Hitler was literally speechless. Eva rose slowly and walked over to Maria and hugged her tight.

Hitler recovered, "How can this be? You are not married?"

I'd been waiting for this! "Neither were you and my mother, yet here I am!"

The quiet thickened over the table. Had my impetuosity ruined everything? Who was I to judge the Fuhrer? All my life I had been cursed by the people of Oberschwarzenberg because my birth mother, Lotte, told them that Adolf Hitler was my father. I had fought many schoolyard battles to protect her honor. I had heard all the Beyerlein biddies calling her Hitler's whore and me his bastard.

I had spent years tracking down the truth, put up with violence, dishonesty, and misdirection only to find the old fraud living a few blocks from his birthplace.

Just one word of acknowledgment from him would have made all the difference. But never a word! Nothing! And now he was judging me.

In the few minutes before dinner when I found I was to be a father I already decided to marry Maria to give her and my child the love and home that were denied me. Never would my child have to wonder who its father was.

I would be different!

Perhaps he read all these racing, raging thoughts in my eyes. Perhaps he was grateful I did not voice them. He responded, "Yes, you are quite right. I did not do as well by you as I would have liked." He rose to hug me. "Please, let me make it up to you, Son. You and Maria can stay with us as long as you want. Forever, if you wish."

I could not help myself. I hugged him back. I was truly home now.

After dinner they both volunteered to do dishes to give Maria and me a few more private minutes. Every time I looked at her I felt the start of tears like an early spring rain that brings forth the flowers. I was going to be a father! How amazing!

We walked, holding hands, embracing before sitting on the loveseat. I had so much to tell her, so much to learn. I knew so little about being a father. I turned toward her, held her hands, and looked into the deep mountain pools of her eyes.

This was going to be hard. In just three days I had become the son of Adolf Hitler, his heir and successor; and today a father. I bucked up my courage. It was time to become a husband.

"Maria, my love, will you marry me?"

"Of course. I would not have come otherwise."

She fell into my embrace, tears wetting our shoulders. I am sure I never loved another person as much nor will ever again.

Then reality. "What about your parents? Your father never seemed to like me."

"I told them just before I left that we were going to be married. Papa was ecstatic like I was giving him just about the best gift ever. Mother was a little more hesitant. She kept glancing at my tummy trying to discover if there was a reason beyond love."

"Eva did not seem upset about the baby," I said.

"She has known from the minute I knew."

I took a minute to process. "You never told me."

"I wanted your mind to be clear when you met your parents."

"You do know who my parents are?"

"What do you mean?"

"They are not exactly who they appear to be."

Just then Adolf and Eva entered the room and sat down.

Dad spoke as Eva and Maria exchanged knowing glances. "Son, your mother and I feel it is our duty to demand … I mean encourage you to marry Maria."

"I've already proposed and Maria accepted. All we have to do is set a date."

"I was thinking next Saturday afternoon would work fine," Eva interrupted, then laughed. "In fact, the invitations have already been printed."

Der Fuhrer and I had been out-flanked! We all rose out of our seats to hug. Eva put her arm around my shoulder.

"Don't take it too hard, my son. I'm used to handling powerful men." She laughed again.

Soon we were all laughing. Dad got out another bottle of wine, poured two healthy glasses and two more with just a sip. He handed Eva and I the full ones, gave Maria one with just a swallow and reserved the other for himself. Maria gave him a look.

The old softie told her, "My dear Maria, my soon-to-be daughter, too much alcohol is not good for my grandchild."

Maria smiled. We toasted in unison and returned to our seats.

I hated to do it but I thought we needed to clear up Maria's misconception regarding her potential in-laws.

"Mom. Dad. I think you need to tell Maria the truth now before we are married."

"What truth would that be," Mr. Innocent asked.

"About who you really are."

Eva said, "Perhaps we should wait until the morning. Everyone is tired and excited."

Maria looked like an opossum caught in the headlights.

"What is going on, dear? Aunt Eva, Uncle Adolf. What is this all about?

Hitler told her, "Nothing of great importance. Your husband sees an opportunity to hurt me again."

"Either you tell her or I will," I challenged.

"Tell me what? I've known your parents my whole life. My parents have known them even longer. I know exactly who they are." We all paused for a minute. "They are," she continued, "my godparents."

I heard myself respond. "He is not Adolf Braun. He is really Adolf Hitler."

"You are lying. Hitler died years ago. In Berlin. At the end of the war. He was a beast, a devil. Everyone knows that."

"Lotte knew he was alive and I needed to know. That is why I searched all those years. The Nazi underground eventually took me to your father. He cleared the way for me to come and find out for myself. Permit me to introduce you to der Fuhrer, my father, Adolf Hitler."

Maria pulled away from me. Was she seeing me as the son of a monster? What had I done? She struggled to her feet and rushed into Eva's arms. My father glared at me, the same stare he had once used to denounce his former friend, Ernst Rohm, before ordering his death. Maria's sobs brought our attention back to our women.

Eva was patting Maria's head as she wept. Had I only known I would have kept my mouth shut. But what right did he have to insult my mother? All the years of struggle, shame bubbled up like a long dormant volcano. I had spewed back to him all the hurt his neglectfulness had heaped upon me. I was just a child, hell long before I was born according to my mother, when I learned that Adolf Hitler was my father. The more I learned about him, especially after the war, the less I liked the idea. When Erich assumed the role of father, even though he and Lotte never married, I gladly nestled in his arms, feeling secure for the first time in my short life. There had been numerous fights trying to protect my mother's honor because she had the temerity to tell everyone who got her pregnant, fathered her child and then abandoned her—Adolf Hitler.

Her strong unflagging belief in the face of Oberschwarzenberg's condemnation was the *raison d'etre* of my struggle to discover the truth.

Upon my arrival I had fallen immediately under his spell. I had lost all interest in anything but learning all he wanted to teach me—until his comment about Lotte. I could finally see the bastard for who and what he really was.

I wanted nothing more than to hurt him as he had hurt me. I wanted to take away from him his only heir, his only possibility for a normal life, his chance to be a grandfather.

What had I been thinking? Could this monster ever be human? Why had I believed in the facade? Was he that good, that overwhelming?

I had to conclude that he was, that I had been duped, that I had exposed my dear Maria to him and his wife, their hands bloodied by the deaths of millions, the suffering of millions more, his power and her acquiescence screwing with the world even now.

All these thoughts flashed by in a second before I got off my duff and went to comfort my dear Maria. I stood by her and Eva, hoping I might get an inkling of how to proceed, how to break their embrace, how to replace Eva with myself. I'm ashamed to admit that nothing came to my mind. I quickly realized I had few resources to call upon when it came to facing the emotionalism of women.

I looked to my left. My father's death-dealing look had softened somewhat. Was he now trying to make peace with me or just on the brink of laughter? I'm pretty sure I would have strangled the old bastard after the first giggle.

He rose, put his arm around my shoulder, and said, "Son, perhaps we should adjourn to my den."

In spite of myself, to my great astonishment, I have to admit I welcomed his touch, his reassurance that I had a father, a home, that my journey was over. Adolf Hitler, der Fuhrer, the murderer of millions cared about me, perhaps even loved me.

Once in his den he ushered me to one of two chairs flanking the fireplace. The room so resembled Erich's living room that for a minute I lost my place in time. His gravelly voice brought me back. "Son, you have had a rough few days. I'm sure that finding me alive and your father was perhaps your dream but that at some level you expected to find me both dead and a cuckold. I regret my comment that you interpreted as being about you and your mother. You must realize I had nothing but the highest respect for your mother. "

"Why didn't you marry her? She asked for so little. Just a nod of recognition that she carried your baby, raised your son?"

"In the present context I know that it looks heartless to you. You were just a child and your mother an unsophisticated country girl. How would she possibly survived in Berlin, among the politics and intrigue?"

"You never gave her a chance."

"You are, of course, correct. However, that is all in the past. I was in no position to publicly acknowledge her or her struggles. Surely, you must be aware that I did make allowances for her and her village. I always made sure they had enough and that my people were watching over you both."

"So, what now? Am I to be accepted as your son? Your heir?"

"I have made preparations for you to accept my mantle at the conclusion of your training."

"The world is to know me as your son?"

"Not exactly. Adolf Hitler died in 1945. His name, his legend, his worldly presence all disappeared in that fiery bomb crater at the Chancellery. The world knows me as Adolf Braun and that will never change."

"Whose son am I?"

"You will become Adolf Braun, Jr. prior to your wedding."

"What will become of Maria? She knows the truth."

"Maria must never tell anyone. Whether she likes the truth or not she must keep it."

"And if she was to decide she no longer loves me?"

"That, my son, would not be a good choice. There are forces far greater than the needs or wishes of a young girl at work here."

I stood up. He put his hands up as to fend off my attack.

"Son, you must make sure Maria understands that it is in her best interest to marry you, have your babies, proudly carry the Braun name."

"And if I cannot convince her?"

"Then I would have to give serious consideration as to who will become my heir. No man that cannot control his woman can expect to wield the power of der Fuhrer."

"But, but ... I've seen how Eva runs things here."

"She has her area—this home. I have mine—the world. You must follow our example. Now go to your beautiful fiancée and ask my Eva to come in here, please."

I followed his suggestion, more of an order, and went to talk with my Maria. Eva arose at once and went to her husband. I sat next to Maria, just holding her for a few minutes until her sobbing eased.

"Maria, we need to talk."

She responded quickly with, "Eva and I already did."

Of course, good old Eva had everything under control. Poor Dad. The man was delusional. "What did you two talk about?"

"What did you and your father talk about?"

"I asked you first."

"Yes, you did. What did you and your father talk about?"

This is the girl I was supposed to control? To prove my mettle? To prove I was able to run the world? I was doomed.

In short order I told her that it was important that we be married, that we become Brauns, that she never tell anyone about the true identities of me or her in-laws.

"Is that all," she said. Very dismissive. Like der Fuhrer and I had been discussing the weather.

"Y-y-e-s-ss. What did you two talk about?"

"Eva explained all that, then we moved onto plans for the wedding and names for the baby."

"But, you were crying!"

"Only for joy, silly boy."

"You are all right with me being his son and heir?"

"If it is important to you, then, of course, it is fine with me."

Whatever or however, Eva had done the hard work for me. Someday, I'd have to ask her how she managed. For right now, it was time for bed. It would be time for sleep a little later.

For the next two months, Maria and I stayed with my father. We married, and Maria spent much time with Eva while I trained under my father, learning the family business.

Then, in late November, I wrote to Lotte.

26 November 1964

Dear Mama and Papa Erich

Great News!

Wonderful things have happened since I arrived in Braunau am Inn. I cannot wait to share my good news with you both. We will be arriving Sunday, 6 December in the afternoon.

Love,

Adolf

33
"You Did This To Me!"

The home of Adolf and Eva Braun
Braunau am Inn, Austria
6 December 1964

I lay on our bed admiring Maria's stretched abdomen. Our baby made swimming motions under her skin. One of my greatest pleasures is playing with my son. I gently push him away and watch him swim back. I could do this for hours except for her need to use the toilet frequently.

Finally after the third interruption, I suggested, "Maria, we should finish packing and get an early start."

"I'm still tired," she responded. "Your son was kicking and squirming all night."

"I know, dear. But in your condition, 106 kilometers can take hours. Besides, I'm kind of excited to be going back home."

"You just want to show off your pregnant wife to prove your manhood to all those bullies."

There was a little truth to that, but I said, "I really want you to meet my mother and Papa Erich."

"I sure hope you are ready."

In fact I had been talking with Dad about this venture so as to limit the risks by subtly shading the truth.

"I have my story ready. How about you?"

"Don't worry about me. Eva and I have worked it all out."

"Smells like breakfast is ready. Too bad you can't handle bacon anymore."

Maria gave me a punch to my arm, a little harder than her love would have dictated.

———

The home of Dr. Erich Schwimmer
Oberschwarzenberg, Austria
6 December, early afternoon

My knock echoed for a moment, then I heard footsteps approaching. I grasped Maria's hand tighter. This was it.

The door opened. There stood my dear mother. Her still-blond hair was pulled into a matronly bun. Her green dress sparkled in the sunlight, matching the magic in her blue eyes. We fell into each other's arms.

"Mama, I've missed you so,"

"My boy, my boy, my boy," she repeated without end until she saw Maria. Papa Erich came up behind Mama and we fell into a manly hug. Finally, pushing me to arm's length, he suggested, "You might introduce your young lady to us."

"She is not my young lady. She is my wife, Maria."

Maria bent a little to embrace Mama as we men looked on.

"In my professional opinion I'd say she is a little pregnant, son," Erich said.

I nodded.

"I presume you are the father."

I nodded again and received a hearty pat on the back, a hand-shake and, "Congratulations."

We adjourned to the living room, which still sported two chairs flanking the fireplace and a couch. Though worn, its back was still covered by the quilt with the blue polka dots on a red background.

Lotte and Maria sat on the couch deep in a light-sounding

conversation punctuated by laughs and finger pointing aimed at Erich and me in the chairs. Though parted for seven years I found I had not so much to share with him. Though he had been my father for most of my life I felt there was a chasm between us. How could he hope to compete with my real father? I now understood why Lotte had never given up her obsession all these years.

"So, my son, has your journey been successful," Erich asked.

"Well, in that I met and married Maria, I can say it has far exceeded my hopes."

"And your search for your father?"

"I'd have to say that I've always hoped it was you."

"You found no trace of him?"

"All were dead ends."

"You are moving back here?"

How could I ever return to Oberschwarzenberg? After my time with my father I felt myself transformed. I was the heir to the greatest man to ever walk this planet. Lotte, Erich and all the others would never understand the new me. I had nothing in common with them. I, and I alone, had been chosen to carry out my father's destiny.

"That would not be practical. Maria wishes to return to her studies and I have apprenticed myself to a painter."

"A painter? You?"

"Turns out I have some talent in that regard. We will continue to live in Braunau am Inn. We have been taken in by my master."

"Who is this master?"

"His name is Braun. They are an older couple, a few years older than you and Mama even."

"They sound ancient."

"Oh, Papa Erich, you know what I mean."

"Have they lived there long?"

"Since before the war ended."

Mama raised out of her seat. "Erich! Why have you allowed me to be such a poor hostess?"

Erich raised his hands. "I allowed?"

"These children must be tired from their trip. Hungry and thirsty, too, I expect."

She bustled off to the kitchen. Erich arose, shrugged his shoulders and followed. I turned to Maria. "How's it going?"

"Your mother is a dear."

"I mean, is she buying our story?"

"Of course. It is the truth…mostly," Maria replied.

"Has she asked about coming to visit?"

"Not yet."

"Remember our house is too small."

"But she will want to visit her grandson."

"I know. Tell me again what we decided."

"It will be easier and more fun for us to come here," Maria said. Then she screamed, louder than one of Wagner's Valkyries, doubled over and tumbled from the couch, writhing on the floor. A stream of clear liquid oozed staining her blue skirt. Again a scream, louder.

"My God, Maria. What are you doing?"

She glared up at me grimacing, hateful. She screamed softly, collapsed, panting, staining the rug. I leaped to her side, dread replacing my shock, prodding me to action. As my knees hit the floor Erich rushed in followed by Mama.

"What have you done," Erich demanded.

"Nothing," I pleaded.

He ordered Lotte to get some blankets and towels as he rolled

Maria onto her back. Through her once-beautiful skirt I could see the turmoil of her abdomen roiling like sea waves crashing about in a hurricane. She gasped and gurgled, blank eyes staring where I could not see.

"Is she dying?"

"Is she dying? Gottverdammt, boy! She's having a baby!"

"Impossible. She is not due for another two weeks."

"Get her a pillow." I rose to leave. "Take off her shoes." I turned around to bend down. "Help me get her skirt off." I turned again ending up right where I had started.

While we struggled with her clothing, Mama returned with a bundle of bedding, a tower of towels, and a pillow. I removed Maria's shoes while Mama placed her head on the pillow and covered her with a blanket.

Erich shouted, "I need towels and my medical bag." Lotte tossed me the towels and rushed off to retrieve his bag.

"Hold her hand while I wash up," Erich said. Now this was something I could do. When I grasped her left hand in mine her eyes flickered open. Though her scream was little more than a whimper, I'm pretty sure I heard, "You did this to me!"

———•———

"OOOOOHHHHH!!!!!" Hour after hour I had to listen to Maria moan. When she wasn't moaning she was cursing me. Me? All I did was have sex with her. Getting pregnant was her idea. Getting married was her idea. All I wanted to do was to find my father. I had not planned on becoming one!

"You're almost there," Erich kept muttering in an encouraging voice. His body bent over the bed, his head perched between Maria's legs near her knees.

Mama, of the boundless energy, bustled around, putting the

same things away she had gotten out just a few minutes ago. Every five minutes since we had brought Maria into their bedroom a half-hour ago she had changed the wet cloths bathing Maria's forehead.

"Things are coming along very nicely," Erich reassured me, "for a first delivery." First? I was never going through this torture again, thank you!

"Ouch!" Gottverdammt, that girl had a grip! "Easy, Maria! You are crushing my painting hand!" From beneath her beetled brow two dark cinders glared at me. "I'm just joking, honey. Squeeze all you want," I soothed my voice, but my face contorted in pain mirroring her's.

Erich dove deeper between her legs, stretching out his hands like an American footballer catching a pass. "Here comes the head! Keep pushing. Now just a little more."

I was not sure how much more of this I could take. The noise and the pain overwhelmed my system. I felt myself going deaf blocking out her moans. And my hands! Luckily I was not an artist or my career would be ended. But, I held on and kept my post at her side. I was a man and I would see this through.

"The shoulders are coming! Push, Maria." Erich crawled out from Maria's legs holding a red, wrinkled, squawking, squirming something. The man was smiling like a deranged Leprechaun. Mama swooped in with towels relieving him of it. Thank God she wrapped it up. I had never seen such an ugly hunk of matter.

After rubbing around on it for a minute she turned to me offering up her burden, a long tendril hanging from its middle. "It is a boy, Adolf. You have a son!" I beheld the most beautiful child there ever was or will be. Together we laid him on Maria's tummy as Erich cut the umbilical cord. Suddenly, I realized the room was very quiet. It was over. Maria smiled like a saint, her eyes bright, holding out her arms to caress her child. My son. Our son, Adolf Braun III, looked me in the eye and I was hooked. Without thinking I determined that hereafter he would be called by those who loved him: Drei.

"Look, dear, he has a birth mark just like yours," my mother said.

St. Polycarp Church
Oberschwarzenberg, Austria
14 December 1964

I gazed out at the gathering of old men seated in the pews. These were the Onkels, the Stadtsteuergruppe. They were the much-respected and feared former soldiers and sailors of World War II Germany. The fire of Nazism that burned white hot in my father's heart had been reduced to a few gray, ash-covered embers matching the hair on their heads.

These few, the Onkels had rebuilt Oberschwarzenberg after the war. They had been responsible for the paved streets, water and sewer systems, most of the new homes and the repair of the old.

Erich assumed his position on the stage in front of the altar. I occupied a hard wooden chair next to him and prayed Drei would not exercise his right to wail.

In a voice as deep and smooth as the Weissbach, Erich began. "Mein Komaraden, my son has returned!" Erich nodded to me. I stood.

The Onkels rose in ragged formation, though their aches and pains slowed their response. They began to applaud until Erich hushed them, "It would not be good to wake the baby, mein Herren."

Egan Beyerlein, always the troublemaker, spoke up. "You call him son, yet his name is not yours."

"Quite right. It is necessary for reasons you need not concern yourself about for him to be called Adolf Braun, Jr and his son, my grandson, to be called Adolf Braun III. We are of different beliefs regarding my son but just as we united in our desire to rebuild our town and to keep it safe we must accept him."

The Onkels gathered to greet me and my son. Deep in their twisted souls many assumed he was Hitler's heir just as I was. They gathered around me as if all the fights with their children over my lineage were forgotten, all their snubs banished to history's trash heap. But I remembered and Lotte remembered even if Erich chose amnesia. Our memories were sharp as the jagged peak which towered over the town.

I recognized I was of the future. These Onkels were history's orphans still believing in a German military victory long after Adolf Hitler had decided his new strategy.

It was obvious the Nazi money still flowed. My father would never turn off the taps. He still took care of my mother and her reluctant people.

Later at home I had to give Maria a recap. Her only response was, "That was nice." I slept well feeling I had passed some test, that even with a different name these old men and the whole town chose to believe what they were told regardless of reality. Maria, however, had to deal with Drei's insatiable appetite.

———

The letter arrived a few weeks following Drei's birth, postmarked Braunau am Inn. I opened it sensing its message emanating like a thick snowy ground fog oozing from the warm waters of the Weissbach River.

I handed it to Maria when she finished nursing our son. Better she should know firsthand. She took it, her eyes with the look of a mouse grasped in the strong sharp mouth of an old farm cat. Her tears showered like a spring rain.

Lotte, my dear mother, bustled in, shaking a blizzard of flour from her apron. She had heard Maria's sobbing and stormed in like a Panzer.

"What is it," she demanded.

Maria made to hand her the letter but I intercepted, taking it and reading it to myself.

Son

I demand that you return immediately. Events are taking place that require our attention. The needs of the German race must be foremost in both our minds and spirits. I take it that your mother, Maria and my grandson are all in good health.

Eva misses you very much, as do I.

A. Braun

"Well?" Lotte repeated.

"Herr Braun," I answered, "wants us to return."

"You cannot! I will not lose you again!"

"Mother, you must see that my future is not here. I must study with my master."

Lotte turned to my wife. "Maria? Please?"

Holding our son to her breast she rose and was enveloped in Lotte's embrace. Together, they cried.

Maria gave me *that* look dismissing me from their presence. I turned, retreating to the living room where I found Erich.

34

"Mein Gott in Himmelhoch!"

The home of Adolf and Eva Braun
Braunau am Inn, Austria
25 December 1964

We were only a few minutes from home when I had an inspiration.

"Maria, did you bring your eyeliner?"

"What in the world are you talking about?"

"Just thinking a little."

"For a new father and the potential leader of the world you should be thinking a lot more seriously."

Her response shut me up but did not change my mind. I did not get where I am by giving up!

"Where is it?"

"In my purse." I was amazed at how much disgust those three words held.

"Just keep your eyes on the road, dear. I have everything under control," I reassured her.

Holding my son in the crook of my left arm I fished in the backseat with my right arm for her purse. A quick glance showed I had the choice of three liners, each a little darker than the next. I settled on the darkest and used my teeth to drag it out.

Maria glanced over just once and uttered a dark threat about how I'd better not be doing anything to harm her baby. Hers? I was the Papa! I continued my work. The life of an artist is never easy.

We arrived just as I applied my masterstroke. Carefully shielding my son from his mother's view, I exited the car and strolled up the walk. I made to knock as Maria bustled up. "Dummkopf! Don't knock! We live here!"

I knocked anyway. While Maria steamed and stamped her feet I waited patient as a cat stalking a mouse. Eva opened the door and Maria rushed into her embrace leaving me and our son in the dust.

Eva regained her momentum enough to embrace me and my son, then held her hands out that I might let her hold him. She pulled the blanket away from his face and screamed. Poor little Adolf Braun, III or Drei, as I called him, let out a wail of his own. Eva glared at me, shouted, "How could you!" and thrust him into Maria's arms.

My wife exclaimed, "You bastard!" But with a smile on her lips.

I followed Eva and Maria, grinning, happy to know I had been successful. It only remained to see how Dad would react.

Our parade came to a halt at his seat. Eva went to stand behind the throne as I stood to the left and Maria presented him with our son.

Adolf Hitler roared out of his seat. "Mein Gott in Himmel-hoch! What have you done?" For a man who had pretty much disregarded religion and any deity he was quick to invoke a higher power when presented with his new grandson.

The look on his face was priceless. The ruler of the world was absolutely perplexed. He held Drei at arm's length, staring at his face. Poor old man, his face was becoming as red as his old Nazi flag.

Eva commanded, "Breathe, you old fool!"

"But … but … but …," he sputtered. Eva pounded him on his back as Maria helped him to sit again and not drop Drei. I could only smile.

Hitler regained his composure at about the same pace a lame old horse hobbles to the abattoir. He pulled in Drei and looked at him very closely, feet to head, and back again noting the birthmark. He just could not give up staring at little Drei's face. After all, how many newborns have bushy eyebrows and a cheesy mustache?

Eva started laughing giving us permission to join in. After a further moment of study even Grossvater Adolf joined in. For the next hour he held Drei close, cooed to him, and acted the most dear and silly man in love with his grandchild.

———

The next morning, Eva brought platters of eggs and sausage, hot stacks of toast, and steaming cups of coffee to the breakfast table. Maria joined us just as we started.

"Where is Drei," der Fuhrer demanded.

"Down for a morning nap, Grossvater."

"He should not be alone. What if he wakes up and is scared?"

Eva interjected, "That boy has the lungs of a Valkyrie. I will get him as soon as I hear the slightest whimper … and bring him to you."

"My son and I will be in the cellar most of the morning. I will have to trust you two to take care of Drei until we are finished."

As if those two would ever trust us men to care for Drei on our own!

———

Following my marriage to Maria and the birth of Drei, I

plunged deeper into my father's world. For twenty-five years we labored together in that cellar, pushing there, prodding here. All the while watching Germany gain strength and prestige in Europe and the world.

In 1989, Drei joined the family business and we succeeded in re-uniting our Germany. Unfortunately for Grossvater Adolf, this very day of his greatest success—9 November 1989—was also the day of his death. My father, Adolf Hitler, died with myself, Drei and Maria in attendance. Eva had succumbed to a painful bout with stomach cancer a decade earlier.

Dad had lived his life to the fullest, enjoyed being a major part in his grandson's life and accomplishing his goal of making Germany the predominant country, economy and culture in Europe. He out-lived his WWII enemies and many of their progeny. He had adapted to the changing world and was in fact responsible for much of it.

I was to discover that my mother also chose this day to pass onto her final reward. She had done her duty and died a hero.

I was thrust into the maelstrom on my own for the first time, though like my father, I had a supportive wife and fantastic son. Unlike myself, my son had known his real father from the very beginning and had the love of his grandparents, Adolf and Eva. Of course, he also had Herr Paschaltz and Francesca as they moved from Italy to Braunau am Inn soon after his birth. And Lotte and Erich whom we visited yearly. He would never have to wonder who he was or from whence he came.

Hitler had laid the groundwork, established the channels, preserved the true believers and added so many more. He corrupted and usurped the leaders of the West and the Communists, Arabia, Asia, and Africa, their youth movements and terrorists to do his bidding. He kept the world focused on these minor irritations while he pulled the strings. For a man with few democratic bones and no sympathy for minorities or liberals, Dad was a major source of their funding.

Of course, his minions were also major movers in the diplomatic and military institutions through their connections with his banking and financial partners. All their arguing and saber rattling only served to reinforce the necessity of a strong Germany to be present to pick up the pieces. Only a man as brilliant as my father could have so engineered the world.

He had no army, no government, no industry, no colleges or intelligentsia, yet he had all he needed to see victory—an indomitable spirit, coldly focused vision, an heir and serious followers who had all pledged their loyalty, their very lives and deaths to him.

Though he, and later Drei and I, and now Vieri, were not able to predict world events we faithfully believed that Germany would reign supreme—not militarily—but financially. For we finally understood that money was not just the key to victory but that in fact it was the very essence of victory. Dad came to realize, and made perfectly sure I understood, that the Jews were not the enemy. He had fallen prey to the common wisdom of his youth and of Christian history. No, the villains were and yet remain the ultra rich. That many are Jews is undeniable but they are a minority even here.

It was his brilliance that he was using these rich bastards to gain his goal without letting them control him, like the Biblical imperative that one should be in the world but not of the world. Several times Jesus had railed against the rich, the money-changers, and the Pharisees of the temple.

Beginning with the German re-unification and subsequent European Union, my focus turned to causing deeper fissures in

Russia, eventually overseeing its demise. Vladimir Putin tried to put it back together, but the west through NATO, dominated by Germany, had already taken in Poland, Ukraine and many more of the Soviet Union's colonies. No matter how hard he might have tried, Putin was no Stalin. He had neither the brains nor the balls.

The United States and much of the West was easily controlled through involving them in the endless wars of the Near East: Afghanistan, Syria, Iraq, etc. Their neglect of their underclass, the influx of Muslim refugees, and capitulation to the rich will only lead to more disruption, quickly becoming Mao's Paper Tiger.

I retired in 2014 after speaking with my cousin, Lorenz Meyer. I agreed with Drei and Vieri that China will be our next target and I am confident they will be able to carry on the family business.

St. Polycarp's Church cemetery
Oberschwarzenberg Austria
17 October, 2016

They are all dead now. All these people who knew Lotte as a child, and tolerated her as an adult lie here together in this cemetery for eternity. Interesting how death is the great leveler of people. All their money or bile did not keep them out of the ground.

It is another cold, blustery October morning, twenty-five years after Erich's death. In another week my book about Tante Lotte, *Hitler, My Father* will be published. Lotte, Little Adolf, Erich and all the others who had taken over the last several years of my life would be enshrined eternally within its pages.

As Hilde requested, I retired from the University a few years ago to write this book. She wants to celebrate our twenty-fifth wedding anniversary on a world tour she has been planning for the past decade. We are to depart for Africa in June. Without children to tie us down we are to become nomads and vagabonds.

Since finishing the book two months ago I sense that I am being observed. I must be getting paranoid in my dotage. The townspeople grudgingly kept Lotte's secret out of fear. After my encounter with Little Adolf I wonder if Lotte's threats were as idle as I'd hoped.

Acknowledgements

Hitler, My Father is based on facts and documented history with the injection of just enough creative fiction to make an interesting story.

I'd like to thank the members of the Yeah, Write! Writer's group in Frankenmuth, Michigan: Brian and Shay, Kit, Colleen, Roxanne, and Lynn for their years of help and support.

I'd like to thank the accommodating staffs of the Tarpon Springs, Florida Public Library, Wickson Memorial Library in Frankenmuth, MI, the Mayville Library in Mayville, Michigan, and the Florence Public Library in Florence, Massachusetts for their quiet workspaces and reference materials.

I'd like to thank the staff of the Burger King restaurant in Frankenmuth, Michigan for providing me space to work, repeated senior drinks, and Wi-Fi.

My special thanks to Robert Reindel for connecting me with my publisher, Ted Parkhurst of Parkhurst Brothers, Linda Parkhurst for the cover and text design, Roger Armbrust for editing, and the Tarpon Springs Friday Writer's Group. Additional editing was provided by Gabe Lewis of Silverwood, Michigan.

And my very special thanks to my muse, Rose D'Alessandro, for her support, input, and acceptance of the writer's uneven temperament.

If you have enjoyed this book, please visit:
www.parkhurstbrothers.com
for more titles that spotlight humanities, folktales, and storytelling.